THE GIRL NEXT DOOR

Center Point
Large Print

Also by Ruth Rendell and available from Center Point Large Print:

The Vault
The St. Zita Society
No Man's Nightingale

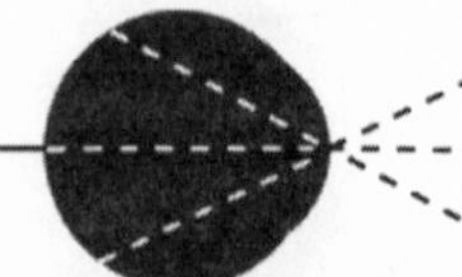

THE GIRL NEXT DOOR

Ruth Rendell

CENTER POINT LARGE PRINT
THORNDIKE, MAINE

This Center Point Large Print edition
is published in the year 2015 by arrangement with
Scribner, a division of Simon & Schuster, Inc,
and Doubleday Canada, a divison of Random House of
Canada, a Penguin Random House Company.

The text of this Large Print edition is unabridged.
In other aspects, this book may vary
from the original edition.
Printed in the United States of America
on permanent paper.
Set in 16-point Times New Roman type.

ISBN: 978-1-62899-471-1

Library of Congress Cataloging-in-Publication Data

Rendell, Ruth, 1930–
The girl next door / Ruth Rendell. — Center Point Large Print edition.
pages cm
Summary: "The discovery of bones in a tin box sends shockwaves across a group of long-time friends"—Provided by publisher.
ISBN 978-1-62899-471-1 (library binding : alk. paper)
1. Large type books. 2. Psychological fiction. I. Title.
PR6068.E63G57 2015
823′.914—dc23

2014046532

For Michael Redington with love

1

HE WAS A handsome man. A handsome boy, his mother called him, because she started praising his looks when he was five. Before that, he received the compliments children necessarily get: “Beautiful baby” and “Isn’t he lovely?” His father was never there. The boy left school at fourteen—you could then—and went to work in a market garden, a slaughterhouse, and finally a cosmetics factory. The boss’s daughter fell in love with him. He was twenty by then, so they got married. Anita’s father said he would stop her having the money her grandmother had left her, but in the event he was too tenderhearted to do so. It wasn’t a large sum but it was enough to buy a house on the Hill in Loughton, twelve miles from London but almost in the country. Woody, as his mother and his wife called him, as someone at school had first named him, hated work and decided never to do any more as long as he lived. There was enough left to live on but whether for the rest of his life he didn’t know. He was only twenty-three.

In those days you had to get married. There were no two ways about it. Living together was not far short of a crime. They were happy enough for a couple of years. His mother died and he inherited her house as well as a small amount of money. Next Anita's father died. People died at a much younger age in the 1930s. She was an only child, so it was her turn to inherit a parental legacy, and it was much in excess of what Woody had got. Because he didn't work, Woody was always at home. He thought he "owed it to himself" to keep a close eye on his wife. She was always going to London to buy clothes, always having her hair done, going off for weekends to stay, she said, with girls she had been to school with and were now married. He wasn't invited.

A woman came in to do the cleaning. Woody thought his wife could have done that and he said so but he couldn't stop it. She paid. She didn't even look after the child, took little notice of it as far as he could see. He had read somewhere that once, sixty or seventy years ago, an act of Parliament was passed letting married women keep the money that was theirs. Before that, they had to hand it over to their husbands. He hated that act. How perfect life would have been when the men got all the money.

When the war came, he was thirty. The horrible possibility of being called up loomed. But he had a stroke of luck. He told the doctor he wanted to know if he was perfectly fit so that he could join up. The navy was his choice. He felt well, he always did, nothing wrong with him—unfortunately. But the doctor found a heart murmur, the result, he said, of pneumonia when Woody was a child. He remembered that pneumonia, remembered most of all his mother's anxiety and terror. But he was overjoyed, too thankful to dwell much on his heart. He put on a show of sorrow for the doctor and said in a regretful tone that he felt all right and would no doubt live to be a hundred.

A lot of his wife's friends were always in the house. One of them was in uniform. He wasn't as good-looking as Woody but the uniform was no doubt a great attraction. Another young man who was staying nearby was often to be found making himself tea in Woody's kitchen or drinking it in Woody's lounge with Woody's wife. He wasn't much to look at.

"You judge everybody by their appearance," said his wife. "That's all that counts with you."

"I judged you by yours. What else was there?"

If his wife wanted to be unfaithful to him, there was nowhere for her to go. But love or something will find a way. How did he know where she really was on these visits to old school friends he was supposed to accept? His wife had red hair and dark blue eyes; her friend, the one in uniform, had eyes the same colour and light brown hair. One afternoon Woody walked into the kitchen to get money out of the biscuit tin to pay Mrs. Mopp, who was really called Mrs. Moss. But Mrs. Mopp was a funny name and Mrs. Moss wasn't. She was just behind him, too greedy for her cash, he thought, to let him out of her sight. His wife was sitting at the kitchen table, holding hands with the one in uniform. Her hand was lying on the American cloth cover of the table, and the man's was lying on top of it, holding it there. They snatched their hands away when Woody came in but not soon enough. Woody paid Mrs. Mopp and walked out, saying nothing to the man and the woman, who just sat there, looking down into their laps.

FOR WOODY, anger was cold. Cold and slow. But once it had started, it mounted gradually and he could think of nothing else. From the first, though, he knew he couldn't stay alive while those two were alive. Instead of sleeping, he lay awake in the dark and saw those hands, Anita's narrow, white hand with the long, pointed nails painted pastel pink, the man's brown hand equally shapely, the fingers slightly splayed. The third member of the family Woody was usually aware of. He doubted that Anita was. She ignored the child. Once he saw her run along the hall towards the front door and not see the little boy. She ran into him in broad daylight, knocking him over, not hurting him, but leaving him there to pick himself up and start to cry. He wouldn't miss his mother, glad to see the back of her, no doubt.

Before Woody did what he meant to do, he took the rest of the money out of the biscuit tin and put it in a smaller one that had once held cocoa. The biscuit tin had a picture of variously shaped shortbread biscuits on it and was quite big, maybe twelve inches by eight and three inches deep. It would be big enough, for their hands were small. Anita came and went, with the man in khaki and maybe also with the other man who wore civvies. Woody didn't care about him. He would disappear when Anita did and wouldn't call round asking for her. Mrs. Mopp came in and cleaned the house. She and Woody seldom spoke. There was nothing to say. The boy went to school and could go by himself; he knew he had to and arguing about it was useless. He talked to Mrs. Mopp and seemed to like her, but that was of no interest to Woody. He thought a lot about Anita's money; it took time, that thinking, and delayed his doing what he had to do. There had to be a way of getting her to transfer those thousands of hers, and there were quite a few thousands, into his bank account, but she had a suspicious mind.

"I'm not having a joint account with you, Woody," she said. "Why d'you want it? No, don't answer. It'll be some low-down thing, some monkey business. The answer's no."

Pity, but it wouldn't put him off. Nothing would do that. The best he could achieve was to get hold of her chequebook and write a cheque to himself for a hundred pounds. More would arouse suspicion. He had no problem cashing it and was rather sorry he hadn't made it out for twice as much. Now he had to do the deed before she got her bank statement.

Woody didn't think about their early days. He didn't think about what he had once called their "romance." He never harked back to even the recent past, saying to anyone who would listen, "It's over, it's not coming back. What's the point of dwelling on it?" However he did it, there mustn't be blood. Telling Anita he was going to stay with his auntie Midge in Norwich. She was ill and was likely to leave him her money—a motive for his visit his wife would be sure to believe. Once he was out of the way, he guessed Anita and the khaki man would share a bed, very likely *his* bed. He would return in the small hours.

Of course he was right. They were there and fast asleep. Having locked the door behind him, he strangled the man first because Anita was a small woman who was no match for him. Then chasing her round the room, he knocked her to the floor and used the same leather belt on her. It was soon over. The only blood was his own where they had both scratched him, and there was little of it. His slaughterman's experience was of great value to him in removing the right hand and the left hand. Before laying the two hands in the biscuit tin he took off Anita's wedding and engagement rings.

This was a bonus. He had forgotten about the rings when he was calculating what money he could forage. Of course he could sell the rings. He could go a long way away, down to Devon or up to Scotland, and find a jeweller who would give him a lot for that diamond ring. Anita had bought it herself. She wanted a diamond ring and he couldn't afford to pay for it.

It was October, better than summer because he need not hurry with disposal of the bodies. Now that he had removed the offending hands, the hands that had held each other, he hardly knew why he had. To look at them? To remind him of his vengeance? But the hand-holding was in the past, and now was the present. He knew he would scarcely want to contemplate those hands in a day or two's time. What he might do was bury them, and knowing they were there, hidden, and whose they were, would be enough. He wrapped the bodies in bedsheets and tied them up with garden string.

The child slept through it. He was only just nine, old enough to see everything that went on even if not understanding most of it. Woody knew he would have to get rid of him. Not that he intended the same fate for him that he had meted out to Anita and her lover. Michael was his son, he knew that, anyone would, for the child was lucky enough to look exactly like Woody. While not feeling anything like love for Michael, he nevertheless had a kind of tie of blood with the boy. Michael was *his,* and now that his mother was gone, the nearest human being in the world to Woody. He could arrange never (or seldom) to see him again, but to shed his blood, as Woody put it, that was not to be thought of.

The bodies in their bedsheet shrouds he had stowed in the summerhouse and covered them with firewood. The lid on the biscuit box fitted tightly, so there was no smell. He kept the box in Anita's wardrobe underneath those dresses she was always buying, but he knew he must find some permanent resting place. He slept in the room where he had killed them, and sometimes he contemplated the box, but he never attempted to remove the lid. Decay would have begun and he was afraid of what he would see and smell if he prised open the lid.

He had known for a couple of months where Michael went when he was out playing with the Johnson boy and the Norris boy and those Batchelors from Tycehurst Hill and lovely Daphne Jones and the little kid Rosemary something. He knew they played underground. Their games were over, time was up. He watched Michael cross the Hill. Woody waited half an hour and then went across the road and up to the entrance to the tunnels. The children were inside but he couldn't see them from where he stood. He shouted out to them, "I know you're in there.

Come out now. Your games are over. Time you went home and don't come back. D'you hear me?"

They heard him. One by one they came out. Daphne stayed behind to blow out the candles. She was the last to leave, and standing on the wet grass at the top, she gave him her mysterious smile, turning her head away.

Next day a policeman came. He wanted to speak to Mrs. Winwood. Woody gave him his prepared story. His wife had been ill and to convalesce was staying with her cousin in the country. The policeman didn't explain why he wanted to speak to Anita or if he was suspicious or what stimulated the request to see her. He went away.

Sending the boy to Auntie Midge was not to be thought of; she was too old and too poor, but how about a cousin of his own, his sort of cousin Zoe? She couldn't have kids and said she longed for them, God knew why. Never mind that, she was thinking of adoption but hadn't fixed on a child, had seen Michael a couple of times, and mooned after him the way some women did. Adoption was easy, more or less the parents' consent had to be secured and you just took the kid over. Zoe had just got married, a bit late in the day but never mind that, and there was plenty of money. She wanted the kid so much she didn't want to know where Anita was or even that she had gone. It was soon arranged.

When the day came, Woody was so anxious to get the house to himself that he took the kid to the station on the underground quite early in the morning and more or less pushed him into the Lewes train. The sandwiches Woody had made he forgot, left them behind on the kitchen counter. But the boy wouldn't want to eat sandwiches in the middle of the morning. Woody had only one regret at seeing the last of his son. It seemed a shame to lose sight of such a good-looking kid. Woody got on a bus and off it when it turned down Knightsbridge. A jeweller in a shop full of rings and pearl necklaces bought Anita's engagement and wedding rings off him for close on a thousand pounds. Enough to buy a fine house with, only he didn't want a house. He had one and would sell it as soon as the war was over. The jeweller asked no questions.

Woody was free. But was he? Not while the bodies lay under the firewood in the summer-house. He was actually contemplating them from the summerhouse doorway when Mrs. Mopp came down the garden to tell him a police officer was at the door asking to see him. Woody shut the summerhouse door and locked it. Not one police-man this time but two. His wife was seriously ill, he said, and he was going up to Yorkshire later that day to join her. They seemed to accept that but made no answer when he asked them, inwardly trembling, what made them ask.

Not while he had the white hand and the brown hand in the biscuit tin. The latter was easily disposed of, secreted in a place where only he could find it when the time came to contemplate those hands again, to remind himself. Since he had driven that bunch of kids out, none had returned, and now it was winter, too cold and wet for visiting the tunnels. One cold, wet evening, pitch-dark in November, he had shone his torch down the steps into the tunnels and followed its beam of light, carrying the biscuit box. In spite of the tarpaulin covering, the whole place was growing waterlogged, the only sound the slow, steady dripping of water onto water. He must be careful. It would be a fine thing if he slipped and fell and, with those hands in his hands, had to shout for help. Would he ever be found?

Woody stood still, thinking, staring down a deep hole, from which the yellowish, clay-thickened water seemed to be draining away. He could hardly see its bottom, only knowing that down there the liquid was finding a way out. Resting the torch on the lip of the hole, he squatted down and slid the tin over the edge. The light showed him that it had slipped down into the muddy wetness, then by its weight pushing aside some obstacle and disappearing from view. He got to his feet, slipped a little, knocking over the torch into the hole. The darkness was absolute. He turned round, telling himself to keep calm, not to panic, and struggled, foot placed carefully in front of foot, hands clutching at the tufts of rank grass that grew here and there from the clayey walls. A little light showed ahead of him, light from the moon it must be, because there were no streetlamps. He clambered up the slippery steps, sliding back once, then again, until at last—and by this time he could see the source of light, a full, round moon—he emerged onto the grass of the field.

By the moonlight he could see that he was caked with mud, yellow filth, his hands and arms, his feet and trousers halfway up his thighs. No one was about. Few people ever were on these wartime evenings. And there was silence, not a light showing, not a note of music heard, not a word spoken, not a child's cry. As he opened the gate and let himself into his garden, he glanced at the Joneses' house next door, at the faint strand of light showing underneath the blackout curtain from what he thought might be Daphne's room. Lovely Daphne—if only she were a bit older and had money, she might become his next wife.

He let himself into the house by the back door, taking a look at the summerhouse from the doorstep. What a way out of his difficulty that would be, to get those bodies, the man's and the woman's, across the road and slide them down the hole as he had slid their hands. But impossible. He would be seen. He had no car, he couldn't drive. The idea must be given up, and the only way would be to destroy the bodies by fire before the police returned to search the place.

Only after the fire had burned the bodies and wrecked the garden did he realise he could never inherit Anita's money because as far as anyone knew she wasn't dead. Officially, to the police or the lawyers or her relatives, she could never die. There was no death certificate, no funeral, no will, no death notice. He looked at himself in the mirror and thought, My face is my fortune, always remember that. A headline in a newspaper told him that a direct hit had destroyed the police station in Woodford, which was only a few miles from Loughton. A lot of officers had been killed, and Woody wondered if this was why the police failed to come back. They had forgotten about him and let him alone. No one ever called him Woody again.

2

IT IS A fantasy many have, a kind of dream, a place to think of to send one to sleep. It begins with a door in a wall. The door opens, confidently pushed open because what is on the other side is known to the dreamers. They have been there before. They have seen somewhere like it, somewhere real, but less beautiful, less green, with less glistening water, fewer varied leaves, and where the magic was missing. The secret garden is always the same, perfect, the plants in flower, the sun always shining, a single bird singing, a single dragonfly in flight. The dreamers never leave the secret garden. The garden leaves the dreamers, replaced with that sense of loss that is sadness and hope departed, perhaps the first they will ever have.

Their garden was not beautiful. It had no flowering trees, no roses, no perfumed herbs. Tunnels, they called it at first. The word *qanat*, an impossible word, was found by Daphne Jones and adopted by the rest of them. It means, apparently, in some oriental language, a subterranean passage for carrying water. They liked it because it started with a *q* without a *u*. Their teachers at their primary schools taught them that no words could ever start with *q* unless followed by *u*, so Daphne's idea appealed to them and the tunnels became qanats. In time to come the qanats became their secret gardens. They were Daphne, of course, Michael Winwood, Alan Norris, Rosemary Wharton, Lewis Newman, Bill Johnson, and all the Batchelors, Robert, George, Stanley, Moira, and Norman and the rest. They discovered the qanats in June in the last year of the Second World War, tunnels that were secret gardens to them or to those of them who had dreams and imagination. They never said a word about them to their parents, and in those days few if any parents asked their children where they went in the evenings, telling them to come home only if the air-raid sirens sounded.

It was not countryside where the qanats were. Building had begun on these fields before the war started and had stopped when the first sirens sounded. They were on the edge of Essex, an outer suburb of London on the borders of Epping Forest. Green meadows still remained, divided by tall, thick hedges composed of many varieties of trees, uncut, seldom even trimmed, squat oaks two hundred years old, screens of elms flourishing before Dutch elm disease was heard of, blackthorns and hawthorns creamy white in spring, crab apples with pink-tinted blossoms. In the fields where hay was no longer cut grew yellow ragwort and blue speedwell and red campion and bee orchis. Painted Ladies and Red Admirals and Peacocks deserted the wildflowers and made for the buddleia in the gardens of the houses of the Hill and Shelley Grove, and dusk brought out the Red Underwing and the Lime Hawk moths. The children thought the fields would always be there; they knew nothing of change. They played in the grass and the hedges, running home to Tycehurst Hill and Brook Road when the sirens set up their howling. Bombs dropped, but not here, not on Loughton, only one in the whole war.

One day, when no siren had gone off for a week, a group of them, several of the Batchelors and Alan and Lewis, came upon a cave, a hole in the ground that looked like the entrance to a tunnel.

June 1944. School hadn't broken up for the summer holidays and wouldn't for another month. It stopped at three thirty in the afternoon and everyone had come home. The Batchelors, Robert and George and Stanley and Moira—Norman was recovering from chicken pox—all went out into the fields, and Stanley took Nipper on the lead. Alan and Lewis and Bill were already out there, sitting up in the hollow oak, in the broad, circular space where someone a hundred years ago must have chopped off the top of the tree and a dozen branches had grown up around it. In summer when it rained, you could sit in there and not get wet, protected by a canopy of leaves. It had been raining that day but was no longer, so Alan and Lewis came down and joined the others in their wandering up the slope on the other side towards the Hill. Would they ever have found the qanats if Moira hadn't spotted a rabbit dive into the hole? Not one of the boys would even have noticed it, not even Stanley, the animal lover, not even Nipper, who had seen the Joneses' dog on the pavement outside the Joneses' house and begun plunging about on his lead, barking and growling. Stanley had to stay outside while the others went into the hole. Someone had to hold on to the dog.

The Joneses' dog was making such a racket that Daphne came out to grab it and drag it back into the house.

Inside the hole were steps, muddy and rain-soaked, cut out of the clay. Who had cut those steps? Who had made this place? They didn't know. A passage led along under the field, under the grass and the wildflowers and through the tree roots. It was dark, but not so dark you couldn't see each other or the tarpaulin roof, but you could tell you'd need candles in the night-time. The walls were just earth, but earth composed of ginger-coloured clay, the kind of clay their fathers complained about when they had to dig the garden. The seven of them, for Daphne Jones had joined them, saying Stanley had told her where they were, emerged into a wide, round area like a room that other passages led into. It was no secret garden, but it had certain secret-garden qualities. It was quiet. It would have been silent apart from the noise they made. It was still and welcoming. It was dark until you lit it.

"We could come in here," George said. "We could bring food and stuff. It'd be good if it was raining."

"It'd be good anyway," said Alan.

"I'm going to explore," said Moira, and they all went with her, discovering what passages there were and how deserted it was, as if no one had ever been there but to dig it out, dig steps down to it where they had come in, cover it up with tarpaulins, then had just gone away and abandoned it to the rabbits and the squirrels.

"Qanats," said Daphne Jones, and qanats they became.

AS YOU GET OLDER, you forget names: those you studied with, worked with, lived next door to, the people who came to your wedding, your doctor, your accountant, and those who have cleaned your house. Of these people's names, you forget perhaps half, perhaps three-quarters. Then whose names do you never forget, because they are incised on the rock of your memory? Your lovers (unless you have been promiscuous and there are too many) and the children you went to your first school with. You remember their names unless senility steps in to scrape them off the rock face. Alan Norris had not had enough lovers to forget the names of those he had had, and his wife had had none. This subject they never discussed. Nor did they think about those people they had been to their first school with, but they remembered the names. They had also been in those tunnels that they gave a peculiar name to, but they had no reason to think about it until it was all over the papers.

"Qanats," said Alan, who something over fifty years ago had married, if not the girl next door, the girl in the next street.

Rosemary said she had always disliked that name, even when she was only ten. "Why not *tunnels?* That's what they were, after all."

The *Daily Telegraph* spread out on the dining table, Alan was reading about a discovery made by three Polish builders under a house called Warlock on the Hill. Reading about it and looking at a picture of what they had found, a biscuit tin and its contents.

"What a name," said Rosemary, reading it over his shoulder. "Zbigniew. Is that how you pronounce it?"

"No idea."

"That's the one who dug it out. They were putting in a basement, it says. That's the last thing we want in Loughton, basements. Those things are hands, are they? Just bones by this time, thank goodness. They'll never finish doing that basement now."

Alan said nothing. He was reading about the builders with the strange names unearthing the tin box with their digger and the police coming and afterwards all digging being made to stop. The tin had once contained shortbread biscuits. When found, it held the skeletal hands of a man and a woman.

"I wonder," said Rosemary, "if they've closed it all up. I mean, put wire all round the garden and that blue-and-white tape you see on TV. We could go up there for our walk and have a look."

"We could." Alan's voice had a faint ironic edge to it, not lost on Rosemary.

"Not if you don't want to, dear."

He folded the paper up. "There's no mention of the qanats—the tunnels, I should say. Only of finding these things under Warlock. We don't even know if it was in the qanats that they were found."

"I do wish you wouldn't call them that."

"The *tunnels* then. We don't even know what they were, tunnels dug in a field and covered up with tarpaulins. George would know. I think he would. If we're going for a walk, why not go and see George and Maureen?"

"If you like."

"Why did we never know what the tunnels were, darling?"

"I suppose we never asked. Our parents would have known, but we never asked them. We never even told them."

"We knew they'd have stopped us going there."

Rosemary went back to her sewing while Alan returned to memories of the qanats. The things they used to do, the games they played, the food they ate that they had brought with them, dense wholemeal bread—how he had longed for white bread—with jam made from turnips and rhubarb, fish-paste sandwiches, potatoes wrapped in clay and baked in an old water tank they found and made a fire in, their fortunes told by Daphne Jones. The name again brought him a shiver of ancient excitement. Acting Mary, Queen of Scots, and the murder of Rizzio. Why Mary, Queen of Scots? Why, come to that, the murder of the Princes in the Tower? Lady Jane Grey? He had forgotten. In spite of those rediscovered memories, so many reasons for things were lost, buried deep underground like those hands. He had a vivid memory of Stanley Batchelor bringing his dog, a white dog with black patches, and Alan had loved it, he and Rosemary hugging the dog and stroking it and saying to each other, "He's so lucky. Why can't I have a dog?" Eventually he could, his beloved Labrador, and Rosemary her spaniel, when the war was over.

He took the paper with him to find Rosemary. She was in her sewing room, sitting at the treadle, her fingers guiding the hem of the dress she was making for Freya. Possessing and using a sewing machine was commonplace when they were first married. Rosemary had made all her own clothes over the years. When sewing grew less common, she made their children's clothes, and now, at least their great-grandchildren's. "Because they're much nicer than anything I could buy."

Alan disagreed but he didn't say so. In one phase she had tried making his shirts, but he put a stop to that. The hand that held the cloth in place was wrinkled now, the veins prominent, but the joints had no sign of arthritis. Rosemary looked up and lifted her foot from the treadle.

“I think we should go and see George Batchelor and take the paper with us,” said Alan. “It’s ages since we saw the Batchelors.” An unwelcome thought struck him. “If he’s still alive.”

Rosemary laughed. “Oh, he’s alive. I saw Maureen in the High Road last week. He’d had his hip done and he was just coming back from St. Margaret’s.”

“And still living in the same place?”

“Not the same phone, though. Maureen gave me her mobile number. Shall I phone them, darling?”

ALONE AMONG THEM, Michael Winwood had a parent still living. They had little contact with each other. There had been no positive quarrel. Neither had ever said to the other, “I will never speak to you again,” but Michael intended never to see his father, and he was sure his father never intended to see him. He wondered if John Winwood had read about the hands, the man’s hand and the woman’s, in the biscuit box, or if perhaps such a discovery would mean nothing to someone of his father’s age. The old man would be a hundred in less than a year’s time and would no longer be compos mentis. Perhaps Michael would have cared if his father had been poor and living in wretched circumstances, but, according to Zoe, he was in the most luxurious old people’s retreat in Suffolk. His home was an apartment with en suite shower rather than a room, and he had everything an ancient human being could require. Michael didn't care, he felt no guilt.

What would Vivien have said about the hands in the box? What would she have said about his father? He would go up to her room, the room that had once been hers, and ask her. Just tell her, really. Lie on the bed beside where she had once lain and talk to her about it. When he closed his eyes, he could see the house called Anderby on the Hill, and on the other side of the road, where there were no houses then, he could see the tunnels, the entrance, and the children gathering. A week after the tunnels' discovery, there were more children, twenty or thirty children. He could see them following each other down the steps and into the long hole, like the Pied Piper of Hamelin without a piper, disappearing into the darkness under the tarpaulin, and then the lights coming on in the depths as someone began to light the candles.

When he thought about Anderby, which he couldn't help doing sometimes, though he tried not to, he usually heard his father singing. That phrase, if you said it to anyone, sounded nice, especially as it was hymns he sang. He wasn't religious, Michael and his mother and father never went to church, but his father had as a child. Hated it, Michael had once heard him say, but the hymns he sang he remembered, the tunes and most of the words. "Lead us, heavenly Father, lead us" and "summer suns are glowing over land and sea." That one about the sun was meant to make you happy, but when John Winwood sang those words, it was preparatory to coming downstairs and snarling at Michael to get out of his sight.

Michael went upstairs and told Vivien about the hymns, laughing as if it were funny.

ALAN AND ROSEMARY walked over to York Hill, having invited themselves to tea.

"We don't drink tea," said Maureen Batchelor on the phone. "George says it's an old person's drink, and when I say we *are* old, he says there's no need to rub it in. Come and have a sherry, why don't you? It's never too early for sherry."

"So sherry's not an old person's drink," said Alan. "I bet you if you went into the King's Head"—they were just approaching this hostelry—"and asked for sherry, the young woman behind the bar wouldn't know what you were talking about."

George, the eldest of the Batchelor siblings still living, was still in the town where he had been born and grown up, a not uncommon phenomenon in outer London suburbs. This was true also of Alan and Rosemary and almost of George's brother Stanley but not of George's brother Norman. So it was a surprise to walk into George and Maureen's living-room in the sprawling bungalow called Carisbrooke and find

Norman sitting beside his brother on a sofa, George's leg stretched out in front of him and supported on what Maureen called a pouffe.

"How are you, Norman?" said Rosemary. "Long time no see." Alan particularly disliked that phrase, which she believed the people she called "Chinamen" used.

"I live in France now. I'm not often here." Norman went off into a gushing eulogy of French culture, food, drink, the countryside, the health service, his house, and transport. A glazed look came over Maureen's face, the expression of someone who has heard it all before. She got up and returned with a trolley laden with glasses and bottles of various sherries, oloroso, amontillado, and Manzanilla among others.

Having accepted a glass of amontillado, Alan handed George the *Daily Telegraph*. "Have you seen this?"

George barely glanced at it. "Sure. We take the same paper." He nodded in a sage sort of way. "I built it."

"What, Warlock?"

"Me and my brother did. Batchelor Brothers. Like we built a good many of the houses on the Hill."

Alan knew he meant not that George and Stanley had built these houses with their own hands, but that their firm had, and on those fields across which they and all the other children had run when the sirens sounded and then the all clears.

"When was it, George?" Rosemary asked.

"Sometime in the early fifties. 'Fifty-two, 'fifty-three."

"Okay. Now maybe you can tell me if you think our tunnels were underneath Warlock."

"Oh, no," said George. "They'd been there, though. That's what they were, the foundations of a house."

Rosemary echoed his last words. "The foundations of a house. I never thought of that."

"They were all gone by the time I acquired the land. We dug new foundations for Warlock. A Mr. Roseleaf had it built. Funny name, I thought, that's why I remembered."

Norman, having found fault with the sherry as being Spanish and not French, had fallen asleep but now awoke with a snort and said, "So that's what they were. The foundations of a house. That was a funny name too, Warlock."

"It means a man who's a sort of witch," said Maureen. "Very funny, in my opinion."

"Nothing to do with witches," said George. "It was because he'd lived in a street called Warlock Road in Maida Vale."

"Well, I never," said Norman. "You were there, Alan, weren't you? And Rosemary. And Lewis Newman—remember him? And do you remember Stanley's dog, Nipper? He was a nice dog. My mum hardly ever got cross with us, not with anyone, but was she mad when she found Stanley'd been taking the dog out in the evening without asking."

Rosemary smiled, remembering. "Nipper was lovely. We longed for a dog, didn't we, Alan?"

"You didn't find those hands when you were building that house, did you, George?"

"I think I'd have said, don't you?"

George softened his scathing tone by struggling to his feet and refilling sherry glasses. Several guests noticed that he was pouring amontillado into Manzanilla glasses, but no one said anything. Rosemary got oloroso instead of amontillado, but she really preferred the sweet sherry, though she hadn't asked for it as it was known to make you fat.

"That was where we met," she said. "In those tunnels."

"What, when you were ten?" George asked

Rosemary nodded, suddenly embarrassed. Met there, lost each other when someone's father turned them out, shouted at them to go home and not come back, met again years later, at a dance this time, dated (though that was a term never used then), and got married. It seemed to her that the others were staring at them as if she had described some tribal ritual, ancient and now unknown. Except for her and Alan, they had all been married at least once before, divorced, moved, even lived abroad such as Norman.

She said brightly, trying to cover a kind of shame, “Who was it that turned us out of the tunnels? Someone’s father? Michael Woodman? Woodley?”

“It was Michael Winwood’s dad,” said Norman. “They lived on the Hill next door to the Joneses, the Winwoods did. And Bill Johnson’s people lived further up the Hill. Winwood found out we were all going into the tunnels in the evenings. I suppose Michael told him. He just walked across the road, found the entrance, and shouted down to us to come out and not come back.”

While Norman was speaking, his brother Stanley had quietly come into the house by the back door. Norman jumped when he felt a hand on his shoulder, got to his feet, and the brothers embraced. Rosemary said afterwards to her husband that she hadn’t known where to look, brothers hugging each other. Whatever next! Alan thought it was rather nice but said nothing. Throughout his marriage he had often taken refuge in saying nothing. They were always weird, those Batchelors, said Rosemary on the way home. For instance, the way Norman, the youngest, used to go about telling people he’d been born on the kitchen table.

George, more conventionally, shook hands with his brother and pointed to his hip with a doleful look. “We were talking about those Winwoods. Remember them?”

"They lived next door to Daphne Jones on the Hill. I remember her all right."

That name again, Alan thought. He'd forgotten her, and now her name had come up three times in—what? The past couple of hours? At least he hadn't blushed. What did Stanley mean by that "all right"? Alan's voice sounded squeaky and he wondered if anyone noticed. Rosemary might. "Is she still alive? She was older than any of us."

"She wasn't. She just looked sixteen when she was twelve. She wasn't really older." Stanley nodded knowledgeably. "I've sort of kept in touch with her." He seemed proud of it. "She's been married three times and now she's called Daphne Furness. Lives in Hampstead or St. John's Wood or somewhere. We don't all cling to our roots."

Aware of feeling envy, Alan wondered what had come over him. How must it feel now to have known and possibly often seen Daphne Jones over the years? He suppressed the thoughts. He was an old man, a great-grandfather, and George was hoisting himself to his feet once more and stood as if about to make a statement, swaying. "It's just come to me. I've got a photo—a snap we used to call them—of us in the tunnels. Well, me and my brother and my sister Moira in the entrance. Robert's not there, he took the snap. Where's that photo got to, Maureen? Can you lay your hands on it?"

"Of course I can. How can you ask?"

Alan expected a little black-and-white or even sepia photograph. Instead Maureen brought an album that looked too heavy for a small woman to lift. It was brown with pages of thick brown card to which what seemed like hundreds of photographs had been pasted. Familiar with the contents, though she hadn't been one of the children in the tunnels, she opened the album at a page with the date 1944 printed on it and laid it on the coffee table. George shifted along the sofa and gingerly set his foot to the ground, lifting his left leg with both hands. Stanley sat beside him, squeezing between him and Norman.

"Now let Alan and Rosemary have a shufti," said Maureen. "You lot can see the pics whenever you want."

Eventually the album was rearranged so that everyone could see but no one could see well. George placed one finger on a dim-looking snap of five children crowded together in what was apparently the entrance to a small cave. Out of focus, it thus looked as if Robert Batchelor had taken it through a thick fog. "Me and Stanley and Norman and poor Moira," said George. He called her "poor" because she, the youngest but one of them, like Robert, the eldest, was dead.

"Who's that?" said Rosemary, pointing to a boy with a mop of curly hair.

"Don't know." George produced a magnifying

glass, enlarging the boy's face to a blur. "Could be Bill Johnson."

The other photographs on the page were of little interest to Alan and Rosemary, being of interiors of the Batchelor house in Tycehurst Hill, of Stanley holding a cricket bat, and, mysteriously to anyone not familiar with Norman's life history, a small shot of a table covered in a checked cloth.

"Look at that," said Norman. "I took that. Fancy you keeping that, George. I was born on that table. My mum was walking about the house, waiting for the nurse to come, in labour, of course, though we were never told that part. It was never put into words, though that's what it was. George and Moira carried it out into the garden for Robert to get that shot on account of it was too dark in the kitchen. Fancy you keeping that. Can you unstick it, George, and let me have it?"

"No, I can't. It'd spoil the album." George looked around him. "You want to see any more? I ask because my leg's giving me hell."

"Give it here," said Maureen. "Let Alan and Rosemary have a closer look."

She lifted the album and laid it across Alan's knees. "Robert took some more of the tunnels on the next page," said George.

Alan turned it over, and there she was, sitting on a pile of bricks with Stanley on one side of her and Michael Winwood on the other. She was wearing a summer frock, and her hair, a nearly black dark brown, hung in ripples over her shoulders and halfway down her back. Alan started at the sight, something like a shiver, sudden enough to make Rosemary turn on him a look of concern. That hair—she sometimes wore it in pigtails, and the waves appeared when the plaits were undone.

"There she is," said Stanley, craning his neck to see. "She doesn't look like that now, but you can still see the young Daphne in her."

Hurriedly, Alan turned the page to a set of some ten or eleven photos of Stanley's dog.

"Nipper. There he is, my first dog. I reckon I've had ten since then, they all lived to a good age." Stanley sighed. "Alfie died last year aged eighteen. I won't have another, not now. It'd be sad for him if I went first, and I easily might at my age."

A thin blight settled on the meeting after that. They were old and hadn't long to last and they shirked facing it. Alan asked where Stanley was living now and was told Theydon Bois, a not-far-distant village in the forest. Alan wanted to ask for more about Daphne but hesitated and asked after Michael Winwood instead. North West London, he was told, and then he got up to go.

"Should we get in touch with the police?"

"Let sleeping dogs lie," said Stanley. "Or bones, should I say?"

"Better let them know." George shifted his bad

leg and winced. “I’ll tell them, if you like. I mean, I built Warlock and I’ve got those pictures. I’m the one to do it. They’re not taking my album out of the house, though.”

“We could try to find some of the others too,” said Norman. “Maureen could do that. Genius with the technology, aren’t you, Maureen?”

“More like the phone book,” said his sister-in-law.

3

ALAN AND ROSEMARY walked back up Traps Hill. In the days when they both belonged to the tennis club, they used to run up that hill. Now Rosemary was proud of walking up without getting more than slightly out of breath. They knew every inch of Loughton, which, when they were children, had been called “the village.” “I’m just going down the village,” you said when you went shopping.

After the meeting at a dance, the remembering knowing each other as children, the going about together and getting engaged, they had married and bought a house in Harwater Drive, and later, when the children came along and Alan was doing well, a bigger and better one in Church Lane. The pretty fields and the woods that had begun where the best road of all met the top of the Hill and Borders Lane had all been built on, acres and acres, miles and miles, and called the Debden Estate. The wealthy people of Alderton Hill shuddered at the coming of this spillover from the East End of London. Living in less prestigious but still admired and sought-after streets, the parents of Alan and Rosemary and their neighbours also shuddered. Some moved away. Out, of course, out into Essex as far as Epping and Theydon Bois, only to be deterred by the coming of Harlow New Town. "Not in my back yard," or NIMBY, was an unknown word then, but Nimbys were what they were.

Alan and Rosemary got married at St. Mary's Church in Loughton High Road, and Alan's friend Richard Parr, who had also been in the tunnels, was his best man. A week later when Alan and Rosemary were away on their honeymoon in the Isle of Wight, Richard immigrated to Canada. He and Alan kept in touch for a while, exchanging airmails handwritten on flimsy blue paper. Making phone calls was far too expensive.

Now great-grandparents—their second great-grandchild had been born three years before—Rosemary and Alan had sold the house in Church Lane, a house they had lived in for nearly half a century. They had bought it for eight thousand pounds and sold it for three million. They moved into a flat, a luxurious first-floor flat in Traps Hill, for they were fit for their age and with a shiver rejected the idea of sheltered housing.

"I'VE GOT SOMETHING to tell you," said Freya, their younger granddaughter. A social worker, she was in Loughton for a conference in the Lopping Hall. "I'm getting married."

Alan said, "Congratulations. Or should I say 'best wishes' when it's the bride?"

Rosemary said, "Is it David?"

In a sharper tone than usual, Freya said, "Well, considering we've been together for five years, of course it is, Gran."

Having no champagne, Alan poured three glasses of sherry. It seemed to be turning into a sherry day. Freya looked at her glass suspiciously before she sipped the contents. It occurred to Alan that she might never have tasted sherry before.

"Mind you come to our wedding. It'll be sometime in July," Freya said as she was leaving.

"It used to bother me a lot," said Rosemary, "her living in—well, in sin."

"That's a very outdated expression. Her parents lived together before they married and so did her sister and Giles. Things have changed. Norman Batchelor lives with a woman he's not married to." Alan searched for a word. "It's perfectly respectable these days."

"Not to me," said Rosemary. "I don't want the

rest of this sherry. We're drinking too much."

Alan said nothing. He had thought of taking Rosemary out for supper, maybe to the King's Head, but her moralistic attitude, very much in evidence recently, changed his mind. "Do you think we've led a dull life?" he asked. "I mean, marrying early, two children, staying married, me working nine till five, you a housewife, gradually moving up the property ladder but never moving out of Loughton. We've been abroad, but only to France and Spain. We've never even been to America."

"What are you getting at, Alan?"

She rarely called him by his given name. It was always "darling" or "dear." "I just asked if you thought we'd led a dull life."

"Well, I don't think so. I'd have said we've had a happy life, not very adventurous, but those sort of lives are full of trouble. We haven't committed adultery or gone in for domestic violence or anything like that. We've brought up our children decently. What's wrong with that?"

"Nothing," he said, but he thought, Everything.

He took a pack of smoked salmon out of the fridge and made scrambled eggs to go with it while Rosemary pinned and then tacked up the sleeves of the dress she had been making for Freya that morning.

GEORGE BATCHELOR COULD manage an invoice or a receipt, but when it came to a letter, he got

Maureen to do it for him. She took the photograph of George and Stanley and Norman and Moira and the possible Bill Johnson to the instant-print place in the High Road and had it photocopied. She addressed her letter with enclosure to "The Chief Investigating Officer, the Metropolitan Police," and took it to the police station in Forest Road herself. Once she was there, she might as well pay the monthly or sometimes weekly visit to Clara Moss, who lived higher up the road. It was a call of duty, not pleasure, and George usually did it. He didn't mind it, enjoyed it, Maureen thought. But he wouldn't be able to do it until his leg was better, so she had taken over. He said it was the least he could do for poor Clara, but Maureen knew it made him feel quite young or at least middle-aged. Though he was old, Clara was even older, must be getting on for ninety.

Maureen pounded on the knocker because Clara was deaf. She came to the door without her stick because she could hold on to the furniture. She said, "Hallo, Mrs. Batchelor," and Maureen said, "How are you, Clara," and stepped over the threshold into the small, dark living-room.

NORMAN WAS STILL staying with his brother and sister-in-law at Carisbrooke, York Hill, and running his bulbs-and-seedlings mail-order company on his smartphone while in constant communication with Eliane, whom he spoke of as his "lady partner." George continued to sit on the sofa with his bad leg up, except when the physiotherapist came and put him through his paces. In the privacy of their bedroom he told Maureen that he was sure Norman stayed and stayed in order to have someone to complain to about the state of this country.

"He hasn't got a woman here, has he?" Maureen asked.

"I wouldn't be surprised. He always liked two strings to his bow. Better ask Stan. Stan always knows things like that."

"I forgot to tell you. Stan's got a new dog. And after him saying he wouldn't have another in case he passed away and it pined. It's a puppy, this one, coal black. Not a bit of white on it but it's called Spot. All the rest have been Nipper. I reckon Spot was the only other doggy name Stan could think of."

INITIALLY QUITE KEEN on the job of finding out the provenance of the Warlock hands, as they were starting to be called, Detective Inspector Colin Quell lost interest when forensics discovered their age. If they had been two or three years in the ground, some challenging investigation would have had to be done, but they turned out to be sixty or seventy years old. This man and this woman had, fairly obviously, been killed. No one, not even a crazy person—a crazy undertaker?—

removes the hands from the bodies of those who have died naturally. No one buries those hands away from their mutilated bodies. Still, he had been assigned the case and he had to do it, no matter that the perpetrator—the killer and dissector—must have been long dead himself.

Quell had received a number of phone calls from people he defined as nuts, psychopaths, and lunatics, describing the find under Warlock as the result of witchcraft, a butcher practising his craft, and the remains of two visitants from outer space. He had received only one letter because few people wrote letters anymore. It was nearly as crazy as the phone call about the witchcraft, but not quite.

"A bunch of kids playing games in the foundations of a house," he said aloud to himself in his office. "What sort of games? And bombs falling all around? Do I believe this stuff?" Nevertheless, he studied this rather fuzzy photocopy of the children poking their heads out of a muddy hole and decided he had better talk to some of these people, all of them as old as the hills now, of course.

He would shortly have to pay a second visit to Loughton, take a look at the workmen and the supervising archaeologist, who were digging away in search of more remains under Warlock. A waste of time, he thought. Who cared after all these years? Pity this Maureen Batchelor didn't give an email address, though she did offer a phone number. A landline, he noted, not a mobile. But what could you expect of someone of her age?

He spoke to George Batchelor. Quell was always willing to admit he had been wrong, and he had certainly been wrong about this onetime builder and his wife. They sounded a lot younger than they must be. They gave him names of some of the other people who had been children in the "tunnels." Having an idea that you should never, if you could help it, speak of death or even "passing away" in the presence of anyone over sixty, Quell didn't ask how many of them were still alive. He didn't have to. George Batchelor equally serenely told him of his dead brother, Robert (the photographer), his dead sister, Moira, and of the still-living Alan Norris, Rosemary Norris, Michael Winwood, Daphne Furness, his brothers Norman and Stanley, and Bill Johnson.

"I think I should see all of them."

George was beginning to enjoy this. "If you're coming to see me, shall I ask all the others round at the same time?"

"If it's not putting you out," said Quell.

"The ones that are still in the land of the living," said George.

He had been bored out of his mind lazing about with his leg up. Now it looked as if he might have a real part to play in this investigation, all these old friends round, the police taking a real interest. He would show them his photographs. It would be a tonic for him. Maybe he could find Michael Winwood or Stanley would. Stanley always kept up with people over the years.

A SMALL CROWD had gathered round his car. Spot was sitting in the driving seat with his forepaws on the steering wheel. Sighs of "Aah" and "Sweet" came from the shoppers who had stopped to stare. Unwisely, Stanley had parked outside the police station on a yellow line, thinking he would only be a minute, but as he approached the car, a uniformed PC preceded him, observed Spot without a hint of a smile, and told Stanley to "get that dog down from there" and move off. He was lucky, he added, that the PC would take no further steps. Stanley put Spot in the back, laid the flowers he had bought for Maureen on the passenger seat, and drove off up to York Hill and Carisbrooke.

Stanley always brought women flowers. Like his brother Norman, he was known as a ladies' man, though, according to his friends and neighbours, there was nothing *wrong*. He bought more flowers for his wife than for any other woman. Stanley always talked to his dogs and he talked to this one, telling him as they got out of the car that he had better behave as a policeman was coming, and a more powerful one than the PC.

Spot wagged his tail. Maureen might have had something to say about Spot's presence but was mollified by the huge bunch of daffodils and narcissi with which Stanley presented her.

"Daphne here yet?"

"No one's here but you and of course Norman," said Maureen. "George can put his foot to the ground now, so mind you tell him how well he's doing."

"Will do. This is Spot."

"So I gathered. He won't pee on the floor, will he?"

"Certainly not. He's already house-trained."

They were still in the hallway when the doorbell rang. It was the Norrises and Detective Inspector Colin Quell, who had met on the front path. Alan and Rosemary had walked to York Hill. All the way Alan hadn't said much because he was anticipating meeting Daphne again after so long and resolving at the same time not to think about it. It would be a long way for her to come at her age. She was two or three years older than he. And how would she come? By tube perhaps. The District Line and then the Central Line. Perhaps Stanley would drive down to Loughton station to meet her. He wouldn't ask. They went into the living-room, the French windows open to the garden, it was such a fine sunny day. Maureen brought in a large blue bowl full of spring flowers and set them on the table.

Spot ran out into the garden, chasing a squirrel.

Because it was nearly lunchtime, George offered Pinot Grigio, which Quell refused. He was driving, he said. Most people think all police officers are traffic cops, and one by one (except for Norman) the others also declined, feeling perhaps that Quell would see the drinking of alcohol as somehow offensive and in some way punishable. Food, however, was acceptable, and even Quell took a smoked-salmon sandwich.

"Well, shall we make a start?" he said. "Don't need to wait for the others, do we?"

George began talking about the tunnels, how he thought he and his brothers "poor" Robert and Stanley had been the first to discover them. Not then but later, when he was in his late teens and went into the building trade, he realised the tunnels had been the foundations of a house, the building of which was stopped by the war.

"So these were the foundations of Warlock?" Quell asked.

"No, no. Michael Winwood's father told us not to play there anymore. He stood at the opening to the tunnels and shouted at us to come out. Kids were obedient in those days. We did as we were told. We all came out and went home. After that we never went there again, and at some point the foundations were filled in. I don't know who took it upon himself to do that and you'll never find out now. It was all farmland up there, and as soon as I could, our firm—that is my brother Stanley and me—we bought as much as we could, and one of the houses we built was Warlock. I reckon that was just sort of next door to where our tunnels had been. That would have been 1952 or '53."

"When you say you were playing there, what did you play? I mean, there can't have been much to do in underground passages. Why did you?"

They looked at Quell pityingly. He spoke from the age of computers and online games, from e-books, DVDs, and CDs, Bluetooth and Skype, smartphones and iPads. They spoke from a distant past when everyone read books and most people had hobbies, made things, played cards and chess, dressed up and played charades, sewed and painted and wrote letters and sent postcards.

Alan had begun describing what they did, how they wrapped potatoes in clay and baked them on a fire they made in an old water tank, played sardines, a constant favourite, picnicked on cheese sandwiches, played cards, acted bits of history they liked, Mary, Queen of Scots, and Rizzio—the mystified Quell had seen *Mary Queen of Shops* on TV but never heard of the Scottish Queen—Henry the Eighth and his six wives, the death of Nelson. There was a fortune-teller, very popular this, who sat in a candlelit chamber of the tunnels and told everyone's future, gazing into someone's mother's upturned mixing bowl. Alan faltered a little when he came to the fortune-teller but scarcely heard the doorbell until a low, somehow thrilling voice interrupted and Daphne Furness, followed by a man who had to be Michael Winwood, came into the room.

Had he seen her in the street, he wouldn't have known her. Of course he wouldn't after sixty years. He only knew her now because who else could it be? She was elegant in a black suit, white silk shirt, and very high-heeled shoes. Rosemary always said that elderly women couldn't wear high heels, their balance was no longer good enough, but she could. Daphne could. Sometimes he glanced at those Saturday or Sunday supplements the newspapers included and it was the trend now to show pictures of grey-haired models in their sixties and seventies along with the young ones. Daphne reminded him of one of those graceful elderly women, long necked and slender. He got slowly to his feet.

She and Stanley kissed, on the cheek, quick pecks and no hugs. Alan held out his hand and Daphne took it. Her fingers were thin and cool. All his memories of her were coming back, but it was the least significant of them that he now referred to.

"I don't suppose you remember, but you told my fortune."

She smiled, showing perfect teeth that were

probably crowns on implants. "And what was your fortune?"

"You predicted a long and happy life."

"It's been long obviously. And happy?"

It was Rosemary who answered, with a touch of asperity, "Very happy, thank you."

Made impatient by the interruption and subsequent delay, Quell said, "I'd like to hear what Mrs. Furness and Mr. Winwood have to say about these tunnels of yours." He turned to Daphne. "Were there any grown-ups—adults, I should say—there with you?"

"They didn't know we were there. They didn't know the tunnels were there, as far as we knew."

"Until my father kicked us out," said Michael Winwood.

Alan said, "I remember one grown-up coming. Just the once, I think." He looked from one to another of the now old children. "It was Lewis Newman's uncle. I don't know what he was called. Lewis called him Uncle James."

"He was young," said Rosemary. "I mean they said he was young. I couldn't tell whether someone was, say, twenty-three or forty. Lewis said, 'Dad says he's young to be an uncle.' I knew my dad was forty and my mum was thirty-eight, so he must have been a lot younger than that." She looked doubtfully at Quell. "Maybe it's not important."

Quell was looking as if nothing he had heard

came into that category. Even so he asked everyone for his or her memories of the tunnels, and one by one they gave him what they remembered. He neither made notes nor recorded what they said. Perhaps he had a good memory. When it was done and he had heard about the air-raid warnings, the bombs they'd expected but which never came to Loughton, the shrapnel from gunfire that lay in the streets for them to collect, the food they ate and hated but got used to, the sanctuary of the tunnels they called, for some reason he never fathomed, "qanats," he asked for mobile numbers or addresses from all of them. He might want to get in touch. He said he'd like to know if they knew of anyone going missing when they were children, anyone disappearing. Please to let him know if they could remember. Rosemary wrote down her home phone number and Maureen produced from a drawer a compliments slip with the name of George and Stanley's firm on it.

Stanley had taken Spot out into the garden as he was in danger of having an accident on the carpet. Michael Winwood said that as they lived not far from each other, she in St. John's Wood and he in West Hampstead, Daphne was going to drive him home. Daphne produced a card from her handbag, and then a strange thing happened. Two cards must have been stuck together, for as she leant across the table to pass one of them to Quell, its fellow detached itself and fell on the floor. While Rosemary was fetching her coat from the hallway, Alan quickly put his foot over the card. He was pretty sure no one but Daphne saw him. She met his eyes and gave him a tiny smile with closed lips. By the time Rosemary came back, he had retrieved the card by dropping his handkerchief and contriving to pick up card and handkerchief together.

DAPHNE'S CAR WAS not the expensive, subtly coloured, high-powered Italian vehicle Michael would have expected, but a silver Toyota Prius and by no means new. The road through the forest was much the same as it had been when he was young, but the old names seemed to have gone. Would anyone now have known what he meant by the Wake roundabout or the Epping New Road? Daphne drove them with ease and speed onto the M25 going anti-clockwise. He had expected her to change her shoes before getting into the car, but she still wore the high heels, her driving unimpeded.

"What did you think of all that?" he said.

"Pretty useless, I should think." They passed smoothly through the Bell Common tunnel, heading for Waltham Abbey. "Your mother had just died, hadn't she? I mean, while we were going to the tunnels. That must have been hard for you."

Michael hesitated. “Everyone thought she’d died. My father put it about that she had, but she hadn’t. She’d gone off with someone. A man, I mean. They’d had an awful marriage. I was only nine but I remember the way they screamed and shouted at each other like it was yesterday. My dad told me she wasn’t dead but I’d never see her again. It’s stayed with me, what he said, all these years. ‘She doesn’t want either of us,’ he said. ‘Just wants to see the back of us.’ ”

“But you saw her again?”

“No, I never did. I was left with my father. He had some sort of heart condition so he couldn’t go into the forces. He didn’t want me either. I was sent to live with my aunt Zoe. She wasn’t really my aunt but my dad’s cousin. Mind you, Zoe was a lovely woman, she was very good to me, and I was all right there with her. I loved her very much. Still do, she’s still alive.”

Daphne nodded but said nothing for a while. They were passing into the sort of countryside Michael thought was probably Green Belt, the edge of Hertfordshire, and the signs were coming up for the A1. “Were they divorced, your parents?”

“Grown-ups didn’t tell children things like that. Not then. Don’t you remember?”

“I suppose I do. What became of your father?”

“He’s in an old people’s home. A care home. I never lived with him after I went to Zoe. My parents must have divorced because he married again. I didn't have a happy childhood up to the time we used to go into the tunnels, but I did after that, near perfect after that."

"I haven't any children," said Daphne. "Have you?"

"Two. One of them is mostly in America and the other one is usually in Hong Kong."

There was nothing much to say to that unless "You must miss them" was something, but Daphne didn't go in for truisms and clichés. She turned off the Hendon Way and took Fortune Green Road so that she could turn into Michael's street, where he lived in a tall, narrow redbrick house.

"This has been very nice of you, Daphne."

"It was on my way."

"Will you come in for a moment?"

"I don't think I will. Not this time. But now I know where you live. Doesn't that sound ominous? I mean that now I know it, we can perhaps keep in touch." She handed him a card identical to the one she had given Inspector Quell. "Good-bye, Michael." She waited until he was in the house. Then she backed out of his garage drive and drove down the hill until she could turn into Hamilton Terrace. There, obliged to park the car in the street, she walked through the glass-roofed way and let herself into the house by the glossy-black front door. As she sometimes did when coming home, she stood in the wide hallway and, addressing her generous third husband, who had left her all he possessed, said to the walls and the staircase as she often did, “Thank you for everything, Martin.”

Up the hill in Ingham Road, Michael was also paying a sort of tribute to a dead spouse. This necessitated climbing three quite steep flights of stairs but seldom made him short of breath. He was used to it and sure the stairs were good for his heart as he did it every day. Not to sleep in this bedroom that covered the whole third floor—it was years since he had done that—but to sit there for a while in one of the little pink armchairs and to check that the room was just as it should be, just as it had been when it was Vivien’s. Mrs. Bailey had been in to clean the house while he was in Loughton, and it was not unknown for her to disarrange things. The pictures, for instance, were sometimes left hanging not quite straight, the cut-glass scent bottles with their silver stoppers pushed too close together, and the brooches and pins in the pink satin pincushion on the dressing table so replaced after the surface had been dusted as to overbalance on the edge and threaten to fall onto the carpet.

He sometimes wondered what Mrs. Bailey thought of this idiosyncrasy of his, keeping Vivien’s bedroom as it had been when she was alive, but he didn’t really care. For some years now he had thought of himself as too old to bother with how the things he did looked to other people.

What did it matter? He could do as he liked at his age. His children probably thought he was senile, but his children were hardly ever here, and when they were, they never went up to the third floor. He didn't think about his father.

4

COLIN QUELL HAD little interest in people, what they might think, how they might act in the future. If he had any opinion of those gathered in George and Maureen Batchelor's living-room, it was to marvel that they had lived so long and apparently (with the exception of George) without handicap or disease.

Quell proceeded with his inquiry on scientific fact alone and, during the week following his visit to Loughton, received various reports on what had been discovered as to the age and provenance of the hands.

That one was a woman's and the other a man's he already knew. It seemed that the woman had been in her late twenties and the man a few years younger. They had not died at the scene but some distance away, perhaps a hundred yards, since the soil with which the hands were filled was clay rather than loam. This satisfactorily confirmed

Quell's view that the hands' original burial site had been in those tunnels the old people remembered. It was no proof, but it made his theory most probable.

As he read the report a second time—it came both on the Internet and as printed sheets of paper or hard copy—he thought once more, the way he had been thinking since he was first assigned to this case, that—well, who cared? These two hands that were being investigated had lain in the clay for nearly seventy years. Someone no doubt long dead had killed the people whose hands they were and placed the hands in a biscuit tin for some unfathomable reason. Quell wasn't shocked by this, he had seen too much of man's iniquity to react in that way, but he was at the idea of the taxpayers' money being wasted on an investigation. If nothing was discovered, so well and good, but if, after months of painstaking examination he found who had killed the two and buried their hands, Quell, recalling a smidgen of sixth-form college Latin, asked himself, *Cui bono*?

AN INVITATION HAD come to Freya's wedding, and it seemed to Alan that Rosemary could talk of nothing else. Like most men, he was not particularly interested in weddings, not even his granddaughter's. No church or even town hall was mentioned on the pretty card, only the hotel by the river at Kew, where both Norrises assumed "the wedding breakfast," as Rosemary called it, would take place.

"I suppose the ceremony will be there as well," said Alan.

"I sincerely hope not." Rosemary scrutinised the card again. "If it's going to be one of those peculiar arrangements in a hotel lounge, I for one shan't feel they're married at all."

"It's their choice. Nothing to do with us. I've heard of this place by the river. It's supposed to be very pretty."

Rosemary said she had better get on with the dress she was making, this time for herself, and headed for her sewing room. Alan stopped her, saying that on a lovely day such as this one they should go out for a walk. He intended to go and he didn't want to go alone. "Buy yourself a dress for once," he said. "We can afford it. We can afford designer—isn't that what they call it?"

She made no reply but agreed to the walk, and although neither of them felt up to their marathons of a few years ago, the round-trip of down the Hill and along Brook Road to the High Road and the cricket field, up Traps Hill, and home, was quite within their power. Alan had told himself he didn't want to go alone but in fact he did want to. To walk in the spring sunshine along these familiar streets, past these familiar houses and gardens, and to *think* was what he wanted. As it happened, Rosemary wasn't saying much. She also was perhaps thinking, and in her case of the lamentable state society was in when it countenanced young couples getting married in hotels instead of St. Mary's Church. But he mustn't be disloyal even in thought.

He put his hand in his jacket pocket to touch the card which had been in there for the past ten days or so. Its presence troubled him a little because it shouldn't be there, he should never have picked it up, or he should at least have destroyed it when he got home. Instead he had read it several times over: *Daphne Furness,* it said, *67A Hamilton Terrace, London NW8*. Then came an email address and a mobile phone number. He thought of her as she had been in George Batchelor's living-room, looking years younger than any other woman there, her wonderful legs, those shoes. Don't go there, he told himself, using an injunction Freya or maybe Fenella had taught him. Don't.

Rosemary laid her hand on his arm, then closed her fingers on it. "You shivered. Are you all right?"

"Perfectly."

"Look where we are. You didn't know, did you? You've been in a dream."

They were outside Warlock. The house looked deserted, all the blinds pulled down at the windows. The great pit, excavated to make a basement, was covered by sheets of tarpaulin in which the heavy rain of a few days before had made shallow puddles.

"Rather sad, isn't it? Such a lovely home. Will it ever be the same again?"

Alan, who usually conditioned himself to agree with everything Rosemary said, found himself violently disagreeing. He wanted to say that with its white stucco and chocolate-coloured half timbering, it wasn't lovely, it never had been, and if it wasn't the same again, all the better. And when did she start calling a house a *home?* But he didn't say any of that. He only wondered if this unspoken disloyalty was going to continue, if he could rid himself of it. He withdrew his arm from her hand and felt into the pocket, where the card seemed to move under his fingers as if it were alive. His fingers remembered the feel of hers when she put her hands into his.

Later, with afternoon slipping into evening, and Rosemary, in spite of what he had said about a designer dress, back at her sewing machine, he told himself he must choose one of two options: throw the card away or call the phone number on it. Like a man who was choosing between faithfulness and infidelity—nothing could be further from his thoughts—he must decide. Of course he wouldn't make that phone call. He looked back on his chaste and blameless life, reminded himself of his age and hers, then thought of the summer when on many occasions

Daphne had borrowed her father's car and parked it under the trees on Baldwin's Hill, and they had made love on the backseat or in the forest itself. *Thou art fair, my love. Our bed is green. The beams of our house are cedar and our rafters of fir.* Where had he remembered that from? He opened the sewing-room door an inch or two, said to Rosemary, "I'm going out for a bit of a walk."

She didn't lift her foot from the treadle. "You've already had a walk."

"I know, but I need another. Don't mind, do you?"

"Of course I don't mind, darling. Remember it's supper at seven, though, won't you?"

There were only the two of them, it would only be cold meat and salad, yet it had to be at seven? Why? Because it always was. He knew he couldn't change it. Down the hill, across the High Road and up York Hill past the bungalow called Carisbrooke and along Baldwin's Hill to that paved apron of land that jutted into the greensward bordered by the forest. Here had been where young couples parked their borrowed cars. But no longer, Alan thought, not these days when a teenage boy or girl brought a lover home to spend the night under the parental roof. In his day parents wouldn't even have considered allowing that. No son or daughter would have dreamt of asking. Thirty years later his own son, Owen, had asked and been briskly turned down by Rosemary.

Alan would have said yes, remembering the secret meetings with Daphne in her father's car and the drive up here. The forest had been dark, car headlights going out one by one.

There were no cars here now. He remembered exactly where Daphne had parked hers, tucking it in under overhanging branches. *Our bed is green. . . .* She was afraid of nothing, or if she was, she didn't show it; he, believing stories of boys and girls being arrested and had up in court for indecent behaviour in a public place, was always fearful. But he was young and his nervousness wasn't enough to impede him when he was in the back with Daphne. He was passionate and greedy and so was she, even when the moon came out from behind clouds and he thought the light was from a policeman's torch. There had been maybe a dozen occasions. Unlike other users of Baldwin's Hill, who were afraid of pregnancy or, in the case of the girls, of not being virgins when they married, he and Daphne went "all the way," as the phrase had it. She didn't get pregnant, though he had done nothing to prevent it.

He wrote to her and she wrote to him, but they were a long way apart, and though her family still lived in Loughton, three months is a long time when you're only twenty. Their letters ceased, though once, two years later, he had a Christmas card from her. Now, standing on the small treeless expanse and looking across the darkening woodland, he wondered what would have happened if he had sent her a card back. But by this time he was going out with Rosemary, his "childhood sweetheart," as his mother embarrassingly called her, and there was no back of a car on Baldwin's Hill for them, for Rosemary was saving herself for marriage.

He turned away and began to make his way back down Stony Path and Harwater Drive. Tiredness hit him as he crossed Church Hill. For an old man he had walked a lot that day, several miles. He was in his seventies. What had he been doing, mooning back to a long-lost youth and a woman who had had three husbands? When he got home, he would get the scissors and cut up the evidence the way you did with an out-of-date credit card and drop the pieces in the bin. Episode Daphne over, he thought. As he unlocked his front door, he heard the soft buzz of the sewing machine and felt a quite unwarranted anger rising in his throat like bile. But he opened the sewing-room door to tell Rosemary he was back.

"All right," she said, getting up, "I'll get supper."

Daphne's card was still in his pocket. Of course it was. Rosemary was the soul of honour, the last woman to forage through his clothes in search of incriminating evidence. What was happening to him that he was thinking of the possibility of deceiving his wife? But he was deceiving her already. That visit to Baldwin's Hill with its attendant reminiscing was itself deceiving her. His thoughts now were a kind of deceit. Suddenly they deflected to the excavation he and Rosemary had gone to look at and to the hands found there. A man and a woman. Had they been lovers, placed there in their grave, by a vengeful husband or, come to that, a vengeful wife? So long ago, perhaps so long that the reason for their burial would never be known.

He was still holding Daphne's card. Instead of cutting it into pieces or otherwise disposing of it, he put it back in his pocket.

5

WHEN JO DIED some few months before, Lewis Newman had received letters of condolence from people he had known during the various phases of his long life—one fellow medical student whose name he couldn't even remember, neighbours from the Birmingham days, those of his friends who were still alive, and his partner in the practice where he had last worked. A letter also came from someone he had been at school with—primary school, as they called it these days. Most of these people, apart from the friends, had read the announcement of Jo's death in the *Times*. That was what such announcements were for, Lewis supposed, and now he wondered why he had agreed to his cousin's ("beloved wife of") insistence that it should be put there.

He replied to these letters, as was polite. In Jo's lifetime, she had replied, and writing to one of the Birmingham people, he thought to himself that this was the first of such missives he had ever written. He saved answering the school friend's letter till last because it was the most interesting. From Stanley Batchelor, it was scarcely a letter of condolence at all. True, Batchelor did say he was sorry to hear of Jo's death, but the tone, Lewis thought, was rather that a man who had looked after a woman "through years of illness" must to some extent be relieved by her demise. This was so much Lewis's own sentiment—something he could never dream of revealing to anyone—that it endeared Stanley Batchelor to him.

The Batchelors. How memories of the family came back to him now across seven decades. His own family had lived in Brook Road and the Batchelors in Tycehurst Hill. Stanley had a dog, called Nipper. Amazing to remember that. One of Stanley's brothers, the youngest perhaps, was called Norman, and he used to boast about being born on the kitchen table. The address on the letter was Theydon Bois. So he hadn't moved far from Loughton or, if he had, had come back again. There was an email address as well. Most people of their age didn't send emails, hardly knew what an email was. The last line of the letter, before the bit about *deepest sympathy,* read, *If you haven't thought about this "neck of the woods" for years, the newspaper stories about Warlock will have brought it back to you. An extraordinary business. It would be good to meet sometime if you feel like it.*

Death, thought Lewis, brought old friends, long separated, back together. He had liked Stanley Batchelor very much when they were children. Would he like him now? Like or not, he was the very person with whom to discuss, if not the Warlock business, the place they called something strange—what was it?—yes, the qanats. He couldn't remember why. That and something else, which, though it had never troubled him, never come near to making him unhappy, had been on the edge of his consciousness ever since he was not much older than the age he had been when he and Stanley Batchelor had been friends. It had bothered his mother. She and Uncle James—no one ever called him Jim—had been close all their lives, though she was seven years older than he. Perhaps because she was seven years older and, as was common in the twenties, had had to look after him when she was a big child and he four years old.

Lewis had often thought about Uncle James.

When Lewis was first married, he had told Jo about him and his curious disappearance.

"He got killed in the war, didn't he?"

"For that to have happened he would have to have joined up, and it seems he didn't."

"It doesn't much matter now," said Jo.

"It matters to me and to Mum. He just disappeared."

"I read somewhere that lots of people did. They were in houses that got bombed. Or they were drafted to work in mines and got buried."

He said no more. He knew it hadn't been like that. Uncle James had been staying with them in Brook Road, and while he was there, he seemed to join the army. Up till then he'd been unfit on account of having some minor thing the matter with him, a badly fallen arch on his left foot. On a second try they took him. He was going to go home to London, where he lived with an aunt and uncle, but he never got there. His uncle tried to trace him. James hadn't told him where he would be stationed, that wouldn't have been allowed, but he did have the names of two men he would be starting his training with and their addresses. Both of them replied. They had never heard of Private James Rayment. The army had never heard of him, though he'd said he had joined up. Efforts to find him had failed. He had disappeared.

That was sixty years and more ago, and Uncle James had never been heard of since. As Jo said, people disappeared in wartime. It was a good time to change your identity or vanish or hide from authority. In those days you had an identity card and you had a ration book, but that was all. No bus passes, no credit cards, no mobile phones, and since you never drove, no driving licence, probably no bank account. You were free. Free to hide, free to be someone else, free to disappear. Lewis's family also did all they could to find Uncle James, but they failed. After a time his disappearance mattered less, receded into a sort of semi-oblivion. It wasn't as if he had died, but rather as if he had gone a long way off, perhaps to live on some distant continent where no one ever went. Perhaps he had. People did rarely go to those places, but sending airmail letters was troublesome and the cost of phoning was prohibitive. Uncle James might have tried to phone but failed to get through, as often happened.

Lewis's mother clung to a belief that he would one day turn up out of the blue and present himself on her doorstep. James had often stayed with them in Brook Road, and Gwen Newman, looking back over the past couple of years, now remembered that while there her brother had gone out a lot in the evenings. Not every evening but often, and she had had a feeling that he only stayed in with her and her husband and Lewis because it was expected of him as a guest. When James couldn't be found, she remarked on this behaviour and what she said had stayed with Lewis all these years.

"I should have asked him where he was going, but I couldn't bring myself to do that. After all, he was a grown man. He used to get back very late, or I suppose he did. I was always asleep."

"Now you mention it," said Lewis's father. "I heard him come in after midnight once or twice."

"I did ask him once if he'd had a nice evening, but he only said, 'Lovely, thanks,' and didn't tell me any more."

"I sometimes wondered why he wanted to stay with us. It must have been rather dull with nothing to do in the evenings."

"He had something to do," said Gwen. "A girlfriend. A woman. He's gone off with her and maybe she was married. That's why he never told us."

THEYDON BOIS WAS one of those suburbs in Surrey or Essex or Hertfordshire on the edge of London. The tube went to Theydon. It was desirable commuter land with shops, big and small houses, a village green, and it was in Epping Forest. Unfortunately, you could hear the distant roar of the motorway, the M25, not yet built when Stanley first lived there in the sixties. Thinking themselves clever and polyglot, visitors pronounced its name Theydon *Bwah*, but *Boys* was correct.

Stanley and George, Batchelor Brothers, had built several of the houses in Theydon, and Stanley and Helen lived in one of the larger detached ones. Stanley had bought it when his children left home, his first wife died, and he married a woman twenty years younger than himself. When he had written back to Lewis Newman and invited him to lunch, Stanley had supposed he would drive, but Lewis, who had given up his car six months before Jo's death, chose the tube. Ealing was at one end of the Central Line and Theydon at the other, so he could sit in the train for an hour or more reading one of his favourite and frequently reread books, *The Count of Monte Cristo.*

Stanley met him at the station with Spot on the lead. Much to Spot's dismay, they sat down on a seat outside the Bull because Lewis wasn't a great walker.

"Quite like being in the countryside," he said.

"We *are* in the countryside."

This was answered by a half smile from Lewis and a shrug from his arthritic shoulders. "My brother George is coming to lunch," said Stanley. "He's looking forward to seeing you again."

George was the only one of the Batchelors Lewis hadn't liked. Too bossy and go-ahead.

"He's recovering from a hip replacement."

"It comes to us all," said Lewis the GP, trying to be generous.

"Not to me, I trust. I try to keep all that sort of thing at bay by regular walks with Spot."

George had already arrived and was seated in an armchair, his leg up and his stick beside him. His big, black Audi, driven by Maureen, was on Stanley's garage drive, and she in what Stanley called "the lounge," drinking sherry with a woman in her fifties with silvery-blond hair, wearing dark green leather trousers and a red satin blouse.

"We built this house, you know," said George when Helen had handed sherry to Lewis.

"And you built Warlock," said Lewis. "You didn't put those hands in the foundations, I hope?"

No one commented on that. Lewis expected someone to say how sorry he or she was to hear of Jo's death, but no one did. Lewis didn't mind, he never knew what to say in response to condolence, but he thought it strange. Helen said lunch would soon be ready. Stanley let the dog out into the garden, and George, opening a huge photograph album, showed Lewis the sole picture of the qanats that existed. The entrance to the tunnels was crammed with grinning children, none of whom Lewis could recognise. George began talking about going there, when they found the place and where it was.

"I reckon I was the first of us to go in there."

"It was quite brave," Stanley said. "The whole thing might have collapsed, the roof fallen in."

"Quell," said George, "was more interested in any adults who might have gone in there, people we'd seen."

"Who's Quell?"

"Policeman. He came to George's and we all went over and talked to him. Well, all—those we could find. Those who are still alive. There was me, Norman, George, and Michael Winwood, Alan Norris and that woman Rosemary he married—oh, and Daphne Jones. Daphne Furness as she is now."

There was a silence, brought about as so often by the utterance of that name. Only Lewis repeated it. "Oh yes, Daphne Jones . . . This cop wanted to know about adults in there? What, brought along by one of us?"

"I suppose so," said Stanley. "Even if we had, he or she would be dead by now." Before he could say more, Helen came back to tell them lunch was ready.

It was a good lunch, much appreciated by Lewis, along with the nicely laid table, the silver and glass and the pink tulips in a Royal Copenhagen vase. Such beautifully prepared food and carefully chosen wine hadn't come his way since Jo fell ill all those years ago. It softened his attitude to the Batchelors without making him wish to disclose who he thought that adult visitor to the tunnels might have been. Yet, he thought, as he increasingly did these days, at his age he hadn't, what he had not long ago taken for granted, an indefinite future. He was one of the oldest of the tunnel occupants and would not, as he put it wryly to himself, eating his crème brûlée with gusto, see seventy-five again. Arthritis wouldn't kill him but his dodgy heart might.

This reverie was interrupted by Helen's offering him a "penny for your thoughts." He responded by asking with a reflective smile if anyone under thirty would understand what that meant. His remark went down badly with Helen, who probably supposed that she was generally taken for coming within that age range herself. Maureen failed to improve matters by catching Lewis's eye and giving him a look that was just not a wink.

"It's my belief," she said as they left the table, "that we shan't hear much more of those hands. Sorry, but I didn't want to mention it while we were eating. The police must know by now that they're never going to find who they belonged to, and anyway, who really cares?"

Nobody replied to that. They all sat down, and George remarked that his leg was giving him "gip." When Maureen was ready?

"I'll just have my coffee now Helen's gone to all the trouble to make it."

Lewis passed the rest of his time in Theydon Bois finding out from Stanley how and where to get in touch with Detective Inspector Colin Quell and, when George and Maureen left, said he must go too. It was a long way to the other end of the Central Line. He thanked Helen profusely for his lunch, but he could tell he had offended her with his comment about the penny for his thoughts. Unexpectedly, Stanley said he would come with him to the station. Spot would enjoy another walk.

"Why do you call him Spot when he's black all over?" Lewis asked.

"I asked my grandson to name him and he's only six. Spot was the only dog's name he knew. I couldn't have any more Nippers."

"Why didn't anyone ask me to this meeting you had with the policeman?"

"Don't ask me," said Stanley. "Didn't know how to get hold of you, I reckon."

Lewis said no more. Instead he contributed the few doggy tales he could remember, and Stanley rejoined with anecdotes of past canines he had owned. The station was soon reached, and Stanley, to Lewis's relief, departed, saying Spot would get fractious if expected to hang about. Lewis had been longing for the chance to be alone and think about George's remark about adults going into the tunnels. It was a fine mild afternoon and sitting on the seat on Theydon Bois station platform no hardship in the sunshine. Even if it took half an hour before the train came, he had plenty to think about.

Whether any of them or any of the others had ever taken an adult into the tunnels, he didn't know, though he thought not. The unwritten law was not to involve grown-ups. Human beings make laws even when they are only ten or eleven years old and take no notice of them when they feel like it. Whatever others had done, he had flouted that rule. He hadn't meant to, or, rather, he hadn't wanted to, but Uncle James had kept on at him about it.

Sitting on the seat in this semirural place, the effort of remembering threatened to send him to sleep. He was old and it was true what they said, that the old remember events of their childhood better than what had happened this morning. He rested his head back against the seat and sleep came. A snore that was more like a noisy snort woke him, and he realised that the woman who had come to sit next to him must have heard it and perhaps been amused. Age also brings something advantageous: old people no longer feel much embarrassment. There has ceased to be any point in it. It's a waste of time, and time is valuable now. What had he been thinking about before he fell asleep? He had forgotten and the train was arriving.

He had also forgotten where he had got to in *The Count of Monte Cristo*, but it didn't much matter as he had read it so many times before and a favourite point in the adventure was soon turned to. By this time he had also forgotten all about getting in touch with Detective Inspector Quell.

HE WOKE UP in the night and knew at once he wouldn't get to sleep again. Four o'clock was the witching hour. There was no hope at four. He could get up and walk about the house, he could make a cup of tea, drink whisky (a fatal choice, this), stay in bed and read some more, put on the radio. If one of those remedies worked and sleep came back until, say, six, he'd think himself lucky and feel quite cheerful. But it seldom did, so he did nothing and thought about Uncle James instead. It was Lewis's fault for telling his uncle something he would never have told his parents, that he went these summer evenings to a secret place to meet a crowd of friends and play all sorts of games. It must have been the end of July or early August. Whether it was after the end of term or before that he couldn't remember, and again he cursed himself for forgetting so much.

Uncle James was staying with them in Brook Road. It was the time his mother noticed how James was often out in the evenings. Lewis saw it too but it meant nothing to him. He was a child to whom the ways of grown-ups were necessarily strange. Lying awake, Lewis looked back across his long life, from twelve years old through his teens and Bancroft's School, Cambridge, and medical school, at last after general-practitioner training, a place in a GP partnership in Ealing. Meeting and falling in love with Alison, the whole thing coming to grief until he settled into marriage with Jo. All the way along the road he must have learned how to live or he should have done, acquiring experience and sophistication. If he had talked to Uncle James then, when Lewis was forty, he would have known where his uncle went and why he wanted to see the qanats, but not when he was twelve. Not in 1944, when, in spite of the war and the bombs and parents' fear for them, middle-class children living in Loughton were naïve and innocent.

Uncle James nagged him about the tunnels. Lewis wouldn't have used that word then, it wasn't respectful, but that is what they were. At last he said yes, but not in the evening. It would have to be a Sunday morning. No one went there on a Sunday, or few did. The English middle class kept the Sabbath holy. All the shops were shut and all the churches were open. Lewis's family went to church only on Easter or Christmas Eve or for weddings and funerals, but he had been sent to Sunday school when he was younger and the prevailing view, held even by non-churchgoing people, was that you respected Sunday, kept your children from playing in the street, and passed a quiet day at home after a heavy lunch. Knowing this as a fact of life, Lewis knew that the tunnels would likely be empty even though it was a fine sunny day.

A walk across the fields, especially with a popular relative, was not only permitted, it was encouraged. He and Uncle James set off up Tycehurst Hill and turned into Shelley Grove, a still unfinished road where further building had been stopped by the war, and where Alan Norris's family lived in one of the few houses. The path across the fields went past the hollow oak, where picnicking children sat in the room-size space between spreading branches and ate bread and margarine and fish-paste sandwiches. No children this Sunday morning, though. Nearby, dividing field from field, stood a great screen of elms, destined to be felled in a few years' time to make room for house-building, instead of waiting for Dutch elm disease to take them. They took the field path that led up the slope to the Hill, and Lewis, remembering a recent visit to Loughton cinema, wished he could do what someone had done to a captive in the film and blindfold Uncle James so that he couldn't tell where they were or see the entrance to the qanats. But he was interested in seeing where they were and paused only for a moment before ducking his head and walking down the steps on the drought-baked clay and under the tarpaulin roof.

Lewis was no sooner inside than he knew—he hardly understood how—that they were not alone. Several habitual "members," as George Batchelor had named them, were already there. Listening,

Lewis heard girls' voices, though not what they said, and then Uncle James, careless of being overheard, stood surveying the clay walls, the wooden boxes and the bricks that littered the place, and let out a loud peal of laughter.

"I don't think so," he said, and Lewis understood exactly what he meant, he didn't have to ask. The tunnels weren't suitable for the plan he had in mind. Whatever use he had hoped for, they wouldn't do. They were too dirty, too *shabby,* to use a favourite word of Lewis's mother's. He knew that but not what that use might have been.

"Come on then," he had said. "Let's go back."

But Uncle James had gone on ahead in the direction of the girls' voices, and the two of them came into a big space where several candles were lit, and from the savoury smell, potatoes were baking in the old water tank. Lewis knew the potatoes came from Bill Johnson's father, who grew them on his allotment in Stony Path. They would have been wrapped in clay and dropped in among the red-hot embers. Three girls were poking at them with sticks to test if they were ready. Now, looking back over all those years, Lewis tried to remember who the third one was, having no difficulty in recalling Rosemary Wharton and, of course, Daphne Jones, she of the height, as tall as any of the boys and with that cloak of long, dark hair. But who had the third one been? He would never know now. The nameless one turned to stare at Uncle James, but Daphne didn't turn. Rosemary bent to try to fish something out of the tank and cried out as she burnt her hand. It was only a tiny scorch, the faintest touch of one of those clay-encased potatoes, but Rosemary began whimpering and Uncle James stepped forward to help if he could. Was she all right? Was there anything he could do?

"She'll live," said Daphne, and then she did turn round, fixing him with all the brilliance of her large, dark brown eyes and compelling admiration for the perfect arcs of her black eyebrows. Did he remember that? he thought at four thirty in the morning. Or did it come later when, attending his mother's funeral, he had walked past her outside St. Mary's Church and she, without recognising him, had taken the arm of the man she was with and walked on.

Uncle James hadn't pressed his offer of help, it obviously wasn't needed, and he and Lewis had gone back the way they had come. They crossed the fields and were halfway down Shelley Grove when Uncle James said, evidently forgetting that his companion was twelve and not twenty-five, "She'll make havoc among the men when she's a bit older."

Lewis didn't know the meaning of *havoc* so said nothing, but he looked the word up in the dictionary when he got home and found it meant chaos, destruction, and devastation. The last thing he saw before he went back to sleep was the sight of one of their neighbours coming down Brook Path from St. Mary's Church with a prayer book in her hand. Perhaps it was that prayer book or the woman's disapproving glance that sent him back to sleep at last.

6

THE NORRISES' FLAT in the block on Traps Hill, though large and with spacious rooms, was not suitable for small children. The windows in the lounge (Alan hated this name for the drawing-room) almost filled one wall and gave onto a balcony. In fine weather these windows were open and there was no danger to adults; the railing on the balcony was an absolute safeguard against falling to the stone-paved terrace below. Not so for small children, who could have slipped through the spaces between the railings or dived underneath them. Fenella, Freya's sister, had a son aged five and a daughter aged nearly three, and when with Fenella's husband, Giles, they all came to visit on a Sunday afternoon, no matter how warm it was and how strongly the sun was shining, the windows had to remain closed.

Only quite recently had Alan resented this. Until a few weeks ago he had gone along with the theory, widely believed, that any hardship grand-parents must endure was not a hardship at all but a pleasure, a treat, a marvellous dispensation of providence for which they should be the objects of envy. And this applied not only to grand-parents—they had after all been through it twenty-five years before—but to the great-grandparents they now were. At their age they deserved a bit of peace on Sundays, not to be besieged by rampaging infants who were being brought up to do exactly as they liked, leaping from one piece of furniture to the next, rolling themselves up in the rugs, hammering on the windows as if this would make them open, demanding Coca-Cola, orange juice, biscuits, and chocolate, which their obedient, smiling great-grandmother ran to fetch for them, and climbing on their great-grandfather's knee to cover up his book or page of his newspaper with sticky fingers. When he mildly expressed this view to Rosemary, adding that having the children here ought to be worth it because it was so nice when it stopped, she reproached him for ingratitude. In her opinion—for she had never forgotten his remarks about their dull life—these kind visits of Fenella and her children were surely enough to dispel any thoughts of dullness. If they were lucky enough to live a few more years, Freya would herself have a young family, and she also would bring them to see their great-grandparents, perhaps on Saturdays.

Freya and her coming wedding was the current most popular topic of conversation in the Norris family, a subject that barely interested Alan. From a small gathering in what he thought of as a glorified pub, it had turned into a party of two hundred people in a riverside hotel. All the more reason, he had said, for Rosemary to buy herself a dress, something she refused to do on the grounds of cost when she could make just as attractive a garment herself. Alan disagreed but he could hardly say so, only continue to press a large sum of money on her, an offer which went against the grain with him, for he was the feminist of the two of them, always disliking the notion of a husband and breadwinner's bestowing cash gifts on his wife instead of the couple's sharing what he saw as their joint resources. It mattered little as it happened, for Rosemary insisted on making this complicated suit from a pattern which he could see, but never say, was beyond her capacity.

He realised then, insofar as he as a man was capable of doing so, that the clothes she had been making ever since they were married had never been very successful. Lapels were uneven, hems longer at the front than the back, necklines, buttonholes, and cuffs not quite symmetrical. The clothes she made were praised because she had made them and not because they looked good. This copper-coloured silk suit would be added to their number but would be worse than usual; Alan admitted to himself that Rosemary, who had never had training in dressmaking, was even less good at it than she had once been because she was getting older. Her fingers were less dextrous and she needed new glasses. Throughout the years when she had made her own clothes, they had seldom attended big parties or important functions. Now they would. This one was very big, and he imagined himself as accompanying Rosemary, as her husband, in a state he seldom experienced. He would be embarrassed. He made the mistake of having a last and more frank and forceful go at persuading her to buy a dress.

"Are you saying I've lost my skill?" she said in response to his telling her that, she having laboured over the neckline of the jacket for half the night, he was afraid it was still crooked.

"Just look in the mirror. You'll see it's not quite right."

"I can see you're determined to make me dress in stereotyped clothes instead of something original."

They argued a little more and then he gave up. He would have to bear that suit and the pitying looks, possibly the thoughts (though these would not be expressed) of guests who might suppose he was too mean to dress his wife attractively. Thus he was falling into the trap he so dreaded of sexism and even misogyny. In the afternoon they went out for one of their long walks, but had to turn back on Baldwin's Hill instead of continuing along one of the forest paths. Rosemary was too tired after staying awake at the sewing machine until past one.

"And after all that effort you don't even want me to wear the thing."

He said nothing. He was looking at the four parked cars on the slope above the green hill that descended past Baldwin's Pond to Blackweir. The occupants of those cars, unlike himself and Daphne, were all behaving in a decorous manner, smoking, one of them looking through binoculars at the spire of High Beech Church, protruding from the dark green woods, another asleep. Standing a little way apart from Rosemary, he thought of Daphne, as he now did every day: Daphne in her father's car, Daphne in his arms, and Daphne in the dark slipping out of those of her clothes that must be shed. Desire drove out fear.

He was wearing the jacket with her card in the right-hand pocket. He shouldn't be carrying it with him. He should leave it at home in a safe place. Rosemary came up to him and took his arm, necessarily his left arm, while his right hand felt Daphne's card. It seemed to him a betrayal, and loosening his fingers, he withdrew his empty hand from his pocket. They walked home.

"I think I'll have a lie-down."

"I'll bring you a cup of tea," said Alan.

Here was another trap he was falling into, that of the spouse who thinks to compensate for his unfaithfulness by performing small selfless services for the betrayed one. How did he know so much about infidelity when he had never committed it? He went into the kitchen and made the tea, a cup for him and a cup for her. She was fully clothed but covered by the duvet, with the almost finished copper-coloured suit lying over the end of the bed. Why? He didn't ask. He went back to the kitchen and laid Daphne's card on the table: an address, an email address, a mobile number, a landline.

Hamilton Terrace was where she lived. In a newspaper he had recently read a piece about the most desirable places in London to live, and the journalist had mentioned Hamilton Terrace as the nicest street. He had never been there but he tried to imagine what the houses looked like. Very different from Loughton, no doubt, and then he saw that Loughton was cited as among the most attractive of the outer suburbs. He hadn't a mobile phone, had never felt the need for one, but if he possessed such a thing, he could make calls from anywhere, he could make, he thought shamefacedly, secret calls. He wouldn't phone Daphne, but tomorrow he would go out and find a shop where they sold such things and buy himself a mobile phone. Meanwhile, he put the card back in his pocket.

THE DNA EXTRACTED from the hands found underneath Warlock was all very well, thought Colin Quell, reading what the pathologist had to say. Most of it was beyond the understanding of even the most intelligent, and Quell considered himself highly intelligent. But he couldn't see the use of it when there was nothing to compare it with. Sixty or seventy years ago that area of Loughton might well have abounded with people whose DNA matched or came close to matching that of the hands. But they were all gone now, all dead. He might, he thought, ask those people called Batchelor to give samples of DNA, ask that exotic-looking woman Daphne Furness, but that would only be of use if one of the hands might conceivably have belonged to a relative of theirs.

IT WAS A SURPRISE to get a phone call from Daphne. She had said she would phone, but Michael doubted that she really meant it, people didn't. Would he come for a drink, just him, no one else? Or on second thoughts, come for supper, she said. She remembered where he lived and said he should take the 189, it stopped just round the corner from her.

Her house was even more unexpected. The drawing-room, as her husband Martin had called it, was all his own work, everything in it chosen by him with care and taste.

"It reminds me of my aunt Zoe's house." He found himself talking about Zoe, how good she had been to him and now she was so old, ninety-six, he dreaded her dying.

"Not many people dread the death of someone so old."

"I don't want to talk about how awful my parents were, though they were. My father was worse than my mother; at least she wasn't violent. Zoe was loving and kind from the moment I went to live with her. D'you know, I couldn't believe at first she wasn't joking or playing some sort of game."

"Do you often see her?"

"She still lives in Lewes. In a cottage but rather a big one. I go down about once a month and it's not a chore, I think we both enjoy it."

"I'll fetch us a drink," said Daphne. "Sauvignon all right?"

When she came back, he was standing by one of the bookcases, reading all the titles. She thought how thin and bony he looked. *Frail* was the word, but not *ill,* his face creased with wrinkles but his hands long and shapely. He took the wine and tasted it with evident pleasure. "May I tell you something?"

"Of course. Whatever it is, are you sure? Don't tell me anything you may regret when you think about it in the long watches of the night."

"I won't regret it."

He told her about keeping Vivien's room the way it was when she died. "I go and sit there sometimes and I talk to her. This room reminds me of it because it's beautiful in the same sort of way. Do you think it wrong of me—self-indulgent, sentimental even?"

"Not if it comforts you."

"I don't know if it does. I don't know if anything would. But I have a sort of feeling that I'd feel terrible if I got rid of it—I mean, turned it into a spare room or something. I'd feel bereft. If one of my children came to stay. I've got two other spare rooms but would I have to offer that room to them?"

"Do they ever come?"

"No. Well, they do. They come for flying visits from abroad—flying in two senses—but they never stay. I feel I ought to mind but I don't really, not while I know they're happy."

"I never wanted children. People say you regret it if you don't have them but I can't say I do. Shall we go and eat?"

She had cooked black-olive pasta with a salad of avocado and artichokes, followed by crème caramel. The cheese was Shropshire Blue, which she said she was hooked on, so she hoped he liked it. He did and took red wine with it. The dining-room had orange walls and black furniture. He wondered if she lived alone or sometimes alone or had someone that a few years ago people would have called a "significant other" but no longer did. She played some Mozart that he had heard before but not for years. That kind of music brought tears to the eyes, and although he loved it, he was glad it didn't last long. He left just after nine, saying he went to bed early and would catch the bus round the corner in Abbey Road.

"I write poetry about buses," he said. "Well, doggerel really. 'A wonderful bus is the one-eight-nine, A special favourite of mine, It goes straight down from my abode, To lovely leafy Abbey Road.' There's more but I won't inflict it on you."

She laughed, kissed him lightly on the cheek, and watched him go until he turned the corner. It was twenty past nine. She was putting the plates and cutlery in the dishwasher when the phone rang. It was one of those calls when you know who it is. She knew. Of course she couldn't have done so, it wasn't the kind of phone that tells you a name, but she knew, though not quite so well as to dare say, "Hallo, Alan."

He didn't introduce himself, he didn't need to. "I'm on the kind of phone that you can carry about but it's not a mobile, so you couldn't know who it was."

"But I could. I did."

"Ah. I'm out on the balcony with a spotty cat."

"You took your time about calling me."

"I know. I was afraid. I must see you. Soon. Friday?"

"Of course. I must see you too. In the afternoon whenever you can."

SPOT SMELT THE smoke as he and Stanley turned the corner. Spot sat down on the pavement and howled. The fire appeared to be in one of the houses in Farm Mead, for by the look of it from the road, smoke was pouring out of the back windows and certainly from the front. A woman Stanley knew by sight came running out of the open front door with a frying pan in her hand. By this time he had called 999 for the fire brigade, as he still called it.

Leaving Spot up the road, tied on a long lead to a pavement tree, Stanley asked the woman how it had happened. She put the frying pan down in a flowerbed.

"I was frying chips," she said, half-sobbing. "I love chips."

You could see that by the shape of her, thought Stanley. "Your smoke alarm didn't go off?"

"I'd taken it out. The noise made me jump every time it went off."

There was nothing to say except reproach, but anything that he might have said was cut off by the howling of sirens from the help that arrived. Firemen—they probably weren't called that anymore—leapt out of their vehicles and rushed up the path with hoses and some sort of fire-extinguishing substance. The woman who loved chips tried to follow them but was sent back again, by which time Stanley had untied the dog and, because Spot refused to pass the house, set off in the opposite direction to take a roundabout route home.

It was only the second fire Stanley had ever seen. During the war when he was a child, Loughton had been a surprisingly quiet place, though only about twelve miles outside central London. The East End had taken it badly, but the East End was nearer than that. He had seen pictures of the Blitz and films, though there was of course no available television. Children, such as Stanley and his brothers and sister, collected the chunks of twisted metal that were shrapnel from antiaircraft shells, they heard distant bombs falling and heard the big guns boom, enough to drive them all crowding into the air-raid shelter, but there was no fire as there appeared to be no incendiary bombs nearby. The fire he saw, the first fire as against this chip-pan one, was big; a conflagration, his father called it when they told him about it.

It was December and it must have been 1944, for Stanley remembered it was the day after his birthday. He and George were walking home from

Roding Road School, the secondary modern, where George had been a year and he had just started. Usually, they'd have walked home up Tycehurst Hill, but this time they took the Hill because George said, let's see what's happened to the qanats. It was after Mr. Winwood had turned them all out but not long after—weeks or months, he couldn't remember. They saw the smoke rising up into the air behind the house called Anderby, the Winwoods' house. It was coming from the back garden and they stood there staring.

"Michael's not there," Stanley remembered George saying. "Mr. Winwood sent him away to his auntie," and Stanley had said, "He's always sending people away."

The fire took a sudden violent turn and flames came, roaring through the gap between Anderby and the Joneses' fence. It had caught the shed that adjoined the fence and the summerhouse beyond, when the fire engines charged up the Hill, bawling with a far more strident howl than these two had made so many years later for the little frying-pan fire. As the men got out with their hoses and ran up the path, Mr. Winwood had come out and led them round the side of the house, no doubt the quickest way. But he came back, waving his arms about and shouting to Stanley and George. "Get off home, the pair of you. What the hell d'you think you're doing gawping there?"

People didn't swear at children then, and *hell* was swearing. They had gone, not lingering long enough to see what had become of the tunnels, not knowing till years later when George acquired the land. Stanley had never discovered how the Anderby fire started, and he had never asked George about it when George might have known the answer. Where had everyone else been? Daphne and her mother and her brother? Perhaps Daphne still remembered.

Stanley apologised for being late home. It was all Spot's fault, refusing to pass a house in Farm Mead where there had been a fire.

"I called the fire brigade."

"My hero," said Helen. "And it's fire *service*. Your dinner's all ready."

He sometimes thought he would have married her even if she hadn't been able to cook, but the cooking helped. This evening it was grilled calamari, coq au vin, and Eton mess or fresh fruit salad if he chose. He chose the Eton mess, pulling in his once-flat belly.

"What do they call fire engines these days, sweetheart?"

"Fire engines," said Helen.

7

DAPHNE DID REMEMBER the fire at Anderby. She remembered the smell before the fire started. The smell is familiar to everyone now, in the world they live in, but not then. Who possessed cars? Even her father, who was (as he put it himself) "quite well-off," had no car until several years later. Petrol was quite hard to get. She had smelt it when her uncle came by car, carried a tank of the stuff, and poured it into the tank. Now she smelt it again. She opened the kitchen window. Outside, the smell was much stronger.

It was twenty-five to four. She had just got home from school, a quick walk up the Hill from Loughton High School for Girls, which was at the bottom of Alderton Hill. On the way up she said hallo to Mrs. Moss, who was Mr. Winwood's char. Everyone called her Clara, but Daphne's mother had told her that at her age it would be polite to call her Mrs. and refer to her as the cleaning lady. In the kitchen a note had been left for Daphne to say her mother had gone to see Granny in Brooklyn Avenue and she'd be back before four. Egg sandwiches were in the fridge.

Fridges were quite rare, Daphne knew. Most people didn't have them. As for egg sandwiches, whatever else was hard to come by in those war years, chickens were always clucking about up here, and eggs, though supposed to be rationed, were plentiful. She took a sandwich outside and saw the flames. Standing on the stone-built terrace, she could see over the fence and the hedge and see the Winwoods' garden a mass of glowing red, crimson where the fire was, and flames shooting up everywhere, now licking the shed on the other side of their fence, threatening the Anderby summerhouse.

She was a bit near the fence for comfort. She ought to phone someone—but whom? Would they expect her to do it, and how would she do it? Just as she thought that she must try and had gone back to the phone, she heard the fire engines arrive. Running into the living-room, throwing open the front window, she saw the fire engines and George and Stanley Batchelor outside. Then Mr. Winwood came out of his house, gesticulating and shouting. For once he didn't see her and wave. Daphne retreated into the back garden. She could feel the heat coming from the glowing fire; it was like being right in front of a powerful electric heater. She found a wheelbarrow on the opposite side of the lawn that their gardener had left on the path, stood on it, and gazed into the glare. The firemen were training their hoses on it now, trying to save the summerhouse; it was too late for the shed and for the ash tree. Its branches had caught and what autumn leaves remained, incandescent and glittering. The flames had crept up its trunk, then burst into a rush of fire, scattering sparks and weaving among the branches of the poor ash tree.

Daphne was just saying aloud, "Oh, the poor tree," when her mother arrived, running across the lawn.

"My darling, are you all right? What on earth happened?"

"I don't know." She wasn't going to mention the petrol. It was just one of the many things she didn't mention to her parents. She didn't want to get anyone in trouble. It was safer for everyone to keep silent on so many things. "It started just after I got back from school. I thought I ought to call the firemen but someone else did."

She had never been frightened or even alarmed. At least, not once the fire engines arrived. What became of Mr. Winwood for the rest of the day she didn't know and didn't ask. Her parents didn't like him, so why speak of him to them? She never mentioned him, knowing of their dislike. Best to be silent on all sorts of awkward subjects. She stood on the wheelbarrow again at dusk just before it got too dark to see. The shed had gone, the summerhouse was charred black on its garden side, the fire was dead, just cinders and ashes. She seemed to remember from earlier short and long whitish sticks and thinner white sticks and something like a long, curved rod with ridges all along its length. By the evening all this had gone, coated with ash. In the morning Mr. Winwood was out there with a torch and a rake—she saw him from her bedroom window—levelling everything and leaving just a round, pale gray patch on the lawn. By the time he had finished it had begun to rain and soon it was pouring.

It was so long ago, she thought as she waited for Alan, and no doubt some of it she had imagined and some of it she had forgotten. Perhaps she would tell him what she remembered and perhaps not. Maybe tell him the whole story when the time was right. Come in the afternoon, she had said to him, and that could be anytime between two and five. It gave him an awful lot of leeway. There was a bit of Browning she remembered, the only bit of Browning she knew except that stuff about *O, to be in England* that everyone knew. *I shall see him in three days, and just one night, but nights are short, then two long hours, and that is morn.*

WHATEVER BECOMES OF US, Alan thought, walking along the familiar roads to Loughton station, whatever becomes of Daphne and me, let us never be the elderly couple sitting in our wheelchairs, hand in hand, in front of the telly. Anything but that. The last thing Rosemary had said as he was leaving was to bid him tell Robert Flynn that he and Isabel must come to them for lunch and to give Alan some possible dates. He could forget that, she wouldn't be surprised if he did. She had lately taken to quoting the Tammy Wynette song and saying he was just a man. The sewing machine had its cover on today, and Rosemary, awaiting the arrival of Freya and Freya's mother, their daughter Judith, was doing the hand-stitching, tacking up a hem she had already pinned in place. Alan had looked up Hamilton Terrace on the London map for the third or fourth time. By now he knew exactly where it was, could have found Daphne's house blindfolded, after dark, and in a power cut.

Like a teenage boy, he didn't know what he would say to her when she opened the door to him. Yet he had thought he could say anything to her. Now as he got out of the train and made his way along the canal to the bridge and Maida Vale, he felt himself struck dumb, like poor Papageno with a padlock on his mouth. Now he was only a couple of hundred yards away, he wanted the distance to be longer, and crossing the street, he sat down on a seat to use up five minutes, breathing deeply before he approached her front door.

"WHERE'S GRANDDAD?"

Rosemary said he had "gone up to town" to see a friend, a Mr. Flynn. "Oh, Ma," said Judith, "not 'up to town.' You sound like Jane Austen. You'll be saying 'five-and-twenty past' next."

"I do say five-and-twenty past. It's five-and-twenty past three now. What's wrong with that?"

"Nothing, Gran," said Freya. "You say what you want. Why not?" They were drinking tea and eating the carrot cake Rosemary had made that morning. "You'll have to tell Granddad my news. We've found a flat and got a mortgage on it, and we hope to move in before the wedding."

Rosemary, who had lifted a forkful of cake halfway to her mouth, set it down again. She was the only one of them to use the fork provided. "Can't you wait until *after* the wedding?"

"We've been living together now for years, Gran, so what's the difference?"

"It seems such a pity. It used to be called living in sin and still is as far as I'm concerned."

This blighted the conversation. After a few seconds of silence, Rosemary made a small effort to put things right, but her wording was unfortunate. "So where is this flat of yours?"

"I wonder," said Judith, "why 'of yours' gives that question such a pejorative sense?"

"All right, Mum. Leave it. It's in St. John's Wood, Gran. More or less opposite Lord's."

"Oh, yes, cricket," said Rosemary. "I'm sure it's very nice."

IT WAS SEVERAL hours before he even noticed what the house was like. He walked through the glass-covered way and pressed the bell. It rang like a bell and not like chimes or a couple of bars of music. When the door came open, he might have regained his voice, he didn't know. He stepped inside, and without those elusive, unnecessary words he took her in his arms, kissed her lips, and held her there as close to him as they could be.

"We have a lot of talking to do," he said when he let her go, "a lot of remembering and reminding each other."

"So that we know about the other one's life, so there aren't any gaps."

"I want to get used to you, I want the details."

"I love you already," she said, and his heart leapt. "I think I've loved you since the car on Baldwin's Hill and the forest. Do you remember?"

"Oh, yes, I remember."

"Let's go and sit down. Come in here. See the big sofa? We'll sit there and we should have some drink. Red wine. I've got a very nice delicious burgundy. Would you like that?"

He nodded.

They sat and talked, each with a glass of wine. They talked about their lives, what they had done, where they had been, Alan saying his had been dull, the same place, the same job, Daphne's anything but. He didn't mention Rosemary, not even as "my wife"; she only spoke of "my first husband," "my second husband." He had always thought of time as being constant, proceeding at the same pace, and wouldn't have believed it could pass so quickly.

"Oh, Alan," she said, breaking into his account of a phase of his life, "never call me darling or dear, will you? Call me by my name."

"Daphne."

"Yes, always Daphne."

He kissed her again then, the two of them slipping back to lie in each other's arms along the length of the deep, soft sofa. He was young again. It wasn't even necessary to close his eyes. He laid his hand on her left breast, but she gently lifted it away. "Not this time, Alan. Next time. Soon."

The latest time he could leave for home was nine thirty. "There's a Persian restaurant round the corner," she said. "We can walk there."

"Why Persian? Why not Iranian?"

"I don't know. But it's always Persian when it's a restaurant. They're the latest thing. We've got a Korean one too, presumably *South* Korean. When you're here all the time, we'll try them all."

Could it ever be? Was it possible? At Warwick Avenue station, just before the train came in, they kissed again, and Alan, looking over her shoulder just before they moved apart, saw that no one was staring at them. They were no more the cynosure of all eyes than if they had been eighteen.

UNLIKE THE BATCHELOR brothers, old Mr. Newman had been a hands-on builder in his youth. While George and Stanley had dabbled with this and that, a bit of bricklaying, a smidgen of touching up the paintwork, enjoying being foremen and bossing others about, Harry Newman had been a general builder. He told his grandson Lewis that he would have liked to have built his own house, a house for himself, but he had never had the time, he was too busy earning his living, supporting a wife and children. When he retired, he had nothing to do, a common complaint among men of his age.

"If you can't build yourself a house, Granddad," said Lewis, "you could build us an air-raid shelter."

Available to the British householder were two kinds of bomb shelter, the Anderson and the Morrison, both named after the politicians who had thought them up. Lewis found a piece in the newspaper about them, the former buried underground and composed of wooden struts, corrugated iron, and sandbags, and the latter like an iron table and kept inside but strong enough to support a collapsed house on its roof. He showed them to his grandfather, not knowing—not believing such a thing possible—that Harry Newman, with the exception of a few large-print words in the *Daily Mirror*, was unable to read. Not that Harry would say so. What he said was that he wasn't going to have any truck with rubbish like that, he'd build his own. And he did.

But for his son and his family, in the Newmans' back garden in Brook Road, his own home being a council house in Roding Road.

It was a good air-raid shelter, and when it began to look as if Loughton would be bombed and the sirens went off every night, sometimes several times, the Newmans, all five of them, descended into its depths with flasks of tea, hot-water bottles, blankets, and eiderdowns and sometimes egg sandwiches. But the work had been too much for Harry. He had some sort of illness, only a small "episode." Lewis the doctor now supposed it had been a transient ischaemic attack, or TIA, treatable today but unrecognised in those days and usually leading to a stroke. It had led to one. Lewis remembered seeing his grandfather's useless arm, his twisted face, and then being told of his death. He had been staying in Brook Road for his last months and had now freed up a room for Uncle James to come and stay when he liked.

Lewis could never understand why Uncle James wanted to stay, and at first he didn't seem to very much. Loughton was boring, there was nothing to do. The East End of London where he went to college and had a room was perfectly safe, there had been no air raids for months. There was no point in him living out here and having to take the tube every day. Lewis liked James and was glad when he "changed his tune" as Lewis's mother put it and decided to stay on. He said that Lewis's father would soon be called up but *he* wouldn't, *he* was in a reserved occupation and could stay here to look after his sister. Most of this, Lewis found out later, wasn't true; there was no reserved occupation and no call-up. Charlie Newman, approaching forty, was too old.

Soon afterwards James started going out in the evenings, sometimes staying out till midnight. No one said anything of this to Lewis, but he sensed that his parents didn't like it. Then came the request to see the qanats. Lewis could no longer remember exactly when James came to know about the tunnels; Lewis must have told him, but if he had, he certainly regretted it. James had said the tunnels "wouldn't do," but still he wondered if James had really liked them, had ever gone up there without him, in the evenings perhaps, in the dark, and stayed out till midnight. But why? If the others, the Batchelors and Daphne Jones and Richard Parr and Alan Norris and Rosemary Wharton and Michael Winwood and Bill Johnson, if they ever found James went there, they would take it out on Lewis, they would punish him. No one was supposed to tell *anyone* about the qanats, let alone show them.

James stayed with them on and off throughout the summer of 1944, the qanats summer, then left, never to come back, at the end of the year. Lewis thought it was November or December, but he could have been wrong about that. His mother was anxious but not really worried. "He's gone off abroad somewhere," she said. "He always wanted to. And not a word of thanks to me after he'd stopped here dozens of times."

Charlie Newman told the police his brother-in-law was missing, but they weren't willing to look for him. They told him they never judged a young man of twenty-five, of sound mind and in good health, to be *missing*. All the chances were that he had gone off of his own accord. Charlie said he had some girl and "shacked" up with her, an expression his wife admonished him for using in front of the child. But Lewis had a secret, he had seen something he hadn't understood and had made a promise to himself that he would tell no one. He never did speak of it to anyone until thirty years later when he told Jo.

He was a child. He knew something about babies being born because Norman Batchelor had told them all about his own birth on the kitchen table, about his mother having a pain and pushing him out. But Lewis knew nothing about how Norman got inside Mrs. Batchelor. For years he had never thought about what he had seen in the air-raid shelter.

"I've read a book about that," said Jo. "Or like that. *The Go-Between*. And there's a film. There's a boy that sees a couple having—well, intercourse, only he doesn't know what it is."

"Like me."

"What *did* you see?"

He had gone down into the air-raid shelter one afternoon to fetch a book he had left down there. It must have been the summer holidays because he wasn't at school. An air-raid warning the night before had lasted only a short time, but they didn't know that it would before it began, and he had taken the book down with him. The shelter should have been in darkness, but through the grille in the door he could see a candle burning. He opened the door a couple of inches and saw two people on the bottom bunk, a woman on her back and a man on top of her, moving up and down, but not hurting her. The man was Uncle James. Lewis couldn't see the woman's face and thought they hadn't seen him. He retreated up the steps, feeling strange, mystified, yet aware that he had seen something he shouldn't have seen. And heard something he shouldn't have heard, a kind of sighing gasp from the woman. Though not a cry of pain.

If anyone had asked him how he felt, he'd have said "upset." He was too old to cry but he felt like crying, though he couldn't have said why. Jo wanted to know why they were there. A bit ridiculous, wasn't it, making love in an air-raid shelter in the middle of the afternoon?

"People had nowhere to go then. This was the 1940s." Jo was younger than he, young enough to have missed that time when the only people allowed to make love were married couples. “They couldn’t go to a hotel. They were quite likely to be asked for their marriage certificate.”

“Did you ever find out who the woman was?”

“I was only a child, Jo. I wasn’t interested in that. I didn’t want to think about it. All I remember about her was that she was wearing stockings and had ginger hair—well, red hair. I think now that James wanted to see the tunnels because he had an idea they might be a substitute meeting place for himself and the woman. When he saw them, of course he knew that couldn’t be. Maybe after giving it a try-out he knew the shelter couldn’t be either.”

“So he and the woman decided to go away together?”

“I suppose so. That’s what the police must have thought when they refused to look for James.”

“What was the book you went down there to fetch?”

Lewis laughed. It was a long, long time since reverting to what he had seen in the shelter had upset him. “Probably *The Count of Monte Cristo*. It was about then that I read it for the first time.”

8

ABOUT A YEAR after Vivien's death, Michael gave up his car. He had only had a car to take her about in it, she and her wheelchair. He seldom used it without her as a passenger, and when she was gone, it brought him additional pain, an actual sharp physical pain in the region where his heart was, to get into the driving seat with no Vivien beside him. His only purpose in keeping the car had become to drive himself to Lewes to see Zoe. The car was parked in the street on the residents' parking, and to keep the battery from getting flat he had to drive it round West Hampstead a couple of times a week: down Fortune Green Road, around those streets named after ancient Greek heroes, Agamemnon, Achilles, et cetera, sometimes down to Shoot-Up Hill and back along Iverson. The battery still occasionally went flat, he had to call the RAC, and they did come at first as part of the deal, but then said if this went on, they were afraid they would have to charge him over the odds. So he gave up the car and it was a considerable relief.

Aunt Zoe, who wasn't his aunt and whom he had never called aunt, lived in Lewes. Now he went down by train and enjoyed the Sussex scenery, as he had never been able to before. Visiting Zoe had always been a pleasure and not a duty, and it was even better when that pleasure was reached in a train. Zoe had put an immediate end to the horrors of his childhood from the first moment he saw her. His mother was gone, departed sometime in the summer of the qanats; dead, his father told him, ill, in hospital, then again dead. She hadn't shown Michael much love but she was his mother, she was all the mother he had. He lived in the house called Anderby with his father, who spoke to him when he had to issue some instruction or tell him off and put food in front of him, mostly fish-paste sandwiches and Spam. Then, suddenly, his mother wasn't dead but had gone away and left them. Michael remembered the utter bewilderment he had felt. His father had found out about the tunnels, come to the entrance, and shouted at them all to go home, never to go there again. He took Michael home with him and thus took from him all his companions. Michael was told he must go away and live with his father's cousin. She had a nice house and a new husband and Michael must learn to like her.

"I never did, but you're not much like me so maybe you will. Like it or lump it. She says she's met you once or twice. I don't remember but perhaps you do. She's no kids of her own and can't have any and she wants you and that's the main thing. You'll go down to Lewes on Thursday in the train."

John Winwood, whom no one called Woody anymore, went upstairs and started singing "Abide with Me." Michael didn't much trust his father, he had no reason to, but he did think his father meant to come with him in the train. But his father had no intention of doing that. He packed a bag for Michael, this time singing "O God, Our Help in Ages Past" while he did so, stuffing the bag with odd socks and clothes Michael had grown out of. His father came to the station with him, saw him on the train, and said he'd talked to the guard and "given him a tip" to see "the boy didn't get into mischief." Then Michael's father went away without waiting for the train to depart, saying as he left that he'd forgotten to bring the sandwiches he had packed up for Michael. That train journey, rain streaming down the carriage windows, cold weather for October, was the worst morning of Michael's life, and he had known some bad mornings. The feeling he had was a mixture of panic and despair. He had a ticket but no money. He needed the lavatory but had no idea where to find it—if it existed on a train. A lady he would and did remember all his life—plump, kindly, with a little dog on her lap—asked him if he was all right and was anyone with him? He brought himself with dreadful shame to ask where the lavatory was, and she offered to show him, carrying the Yorkshire terrier with her. After that, relieved and comforted, he stroked the little dog and talked to it all the way to Lewes.

She shepherded him off the train, carrying his suitcase for him—he was not able to lift it himself—and said she would stay with him until they found whoever—his auntie, was it?—was due to meet him. But no sooner had she spoken than a small, trim, pretty lady in a flowered frock was bending down to greet him, asking if she might kiss him and doing so, wafting over him the most delicious scent of roses.

"You came alone?" That was the nearest to criticism of his father he ever heard from Zoe for a long time. She said profuse thank-yous to the lady with the little dog, then they went in a car to Zoe's house. In a car! Which she drove! She wasn't the first woman he had known to drive but almost the first. She was so gentle and kind, asking him all the things he liked to do and eat and play with, that he thought at first it was some kind of game she was playing, not real. But it was real, and from the worst morning of his life succeeded the best afternoon, and ever since then Zoe had given him a happy life with her and her husband, Chris, and a dog of his own, happiness that went on, punctuated by the minor troubles that flesh is heir to, until the terrible thing happened and Vivien died.

Among the minor troubles was his first marriage. Babette was a mistake. He had married her because when he was twenty-four, you got engaged to, then married, the first girl you went out with, usually one of the typists in the office. In his case, the secretary he shared with the other newly fledged solicitor in the Lewes law firm he joined when he was qualified. Babette was pretty and chatty. The word for her that came to mind was *skittish*. At the end of every sentence she uttered, she giggled. For a while he found it charming. Now, if he thought of her at all, it was to reflect that these days and, for twenty or thirty years past, they would have lived together for a while and, when her giggling shredded his nerves and, to be fair, his grim sarcasm drove her to tears, split up with no or not much harm done. Cohabitation but no marriage—who but a puritanical bigot could fault such a system? In his and Babette's case, when it seemed separation might be difficult, for neither of them had committed adultery or acted with cruelty, Babette fell in love with a silly, pompous man who adored her and ran off with him. The law changed and easy divorce followed swiftly under the Matrimonial Causes Act of 1973.

Vivien was Chris's cousin's daughter, seventeen years younger than Michael. They met at a family wedding. She was as unlike Babette as could be, tall, slender, olive-skinned and black-haired, quiet, a woman who laughed only when there was something to laugh at. She was the headmistress (as they were called then) of a primary school in West Hampstead, and Michael had joined a law firm with premises in the Finchley Road. They bought the house in Ingham Road where a bus passed by and furnished material for Michael's poetry.

He sometimes thought that he had loved her too much and their children not enough. That was not to say that he hadn't cared for them enormously more than his parents had cared for him. They were never neglected or ignored as he had been, and Vivien made up for his occasional indifference by her adoration of both of them. Guiltily, he confessed to himself alone that he wouldn't have much cared if he and Vivien had had no children. He was jealous of them too because of the love she had for them, though she took none from him, he knew that. The difficulty was—he discovered this by self-analysis—that he had a problem with love, giving too much of it or not enough, not knowing how to *handle* it.

She died young, or forty-nine seemed young to him. Breast cancer. Both children were at university. Both were clever, got good degrees; his son went on to graduate studies, and medical school for his daughter. They sometimes came home, but because (or so Michael thought) they associated Ingham Road with their mother. They never went up to the third floor to Vivien's room, the bedroom he was keeping as she had left it. As for him, he went on dully conveyancing (as he put it), having searches made and drawing up contracts for his clients. As he also put it to himself, his heart was broken. But it had never been much of a heart, damaged early in its life, kicked around by his parents. Only Vivien had been able to mend it, and now she was gone. As a child he had never cried, he knew it would be useless, but since Vivien's death he cried, learning how to do it in the long, sleepless nights. Self-pity? Maybe. Those who deride it are the ones who have never had cause to feel it.

ALL THE NEWS he ever had about his father came from Zoe. Not well-off when Michael was a child, he married twice more. The first of these women was called Margaret and she too died. But death came after a long and apparently happy life. His third wife was wealthy, rich, and her death made him a rich man. Michael met Sheila once on one of the rare occasions he and his father encountered each other and liked her. He was old enough by then to be a judge of character, and this woman impressed him as being utterly unlike what he could remember of his mother. When Sheila died, she left his father everything she had, including the manor house in Norfolk they lived in and all the money, much increased by then, her father had left her. Zoe told Michael that this enabled his father to install himself in a care home. Not at all the kind of residence one associates with such places, but a luxurious refuge comparable to a hotel in some Italian resort, though its residents were all over the age of sixty. Michael didn't want to know. He remembered his father with dread and a kind of disgust.

He was a solicitor, partner in a law firm on the Finchley Road, and married to Babette. She was fascinated by John Winwood—largely, Michael thought, because he was rich and there might be money to be got out of him—and constructed scenarios about Urban Grange, the luxury home, its inmates attended on by nicely dressed young women who looked very unlike nurses, doctors who looked like businessmen, cooked for by a chef who also wrote culinary features for a glossy magazine, and with colour TVs and Jacuzzis in en suite bathrooms. He barely listened until she suggested they have his father live with them. Michael could "update" their house and make a luxury apartment in an extension built on to it for his father. It was partly his vehemently expressed disgust that drove her into the arms of the car salesman she went off with. When Zoe told Michael she had heard from Urban Grange that his father was ill and near to death, though, he realised he had better go up to Norfolk to see him, but it never came to that.

John Winwood recovered—he was always recovering—left his bed, resumed occupancy of a wheelchair, and was taken outside among the zinnias and the rhododendrons. But he soon started dying again and was once more at death's door. Again Michael thought himself bound to go there, again waited a day, then two days, and again John Winwood recovered. The wheelchair was discarded and he experienced a new lease of life, dressing in garish clothes he had one of the staff buy for him, exercising in his room, then running round the grounds like a young man. Michael had never known how old his father was and was never interested enough to ask Zoe. When he was a child, parents went to great length to avoid telling their children their age. Michael could remember to this day how surprised he had been when Norman Batchelor told the rest of them that his father was forty-two and his mother thirty-eight. That John Winwood was now very old, Michael knew, but no more precisely than that. He knew too that he was a dying man who never died.

Apart from himself, Zoe was his father's next of kin. She alone, it appeared, received news of him. From Urban Grange or from himself? Perhaps both. Michael told himself that he was uninterested in his father's fate. He was uninterested in his father. Of all the cruelties and neglect John Winwood had inflicted on Michael the worst in his memory was not failing to call the doctor for three days after Michael broke his ankle, not taking him to and showing him over the abattoir where John had once been a slaughterman, not leaving Michael in bed without water when he had measles—but abandoning him on Victoria station without money or food. That was the worst act, and he could never forgive it. He still remembered every detail of that day, the train journey, his fear and his utter loneliness, the kindness too of the lady with the little dog, but even that had never been able to assuage the horror he felt for a father who could do that to his small son. Any love Michael had for him—not much—was extinguished that day when he met Zoe and learned what love was.

So indifferent to his father? Was he? No, he thought as little about him as possible now because he had been shown by Vivien that hatred, which was what he really felt, corrupted the mind and spoilt the character. "Don't hate anyone," she had said. "It's quite useless and harms the hater while it does nothing at all to the hated." So his dwelling on his father's iniquities and even some desire he had had for revenge faded away. Sometimes he even found himself humming one of the hymns his father used to sing. He tried to think of John Winwood as dead but failed in this attempt.

"Your father," said Zoe, "was one of those

people who are always having money left them. His own parents had a lot of siblings. Only one of them married, and that was my mother. The rest died intestate—one of them never even knew your father—and their money automatically went to him. It wasn't dribs and drabs; one legacy was ten thousand pounds and another nearly five thousand. He used some of it to buy the house called Anderby. A house on the Hill in Loughton would have cost a thousand just before the war when he bought it. He didn't exactly fit in."

And my mother? Michael had thought, but didn't say. Anita. She was a dim, vague figure from the distant past. Where John Winwood had met her, why he had married her, if she had any relatives still living—Michael had no idea of the answers to all this. All he could remember was her face. That he could still see when he closed his eyes, a face that epitomised not beauty but exquisite prettiness, the tip-tilted nose, the short upper lip, the baby-doll eyes, the round pink cheeks, and the abundance of red-gold hair. His wife Babette had a similar facial construction and the red hair; his wife Vivien, the antithesis, grave, austere, until she smiled and the sun came out.

"He seems to have been fond of her insofar as he could be fond," said Zoe, who had lately given up never criticising his father. Perhaps she realised Michael was no longer the child she had to protect from an ugly truth; had she known it, he knew better than she. “Anyway, he may have had a bit of a guilty conscience. Sheila probably took an overdose on purpose, whatever the inquest said. She seemed very unhappy to me.”

“Yes, she did,” Michael said, waiting for more, but none came. What did it matter? No more revelations about this father could shock him now. Any connection with himself had come to an end on the platform at Victoria station six decades ago. He had just one question, the one he had never before asked.

“Just how old is he?”

“He’ll be a hundred next January.”

AT NO TIME in his life before had Alan ever concentrated his thoughts on one person in one situation and done so for day after day. He thought of Daphne when falling asleep, and Daphne was the first to come to mind when he awoke. He set her in her house and saw her moving among the rooms—even those rooms he had never yet seen—he saw her walking up Hamilton Terrace and walking along St. John’s Wood Road, stopping sometimes to talk to some faceless neighbour. He saw her reclining on the sofa where they had lain, a book in her hand, and then she laid the book aside to think—perhaps—of him. Most of all, when dwelling on her, he was asking himself what they were going to do. Would the sort of promise she had made to him ever come true? It was so unlikely, he was too old; and this too had to be faced, *she* was too old. People didn't fall in love at their age—but they do.

He had supposed, and in a way hoped, that setting eyes on Rosemary after he returned from his visit to Hamilton Terrace would bring guilt, enormous guilt. He might, he had considered while sitting in the tube, even feel a kind of relief that Rosemary's presence, Rosemary's existence, would show him his and Daphne's folly, the impossibility of what they had half planned to do and the sheer wrongness of it. But this had passed in a moment to be replaced by a thought that it would be wrong, even if possible now, to dismiss this joy he and she contemplated. It was something he would bitterly regret for the rest of what life remained to him. Telling himself that he would be a useless companion to Rosemary now, no husband, a shell, his whole mind and heart given to another woman even if he looked like the man she was married to—that was a hypocritical let-out.

Rosemary was a good woman, he repeatedly told himself, devoted to him, a homemaker, his carer, the mother of his children. Then a small voice inside him said that of all that, only the last was true. An image of the sewing machine appeared in his mind's eye. A song from some musical had been about the sewing machine being a girl's best friend. How ancient that seemed, how antediluvian. Rosemary's sewing machine had been his worst enemy. The sound it made, that buzz that was unlike any other, got increasingly on his nerves. No other woman he knew possessed a sewing machine, though many had done so when he was young. The only other one he knew of was in the dry cleaner's they patronised in the High Road, where a woman in a sari sat in the window stitching seams. How grossly unfair he was being! He couldn't leave Rosemary, anyway. It was unthinkable. Yet he was thinking of it as often as he thought of Daphne.

He continued to make his excuse of a meeting with Robert Flynn, though growing aware that he would have to think of some alternative reason for going out without Rosemary. Now he needed a new pretext, this time for staying away overnight. Lying, which he had once believed he found difficult if not impossible, had become simple, largely because—and this was an additional trouble to him—his hearer was so innocent and so trusting. That made untruthfulness so much more outrageous. Yet he and Daphne couldn't go on as they were, kisses and afternoon visits, however delightful. He knew himself and was aware that for him love-making should take place at night-time, not necessarily in the dark, but at least in artificial light. And in a bed if possible, not on a sofa. It was his age. Wasn't it true that for this fundamental aspect of our being, for sex and love, we want the circumstances, the setting, and the very sounds and scents of our youth? That might well be why some marriages endured more or less for ever. He thought, as he often did, of Daphne's father's car at dusk on Baldwin's Hill. The smell of her now was the same, the feel of her. She was the first woman he had had and would, if all could miraculously go well, be the last.

He would be found out through Robert Flynn. That was why he must think of another excuse. He thought of all this as he told his usual lie to Rosemary and set off for Loughton station. Robert would phone or his wife would or someone else who knew them both would phone and tell Rosemary that Robert was complaining he never saw Alan these days. Coming home in late evening, he often thought of that. But he need not think of it now, not now.

RISOTTO IS A DISH notoriously difficult to make or if not that difficult, time-consuming. Once you have started it with your rice and mushrooms, say, in the pan, stock added and more stock waiting to be added, you cannot leave it. Constant stirring is essential or disaster ensues. The chef at Lotario's restaurant in St. John's Wood High Street was a superb cook and his risotto was famous, thanks in part to culinary features in glossy magazines. The restaurant was always full by eight thirty, but those who booked for seven—the locals and the elderly mostly—found space and soft music, pink tablecloths and napkins, always the best colour, and courteous service. And of course the risotto.

Freya and David had been visiting the flat in the block opposite Lord's, of which they now had possession. They would move into Oak Tree Court on the following Saturday, but today they were measuring windows for blinds and calculating whether the second bedroom would take a queen-size bed. They arrived there later than they had expected and, once inside, made two discoveries: the previous occupants had removed all the light bulbs and they themselves were highly incompetent both with tape measures and rulers. Near quarrelling, they sought their usual remedy for ill temper, sat down on the newly carpeted floor, and drank a couple of glasses each of the bottle of merlot they had brought with them. This restored their equilibrium, and as it was getting on eight thirty and growing dark, they set off to find a restaurant.

"Why not try Lotario's?" said Freya. "He's the man who makes the marvellous risotto."

"I hate risotto."

"Then you can have something else."

The place was crowded. They hadn't booked, but one table was available to them, the sort no one wants because it is just inside the door and liable to draughts.

"I think we should have a pink tablecloth like

these, don't you?" said Freya, who had something of her grandmother in her.

David was not a talkative man, something which seldom bothered her. They ordered another bottle of merlot, risotto for Freya, spaghetti vongole for David. He was not a people-watcher either, in her opinion, like most men. Her eyes roved round the diners and came to rest on a couple seated at a table diagonally opposite theirs. The man was facing them and the woman had her back to them. Far from young or even in their middle years, they might have been described as in the prime of old age, straight-backed and both with good heads of hair. It seemed as if they had finished eating, but two half-full glasses of wine were still in front of them. The man, whom Freya immediately recognised, had his right hand covering the woman's left hand across the tablecloth, and now he raised it to his lips.

Freya said faintly, "I don't believe it."

"That always means you do."

"You see those people—the woman in the black and white—that old man with her is my grandfather."

"D'you want to go over and say hello?"

"Are you kidding?"

Their food came, the risotto and the spaghetti vongole. Freya took a larger-than-usual swig of wine. "I rather hope they don't see us. That isn't my grandmother, you know."

"Some business acquaintance, I expect."

"He doesn't have a business."

David smiled, then laughed. "Well, good luck to him."

"It isn't funny."

The old man was paying his bill. They finished their wine, got up, and began walking towards the door, quite a long way from Freya and David, who kept their eyes downcast. But in Freya's case, not enough to avoid seeing their departure. "Did you see that?" she said as the door closed behind them. "He had his arm round her like they were young."

"Maybe they feel young."

"It's upset me a lot. I feel sort of disillusioned. I mean, I never dreamt of anything like that. Not Granddad."

"It's not our business, Freya."

"Of course it is. He's my *granddad.* I really need a drink, something stronger than that red stuff. A grappa. D'you want one?"

"I'm okay. It hasn't upset *me*."

"NEXT TIME," said Alan, "I'll stay the night."

"Good."

Daphne wouldn't want to know how he would manage to stay the night, what far greater prevarication would have to be employed, what far bigger lie be told to explain his absence for perhaps twenty-four hours. Not Robert Flynn this time, Alan was growing frightened of Robert Flynn, that this innocent and blameless man might suddenly surface like a monster from a calm sea, rear his ugly head (though Alan remembered him as rather a handsome man) and gnash his shark-like jaws, robbing his quarry of an arm or a leg. For to lose Daphne now would be like the loss of a limb. Of all that Robert Flynn might do, he must not be allowed to take Daphne from Alan; better break up his marriage. But that was already broken, wasn't it?

Worries, mostly related to Robert Flynn, whose function as an alibi Alan felt he had overused, beset him all the way home in the tube train. He even envisaged walking into the flat and finding not just a wakeful Rosemary sitting there but also Robert Flynn and his wife, whatever she was called, the three of them assembled to examine his lies and excuses and confront him with them. Of course there was nothing of the sort. Rosemary was in bed and presumably asleep, and the copper-coloured silk suit, finished at last, was on a hanger in the hallway.

9

MICHAEL CARRIED WITH him a large box of chocolates. The flowers he would buy in Lewes, if necessary getting the taxi driver to stop at a florist's on the way to Zoe's. A phone conversation two days before with Brenda Miller, Zoe's carer, friend, and companion, had told him there was nothing to worry about. A woman of ninety-six was bound to grow weaker, bound to be frail, but Brenda believed that the doctor, who had called that day, was exaggerating when she said his aunt was in the early stages of Alzheimer's.

"I thought, but I didn't actually say so, that someone of her age could hardly be in the early stages of anything."

"I'll be down on Thursday and we'll see," said Michael. "She doesn't want Zoe to go to a—well, a nursing home or a hospice or something, does she?"

"That wasn't mentioned. That would kill her, we both know that."

So here he was with his chocolates and his flowers, golden roses and pink and yellow lupins, kissing Zoe, who was smiling at him as she always did. Her voice was a little weaker, her movements a little slower. Instead of a stick, then two sticks to walk with, she was using a walking frame.

"People have stopped called them Zimmer frames," she said. "Have you noticed? I think it's something to do with anti-German prejudice or maybe dislike of the EU."

That didn't sound like early-stage Alzheimer's.

Brenda served lunch, and afterwards the two women ate a couple of the chocolates each. While he was visiting, Zoe omitted her afternoon nap. She would go to bed earlier, she always told him. She didn't want to sleep while he was there. Besides, today she had something to tell him, it was important, it was private, and she had asked Brenda to leave them alone together for half an hour. Well, twenty minutes. They could ask anything of each other, she and Brenda, offence would never be taken or hard feelings.

Michael saw how little she had eaten, not much more than a scrap of the grilled sole, a wafer-thin piece of bread, and the two chocolates. He noticed too how white she had grown, the skin of her face blanched to a pallor only seen in the very old. It was new, though, as was the loss of colour in her eyes, which were no longer blue but the grey of still water. The blue of her eyes was the first thing he had noticed about her when she'd kissed him on Lewes station.

"Sit down, darling," she said when they were in her little sitting room, her own private room where people had to be invited in. "My son. I have always thought of you as that. I hope you don't mind, I won't labour it." He reached for her hand and held it. "At my age, Michael, one must always think of dying. One ought to, no harm in that. Every time I see you, I know I may never see you again. I don't want to talk about your father, and I'm sure you don't, but there is one thing about him I need to tell you. Well, two things really.

"It was the last time I saw him. He was alone, having left Sheila at home. Poor thing. I hadn't liked her but I pitied her as once I pitied you. But I think you were lucky, Michael."

"I know that. Because you found me and brought me here." He wanted to add, *And made yourself my mother,* but he was afraid he would start crying if he said that.

"I didn't mean that. I meant because you escaped him. I will tell you quickly what he asked me. I think the word would be *alibi*. I know what it is but not what it means. You're a solicitor, you'll know."

"It's Latin for 'elsewhere.' "

"Is it? That's what he asked me when he came here alone. Would I give him an alibi."

Michael felt like saying he wasn't hearing this. He didn't, but he thought that, against nearly all evidence to the contrary, Zoe was succumbing to senility. "An alibi?"

Her old face, already deeply lined, crunched into a mask of wrinkles as she seemed to make a concentrated effort to define what she had said. " 'Elsewhere,' you said. He wanted me to say he was elsewhere. If anyone came asking, I was to say he was here with me."

"But when, Zoe? How?"

"It was twenty years ago. I was to say that he was here with me, spending the day here, on a specific date in May."

"You must have asked why?" Michael was starting to feel sick. "You must have asked who would do the asking?"

"I didn't want to know. I knew it was something awful. I knew him. I just said there was no question of lying for him. He seemed surprised. He said, 'But you're my cousin, you're family.' " She gave a deep sigh. "I've seen him since, occasionally. He wrote and told me about going into Urban Grange and telling the company that runs the place that he had no next of kin except me. It suited him then to say I was *only* a cousin."

"His wife was dead by then?" Michael didn't care, he didn't want to know, but she seemed to want him to ask.

"She died in June 1985, a few weeks after he asked me what I told you he asked me. Five or six years later he went into Urban Grange. Sheila had become a heavy drinker and she used an enormous amount of what they call prescription drugs. There was an inquest and the verdict was death by misadventure." Zoe wiped her upper lip and her forehead with a tissue. "That's all. I don't want to say any more. But someone had to know, and who but you?"

These visits always terminated in Michael's leaving in the early evening. Zoe needed to be in bed by eight. Michael and the two old women sat by the French windows in the sunshine and talked about what they had been doing in the weeks since his last visit. In the case of Zoe and Brenda, what they always did was read the papers and novels, watch television, go for short walks, Zoe in the wheelchair, Brenda pushing it. They repeatedly said how lucky they were. To be living here, to have their own home still, for Zoe's carer shared everything with her, happiness and gratitude as well as material things. Michael told them about his reunion with friends of his childhood, but said nothing about the discovery of the hands, which they seemed not to have heard of.

Brenda left the room to make tea, and he said quickly and breathlessly, "Zoe, stay alive for me." He could hardly believe he was saying this, but he went on in this uncharacteristic way, "You are all I've got."

"That's what I should be saying to you. Anyway, you have your children."

"I know. I'm very lucky." Strange how little he thought about them. "Forget what I said."

"I don't think so." She laughed. "It's not very often one gets such things said to one at my age."

He kissed both women before he left, giving Zoe a hug as well and letting his cheek lie against hers for longer than usual. He might never see her again.

"WHAT SHALL WE DO?" After three days, Freya was still indignant.

"Well, nothing," said Judith. "I don't suppose it will come to anything. You're getting married in two weeks' time. We don't want some family upset, do we? And, my God, there would be one if you were thinking of telling your grandmother what you saw. It'll all blow over anyway."

"He had his arm round her, Mum. He kissed her hand."

Judith started laughing.

"It's not funny. These are your *parents*."

"It just goes to show how enormously things have changed. Even when I was your age, and that isn't as long ago as you think, old people didn't have girlfriends and take them out to dinner in London restaurants, the girlfriends didn't wear four-inch heels, old men didn't put their arms round them in public. The old men might have been sugar daddies, but not with women of their own age. You did say she was about his age?"

"About that. Very good for her age but about that."

"You should see how good that is for women in general, Freya. You won't always be young, you know, and you'll appreciate having a boyfriend when you're seventy."

"But what about poor Gran?"

"What the eye doesn't see, the heart doesn't grieve over." Judith paused to consider. "You're sure it was him?"

"Oh, Mum. *Please.*"

A GREAT MANY budding romances must be broken up by the couple's having left the school they both went to, parted when they went to separate universities. More now than when he was young, Alan was thinking, because at that time fewer girls went on to higher education. But Daphne had gone to Cambridge and he had gone to Reading, and though they had made promises to write—very few expensive long-distance phone calls in those days—their letters dwindled until they ceased altogether. Besides, their relationship—not a word ever used then—was strange. Because of the strong sexual element it necessarily had to be private. Not for them the going to the cinema in the evening, followed by the good-night kiss. Love-making was what they did, kissing yes, adoring yes, with the sighs and gasps of passion, the talk that followed consisting mainly in planning when they would next meet, where she could park her father's car so as not to be seen by the neighbours, where he would wait, but not where they would go. That was always the same. Up to Baldwin's Hill and the enclosing forest. On warm summer nights, the forest floor itself, in leafy caverns made by arching roofs of branches. In green clearings and sometimes, adventurously, against the smooth sealskin trunk of a great beech tree.

Where did her parents think they were? They never talked about their parents, of course not. But once he asked, and Daphne said, visiting a friend of hers, a girl she had been at school with, who lived in St. John's Road, sufficiently far away to warrant taking the car. Apparently, her father and mother never checked up on her. It was a foretaste of his own insecure alibi with Robert Flynn. *What goes around comes around* was a phrase he had never liked, but here it was apposite. Suppose there had been gap years in those days, suppose she had gone with him to Reading University. There had been some question of it, but her getting to Cambridge was what her parents had wanted, and the prestige of it overcame her—what for him?—love? Lust? Excitement? All those? And to Cambridge she went. He turned to Melanie, but her laugh got on his nerves and he gave her up for Rosemary, who he hoped would be as anxious for sex as Daphne had been. It seemed to him that he had established himself as her boyfriend and Rosemary as his girlfriend with the sole aim of getting her into bed or into the back of some borrowed car. But she held out—oh, how she had held out!—and finally gave way on a painful and messy wedding night in a hotel in Torquay.

Things got better in that area (as Rosemary called it), and he had no complaints. As far as he knew, nor did she. As far as he knew because they never discussed it. Rosemary wouldn't, the whole subject embarrassed her. Should he have married Daphne? Found her again? After all, he knew where she lived or her parents lived. On the Hill, opposite where the qanats had been and by that time Warlock stood, next door to Mr. Winwood, who had lived alone without wife or son. He could have found her. It would have meant jilting Rosemary and the consequent terrible fuss made by her parents and his. Besides, life hadn't been unhappy, only dull. And he had his children and grandchildren.

He was in the tube train on his way to Hamilton Terrace to spend the night with Daphne. That was how he put it to himself, the expression *have sex with* or something more explicit not having been in use when he last made love to her. He had been young then and he was old now, but this troubled him less than the lie he had told Rosemary. Robert Flynn was not much good to him this time, the tubes ran so late, and why on earth would he stay with Robert? The whole thing was absurd. It was some years since he had seen Robert or talked to him, yet he and Rosemary had discussed the man, he to give verisimilitude to his fabrication, even describing Robert's home because she liked hearing about domestic interiors, his health in comparison to Alan's fitness, and his loneliness since his wife went away on holiday with her sister. Ridiculous and very wrong. No more Robert now but a visit to an old school reunion to be held, not at Bancroft's, where he had been a pupil, but for some mysterious reason, in Dorset. In one of those refurbished barns tarted up with a bar and grand banqueting hall in the middle of Hardy country. It almost frightened him thinking of the description of this place he had given. He was afraid of his skill at mendacity. It seemed almost criminal to do it so well.

This evening he and Daphne were not going out for dinner. She would cook for him.

"What do you like best to eat?"

"Oh, anything," he said. "It doesn't matter."

"What do you like best?"

"Something no one makes anymore. Steak and kidney pie."

He was sure she would forget. His choice seemed as unlike anything she might cook as possible. Surely she was a grilled-calamari woman or a creator of risottos like the restaurant they had been to the previous week.

She hadn't dressed up for him but wore the simple frock he had so admired her in on their first date. He could tell she was avoiding any appearance of festivity or occasion. They had kissed when he arrived, then lain on that sofa in each other's arms, whispering what were once, long before his time, called sweet nothings. Sherry was drunk, quite a lot of it, and lines came into his head—Shakespeare, of course—about alcohol provoking the desire but taking away the performance. He needed no aphrodisiac to encourage the desire. As for the performance, he had resolved not to think about that, but he did, inevitably.

The steak and kidney pie was excellent, all it should be, and it was a shame he did less than justice to it. Afterwards they drank red wine with their cheese and then she put on some Bach. He had never associated her with Bach or indeed any kind of music, but it calmed him, which was perhaps what she intended. Apropos of nothing, no words they spoke leading up to it, she said, "It doesn't matter at all. Remember we have been there, done that."

"I know."

They went upstairs with their arms round each other. She turned the lights off, all but the bedside lamp. He could see the forest and its green floor, bracken fern coming into leaf, and the woven tree branches overhead. *The beams of our house are cedars; our rafters are fir. . . .* He held her in his arms and her face against his had the skin of his young lover. It was all right, it was going to be and remain all right. *Behold thou art fair, my love, and our bed is green.*

"YOU'RE A PSYCHOLOGIST," said Freya. "You're better fitted to do it than I am."

Her sister cast up her eyes, a habit of hers. "You mean you're passing the buck."

"Well, I can't do it, can I, Fen? I'm getting married on Saturday and I'll be away in Morocco for a fortnight. That would really be passing the buck. It would be best to wait till I'm gone. Pick a time when Granddad's not there, that's essential."

"Obviously," said Fenella. "This is all very difficult for me. I shall have to find someone to be with the kids, I can't take them with me. Suppose she—well, bursts into tears?"

"Mum'll take the kids. She'll be so thankful not to have to tell Grandma herself."

"You'd better give me the details all over again. I don't want to get it wrong."

IT HAD LONG been a principle of Rosemary's that it was not for a wife to concern herself overmuch with what her husband did. This had always included how he passed his days while at "business," while with his male friends—he would have no female friends—what his interests were, anything to do with politics or the inside of a car engine. This was why she had never asked him about Robert Flynn, what Robert had said and what Alan had said. Alan's doing his best to memorise the details of a house he had never been in had been in vain because Rosemary had never asked him what it was like. So when he returned from Dorset and the old school reunion, she asked him only if he had had a nice time. She was a little surprised because he insisted on telling her what they had eaten at the reunion banquet in the great hall and how pleased he had been at not having to share a room in the hotel booked for them. But she merely said how glad she was he had enjoyed himself. She had learned on the BBC's early-evening news of a serious delay on the Great Western line on Saturday afternoon, and she hoped it hadn't made him late, but he had only given the perfectly acceptable answer that the Penzance train was held up, not his.

The copper-coloured silk suit was no longer hanging up in the hall outside the sewing room but had been moved, still suspended, to their bedroom. Like Ahab to Elijah or Orwell's Gordon to a houseplant, "Hast thou found me, O mine enemy?" said Alan aloud when he saw it. But he didn't mind it, he didn't mind anything. He was happy. He knew he shouldn't be. Taking Rosemary out to dinner that evening was a monstrous thing to do. You don't compensate for adultery by such acts, but he had already asked her and she had accepted. She might, she said, even wear the suit—but better not perhaps. It must be worn for the first time at Freya's wedding, that had been her original intention and she must stick to it.

He had forgotten all about Freya's wedding, and for a moment a cloud passed across his sunny sky as he remembered he had promised Daphne to spend Saturday night with her. But how he was going to manage this, he had had no idea. On the other hand he had had a good idea that at the wedding he would get a chance to talk to Rosemary's sister and suggest to her that she and Rosemary should go away somewhere on holiday together. France, maybe. He wasn't fond of France, a good reason for Rosemary, who loved it, to go with Elizabeth instead of him. The copper-coloured silk suit fluttered a little in the breeze from the open window, showing with irritating clarity the asymmetry of its lapels.

Out for a walk later in the day, he sat on a log under the forest trees and tried to phone Daphne, but failing to get a signal, the mobile made no more than a shrill noise. In the evening, secretly out on the balcony, he managed to speak to her, arranging that "come what may" he would spend Thursday with her, though not, alas, Saturday night.

It was an unfortunate day to have chosen, or perhaps other choices he made were unfortunate. Having spent a lovely day with Daphne, forgetting his resolve not to make love on a sofa in the afternoon, he might have left an hour earlier but instead got into the tube at Warwick Avenue at half past seven and changed at Oxford Circus onto a Central Line train bound for Theydon Bois. West End shops stay open much later than usual on Thursdays, and the overdressed woman laden with bags from Selfridges and Zara, sitting in the far corner of the carriage, passed unrecognised by him. He, however, was spotted by Helen Batchelor, who quickly made up her mind not to "see" him.

She would probably have done nothing about it had she not come into Loughton the next day to visit her brother-in-law George, who was recovering at home from a heart attack, a mild one but still not to be dismissed. Having handed over the obligatory bunch of flowers and box of Quality Street, she wished George a rapid improvement and left to do some shopping in the High Road, leaving her car on the only parking place she was likely to find on a Friday afternoon. Rosemary was also out shopping, to buy a spare pair of tights lest the ones she would be wearing for the wedding spring a ladder at the crucial time.

They had met only once before. Rosemary would have passed her by with a vague sense of having seen that woman somewhere, but Helen, who was more observant than Rosemary and had better sight, greeted her with a "Hi, Rosemary, how are you?"

Rosemary said she was fine, thanks, thinking what else can you say and why do people ask?

"What a coincidence," said Helen. "I haven't seen either of you for years, and then all of a sudden I see your husband"—she had forgotten his name—"in the tube on Thursday night and you in the High Road on Friday. I'd got in at Bond Street and he got in at Oxford Circus."

Rosemary said nothing. She gave a vague nod. The other woman—was she called Helen?—began telling her about George, poor George, and his heart, which he never took care of as he should. Rosemary excused herself by saying she must get on and went to buy her tights in a kind of daze. This Helen must be wrong, of course. She probably drank, she looked as if she did. Alan was at home. She took the new pair of tights into her bedroom and came out to find him on the balcony, reading something. It might be poetry or some "classic"; she took little interest in what he read, it always seemed such a waste of time. He looked up, smiled at her, and said something about how nice it was to be able to sit out here in the sunshine.

"Whatever were you doing getting into the tube at Oxford Circus last night?"

Instead of blushing, which wasn't his way, he turned white. She didn't notice but he did, or, rather, he felt it happen, a shuddering withdrawal of blood from his cheeks. Unable to speak, he clenched his hands, then managed, "I went to Robert's club, left him there. Cavendish Square."

"I thought Owen was driving you out to the Norfolk Show."

Why would he ever have wanted to go to an agricultural show, and why would their son, living and working in Winchester, have driven him there? It was the feeblest and most unlikely excuse. But he had made it and she remembered.

10

POSSESSING NO GRANDER CLOTHES, Alan had worn a suit for the wedding, probably his best suit if you categorised such garments, but the first man he saw when they arrived was in morning dress. The day was beautiful, warm and sunny. He hadn't envisaged a garden, but the hotel had one, large, with lawns, rosebuds, shrubbery, tall trees, and a river frontage.

A man dressed like a Yeoman of the Guard whom Rosemary called a master of ceremonies was ushering guests in through a kind of tent or marquee attached to the back of the hotel. Taking their places in a queue, Alan was conscious of women ahead of them, and soon behind them, dressed elegantly compared to poor Rosemary. He suddenly felt enormous pity for her along with his guilt. If only someone would come up to them and tell her how nice she looked, even ask her where she had bought her suit. But no one did, and they were soon shaking hands with David and kissing Freya. Rosemary, who had already told Alan how odd it was to see the bride and, come to that, the groom before the ceremony had taken place, said, "Happy is the bride that the sun shines on."

Alan doubted that he would have winced at that six months ago. He did now. Was he imagining the look Freya gave him? There she stood in a white-lace creation, cut low, her left arm full of white roses, her eyes penetratingly on him for no more than a few seconds but narrow with condemnation. Or so he thought, his guilt thinking for him. Back in the garden, Rosemary had spotted Judith and Fenella and Fenella's husband, Giles, and homed in on them. It would have been better to have approached people they *didn't* know and introduced themselves, but Alan knew Rosemary would never do that. He thought, perhaps again imagined, that his other granddaughter gave him a look that was not exactly hostile but rather of the reproving sort a mother reserves for her disobedient child. Judith, on the other hand, had an ironical smile on her face, sheltered by a cartwheel hat. He dipped under the hat to kiss her, thinking, They know. My daughter and my granddaughters know. Just as Helen Batchelor knew.

A net was closing in. He felt a real shiver of fear. Not for himself but for Rosemary and what she might do, something he couldn't envisage. He was realising that it is impossible to imagine how someone, however well you know her and for how long, when confronted by a situation quite alien to her, quite outside her way of life and that of everyone she knows, will react. It could be with tears, with screaming, with loud-voiced threats, with—please God, not that—the declared intention of suicide.

"A penny for them," said Rosemary merrily. A woman had just approached her, been introduced by Fenella, and remarked on Rosemary's "beautiful suit."

Alan said nothing. What could you ever say? Certainly not the truth. Another introduction followed, Fenella presenting the woman's husband. "Grandma, Granddad, I don't think you know Sir William Johnson. He's my godfather."

Had Alan and Rosemary been at Fenella's christening, thirty-five years before? He had no memory of it, nor of anyone before that or later mentioning this tall, distinguished-looking man in a morning coat with a gardenia in the buttonhole.

He had a fine head of curly hair, close-trimmed and white as snow. Something about him, something distant and remote, rang, as Rosemary would say, a bell. Alan tried to put his finger on that bell, make it ring again, but the faint recognition was gone. All he could think was that Sir William (now addressed by Fenella as Uncle Bill) was about the same age as himself.

They were filing into the hotel for the ceremony, to be performed by a registrar. Alan hadn't been to anyone's wedding for years; perhaps Fenella's had been the last, but that had been in a church, an unfamiliar service certainly and probably from the *Alternative Service Book*, but this was, while of no great interest to him, a "travesty" according to Rosemary's whispering. He was relieved when the limited vows had been made and the last poem written specially by a relative or friend had been read.

Lunch soon followed, not a help-yourself affair, but a series of courses of the stuffed-courgette-flowers, black-pasta-with-prawns, roast-grouse variety, served at tables each for four. Alan felt a heavy depression begin to settle on him, a condition he was occasionally subject to but had never experienced since his reunion with Daphne. Coupled with it was a sensation of horror that he might never see her again, that his own relations at this wedding, his son, his daughter, his granddaughters, and their husbands would close round him and, uniting with Rosemary in consolidated love, crush his and Daphne's joy or dismiss it as an unsuitable "fling" already over.

Sir William and Lady Johnson were the other guests at their table, this placement arranged probably by Freya because all four were much the same age. Again Alan felt he knew William Johnson, though the deep, rather slow voice was unfamiliar. Lady Johnson, younger than her husband and addressed by him as Amanda, was thin, blond, and beautifully dressed in a gown of much the same colour as Rosemary's suit but bearing, to Alan's untutored eye, the unmistakable stamp of Paris. Her small, head-clinging hat he thought a wise choice at a gathering where obstruction of the view of the principal players was unfortunate. It was upsetting to realise that he had begun comparing Rosemary to other women, most of whom he was now seeing as more attractive and better dressed than she. This unpleasant reverie was interrupted by Sir William's saying, "I believe I know you from somewhere, but it's a long time ago."

His voice was cut off by the master of ceremonies' announcing a speech to be made by a friend of the bridegroom's, a man who would once have been called the best man. Alan glanced at Sir William and nodded, but no more talking was possible. The speech was short and without facetiousness or obscene jokes. It is hard to make arch sexual references when the couple you are toasting have been living together for five years. Everyone wanted to start eating but weren't averse to champagne first. Apparently, apart from a rejoinder from the bridegroom and a rather surprising raising of glasses to the Queen, there were to be no more speeches. A bottle of white and a bottle of red wine arrived at their table, and Alan said, "I know you from somewhere too. I knew you as Bill. Your voice deceived me but I realise it must have broken a couple of years after we were all in the"—Alan hesitated—"the qanats."

Bill Johnson began to laugh, the kind of laughter that arises not from amusement but from appreciation of a question answered.

"The qanats, yes. A long time since I heard that word. We were only there a couple of months, but I often think of the qanats. I even dream of them." His deep voice sounded deeper but, strangely, more like the tones of the boy of long ago. "My family lived on the Hill at the top and you in Shelley Grove, I think. I remember you now and one or two others. There was a rather glamorous girl called Daphne something, and a boy with difficult parents and all the Batchelor family."

"I was there too," said Rosemary.

Alan detected a note of resentment in her voice, but more than that, something of anger at the mention of Daphne's name. Bill Johnson's wife heard it too. She looked concerned, glanced at her husband, and Bill responded with the tact Alan associated with the diplomat he later learned his old friend had once been. "Of course you were. Rosemary, the only girl who was a regular attender. Did you two meet there?"

"That's right," she said none too pleasantly. "We've known each other all our lives. We were inseparable, weren't we, Alan?"

Although it had little to do with the ceremony they had just witnessed, a line from the old marriage service came into Alan's mind: *Whom God hath joined together, let no man put asunder.* It wasn't comforting. They ate their lunch, an unsuitable time to raise the matter of the hands discovery. But Bill Johnson mentioned it afterwards. He also said that he had been at Cambridge with Daphne. Alan felt a surge of jealousy, quietened a little when Bill said they had had almost no contact while at the university but hers was a face you would never forget. Amanda Johnson, who had taken little part in the conversation but listened pleasantly and occasionally exchanged a word with Rosemary, said that they must all meet again. Dinner perhaps. She would phone. Alan had no faith in that kind of promise of invitations and reunions. They were always forgotten. Rosemary would veto it, anyway.

They parted for more walking round the gardens and watching Freya and David depart for their honeymoon flight to Morocco. The usual lowering of spirits which always comes at weddings when the couple have left settled on the company. People began to leave. Alan found himself and Rosemary close to Judith, and Alan asked her about Bill Johnson.

"When Maurice and I were in Sudan, Bill was our ambassador in Khartoum. We were very much thrown together, there weren't many English people there then, probably thousands now. Maurice asked him to be godfather to Fenella. He's been a very good godparent, always remembered her birthday and whatever."

"A godparent," said Rosemary repressively, "is supposed to bring the godchild before the bishop at a suitable age for confirmation."

"Oh, *Mum*. No one cares about that sort of thing anymore."

"We all knew each other slightly as children." Alan knew he had spoken of "all" and "slightly" to mollify Rosemary and despised himself for it. "You never mentioned him before."

"I did, Dad, but you weren't listening. I never knew about you all being mates as kids, did I?"

It hadn't been a successful day, not for some of the guests. To his shame, Alan thought that the one thing he had got out of it was the chance, perhaps, to use Bill Johnson as a future alibi. He felt his phone in his pocket, the smooth, rectangular shape of it, and thought, Let me have a moment alone and I will phone Daphne, but there was to be no moment of solitude. Fenella ran up to them just as they were leaving.

"Oh, Grandma, I've got an appointment in Epping next Wednesday afternoon and I thought I might pop in and see you on the way back."

Rosemary said that would be lovely, darling.

"And you too, Granddad?"

No one ever had appointments in Epping, Alan thought, not unless they lived there and went to the dentist or to have their hair done. And why ask if he'd be there? Because she wanted him to be or didn't want him to be?

He nearly said he didn't know. But, no, he wouldn't be there, he'd go and see Daphne. "No." His voice was chilly. "I won't be there. I won't be back till late."

11

WHEN HE THOUGHT about it, which wasn't often, Michael told himself he got on well with his children. If he had to think of a word to describe Jane and Richard's attitude towards him, he would have come up with *dutiful,* and his to them with *undemanding*. They always seemed to be in different parts of the world, and since they communicated by email, it was difficult to tell where they were. He never asked them to come home, but part of their dutifulness was that occasionally they did, usually bringing him a present, once an iPod (Jane) because he liked listening to music in private, and on another occasion half a dozen handmade silk shirts from Seoul (Richard). Both were in their forties. Jane, divorced, had two children, both grown-up now. Richard, who had never married, Michael supposed was gay, but the subject had never been discussed. Many subjects were not discussed in the family, such as life and death and family relationships. When the two came back to this country for four or five days at a time, they invariably stayed in hotels, dutifully visiting Michael every day of their stay. This time, for Jane, it was different. She said so in an email.

She would like to stay with him. It seemed ridiculous, he having this big house and she staying miles away in a "soulless" hotel. She didn't mention the expense, she wouldn't. Neither of his children ever spoke of money in his presence. When he had read the email, he went upstairs and had a look at the bedroom on the second floor next to the one he slept in. It was quite all right, rather small with a single bed and a tiny, freestanding cupboard for clothes. The occupant would have to share his bathroom. He went on up the stairs and into Vivien's room. Naturally, Jane would expect to sleep here.

Removing his shoes and carefully folding back the white silk quilt, he lay down on the bed on the side that had always been his and, with his eyes closed, put his arm round her ghostly body, imagining he felt her warmth. He seldom spoke to her but he did now.

"Shall I let your daughter sleep here, my darling?"

Of course she would. There was no question. Jane would take it for granted, perhaps not even noticing the shrine aspects of the room, the peculiar care that had been lavished on it. His children were not observant, they were not sensitive. He blamed himself, reflecting that he hadn't been sensitive with them. Kind enough, yes, indulgent and generous, but not understanding. He had kept all that as well as love for their mother. Yet he could easily be hurt. He foresaw how he would feel when Jane marched into this room and exclaimed that it was "just like it was when it was Mummy's. Why don't you sleep here?"

Jane's reaction was in fact very like that. She stepped over the threshold and, having inhaled the scent of the white roses he had put in a vase to greet her, flung her arms round him and cried, "Oh, Daddy, am I intruding? You've made this your private place for communing with Mummy."

Later, when she had settled down in what she called "the sacred room," he took her out to dinner, not willing to cook for her and sure she wouldn't welcome it. They talked about her children, whom he barely knew, and about her new job. She was a doctor, a high-powered paediatrician. He told her about Zoe, and Jane made him wince by saying she was surprised "the old dear" was still alive.

"Then you'll be even more so when I tell you my father is."

"Too right I will. He must be a hundred years old."

"When people say that they think they're exaggerating, but in fact he is. Well, ninety-nine."

"You never see him, do you?"

"I almost never see him," Michael said. "Ever since his wife died, he's been living in a luxurious old people's home where everyone has a personal butler and a Jacuzzi."

"You're joking."

"I've never seen all this, of course. I get it from Zoe."

Next morning Brenda Miller phoned to say Zoe was ill and had gone into hospital. She had pneumonia.

"I'll come straightaway."

Jane said briskly, "What a shame when I've just come," but seemed quite resigned to his absence. She had lots to do, she said, and hundreds of people to see.

"I won't stay there," he said. "I'll be back this evening."

"Mind you say hallo to her from me."

Zoe would be beyond greetings of that kind, he thought, but he promised he would. Pneumonia, which was once called the old man's friend because, without drugs, painlessly and slowly it gently carried him to his end. They would try to keep Zoe alive and no doubt succeed for a while. But perhaps she had asked not to be resuscitated.

She had said he was her son and she his mother. Those emotive words brought the tears to his eyes that had been withheld while he was with her in her house. He wept in the back of the taxi on his way to the hospital. She was conscious, propped up on pillows, and Brenda was with her.

"I'll go," Brenda said. "I'll leave you alone together."

He held Zoe's hand. Her voice had sunk to a whisper. She was lucid but forced to be sparing in what she said.

"Your father. When I'm gone, he will be quite alone." She paused, looked searchingly at him. Her eyes were still clear. "I have said harsh things of him. Maybe I have been wrong. The alibi—did I dream it?"

"No, no, Zoe, of course not."

"I don't know. When I'm gone, will you tell Urban Grange? Tell them you're his son? They don't know you exist. Tell them you do, that's all."

It had been a huge effort for her. She closed her

eyes and rested her head back against the pillows. Michael thought for a moment she was dead, but the hand he held was not only warm but the fingers moved and pressed against his palm. He brought it to his lips and she smiled, a tiny ghost of a smile. Sitting at her bedside, still holding her hand, he thought about his dead, his poor pretty, red-haired mother, unkind though she had been; he thought about father-like Chris, Zoe's husband, who always had time for the lonely little boy; Vivien, always Vivien, her death unbelievable for month after month, her ghost always with him.

A nurse came up to Zoe's bed. He relinquished her hand and the nurse took it, feeling for a pulse. She smiled, told him to stay for as long as he liked and she would bring him a cup of tea. Hours went by, he didn't know how many. The tea had been drunk and another cup brought, her hand restored to his hand. And he too slept, still holding it, to wake up and find the nurse there beside him.

"Your mum's still sleeping," she said, embarrassed because her words had called forth more weeping and driven him to touch Zoe's forehead with his lips before turning away. He was back with her when she died on the following day, in the afternoon. She had had one last wish, uncharacteristic as it seemed, and he carried it out once he had registered the death and made funeral arrangements. The first thing he did when he reached home was to tell Jane she was dead.

"Oh, Daddy," said Jane. "Would you like a hug?"

What can you say? It's an offer you can't refuse. He submitted to the hug. She told him she had passed the news on to her brother and Richard would be there next day. "To be a support," she said.

Richard came, as cold and practical as his sister was emotional. Both returned for the funeral, sitting on either side of him in the crematorium, literally and physically supportive as each held an arm when the coffin disappeared into the fire.

Only when they were both gone and the bedrooms vacated was he able to creep up to the top floor and open Vivien's door, doing so literally in fear and trembling. He stood there, his hand still on the door handle, telling himself to expect a disarrangement of the room, the bed disordered, the flowers he had left still there but drooping and dead in a vase half full of smelly yellow water. Don't be angry, don't upset yourself. He opened the door and, taking in the precious room, instead of feeling distress was moved by gratitude and, yes, by love. The dead flowers were gone, there was no mess, no dust, and lifting back the quilt, he saw Jane had even put on clean sheets. His good, kind daughter . . .

These days he was always crying. Making up for not crying much as a child when he had cause to cry. What he needed was someone to talk to, someone who would listen and be kind but not—that childhood word—soppy. Impulsively, he picked up the phone and called Daphne's number. A voice that wasn't hers said no one was available to take his call and to try again later.

THE CALL HE should have made, though what "should" meant in this context was hard to say, was to his father's luxurious sanctuary, Urban Grange. Michael didn't even know where the place was. Asking Google to find it gave him something to do. That was easy. He hadn't expected the website, page after page advertising the place. It was described as the most luxurious (there was that word again) haven for discerning seniors in the United Kingdom, a sanctum and a retreat, a grace and favour residence of seclusion, an exquisite Palladian mansion in the Suffolk countryside. Photographs abounded in hot colour. The gardens overflowed with blooms or in other parts of the grounds with exotic trees and shrubs. There were gazebos, follies, temples, and even a ha-ha. Each suite had its own small garden, approached from a glazed-in patio furnished with cane, quilted silk, and silver. What did it cost? No mention was made of money. Money was vulgar. On the other hand, Michael thought, wasn't it vulgar to show testimonials from satisfied residents? One was from a certain Dame Doris Perivale ("Lovelier than any home I have ever had") and Prince Ali Kateh ("Number one in palace category").

There was a phone number and an email address. Michael wrote the number down on the back of an envelope, the only piece of paper to hand, put it in his pocket, and forgot about it. But he didn't forget to phone Daphne, and this time she answered.

JOHN WINWOOD HAD never been prone to worrying. If something to come was unpleasant, he pushed it out of his mind and ceased to think about it. This had not been possible in regard to his married (or unmarried) status. Back in the late 1940s it troubled him, if not all the time, for a few minutes and sometimes longer every day. His wife, Anita, was dead and he told people she had died. He was a widower. That was true and he knew it, none better, but he had no death certificate and never could have.

He wanted to marry again. He had no one specifically in mind but several he was considering. The war had been a widow-maker. Margaret Lewis's husband had died in the Egyptian desert; another one called Beryl Nichols, who was left alone when Gary Nichols failed to return from Dunkirk; and a third called Rita, who served in the bar at the Hollybush and took off her wedding ring after Arnhem. Of these three, all of whom Woody more or less courted, only

Mrs. Lewis had money—real money, that is.

He had sold Anderby and rented a small flat over a shop in Leyton. It was not the kind of place to which he could invite a woman. Certainly not Margaret Lewis, who lived in a big house in Chigwell. His money was running out but he stuck to his resolve never to work. His few years of labour in the factory and the abattoir had taught him never to get a job again but to find a way of living without employment. Another lesson he had learned was that a woman's jealousy will cause her to behave recklessly and do things she would normally never have dreamt of. A man's too, for all he knew. For all he knew because he had never been jealous. Rita was better-looking than Beryl, and both were better-looking than Margaret. She had lain too long and too often in the sun of Nice and Corsica when her husband was alive, and her face and shoulders were creased up and blotched with the remains of sunburn. She was over forty and putting on weight. But she had money. She had a fine big house and a fine big car and a large income, from what source Woody had been unable to find out until the jealousy began.

Their relationship had never been what Margaret called "an intimate one," unlike the situation with both Beryl and Rita. He told Margaret she had driven him to spend nights with these two women because, he said, "a man has certain needs." Jealousy consumed her. She was foolish enough to stand in front of a mirror, call him over, and point out to him the wrinkles and blotches while asking him if that was what sent him to those other women. Foolish perhaps but not silly enough to have any effect on Woody. He closed his eyes to what the sun had done and Margaret's silliness and asked her to marry him. There would be no other women if she married him, no looking at other women. Of course she said yes, leaving Woody in a state hitherto unknown to him, anxiety. Suppose the vicar or the registrar asked to see his first wife's death certificate? He continued worrying throughout his engagement, which, fortunately for him, lasted no more than six weeks. It was a vicar, not a registrar, and he didn't ask.

Margaret had always had money, was born to it, and Major Rory Lewis had always had money. Neither of them had ever worked in the sense that Woody thought of work. So Margaret never asked him why he hadn't a job or a private income. She assumed that everyone in her circle had money. Eventually he told her he had nothing, for the house money and the jewellery money had come to an end. Margaret, still in love, said not to worry as she had plenty for both of them. That was in their early days. She fell out of love and began to ration him. He had the Chigwell house and the Lagonda, and if she gave him ten pounds a week, wasn't that all he could expect? There was no joint account and he couldn't touch her private account. He sometimes thought of how he had strangled pretty Anita and sold her rings and necklace, but those days were gone. He was afraid that if he tried something similar with Margaret, the police would suspect him—they always first suspected the husband—and begin to investigate his past. They would ask when and where Anita had died and ask for her death certificate. His old trouble returned. There were no answers. The only thing was to carry on as they were, Margaret calmly happy, he with his ten pounds a week. An idea of taking some of Margaret's jewellery and selling it flitted across his mind, only to be dismissed as impractical with a wife who was still alive and who had learned from being married to him to be suspicious of almost everything he did.

He was nearly sixty and she some five years older when she died. It was cancer, in nearly all cases in those days incurable. The surprises started at her funeral. A mystery woman (so called by Woody) turned up and seated herself in the front pew, the one set aside for relatives and close friends. She was about fifty, he thought, and she reminded him of someone. He couldn't think who. She turned up at the wine-and-sandwiches party Margaret's friend from Chigwell put on, but since she didn't introduce herself to Woody, he thought no more about her. Until he awoke in the middle of the night and realised that the someone the mystery woman reminded him of was Margaret. Some niece? Perhaps. He sent himself back to sleep by thinking contentedly about Margaret's shares, her bank accounts, this house, and the Jaguar which had replaced the Lagonda. Presumably, she had made a will, but it was of no importance. Everything would come to him.

The will turned up and was a rude and distressing awakening. Woody got the house, that was all right, but nearly all the money (the ten pounds a week continued) and the shares and the car and the furniture went to a woman Margaret hadn't seen since (the will said) "she was taken from my arms at the age of three months and given to a couple called James and Stella Brotherton for adoption."

Another woman who came to the funeral was Sheila Fraser, even richer than Margaret. Woody, no one called him that anymore, did his usual researches and discovered the extent of her wealth. She wasn't pretty or clever and she was obsessed with natural history. They had almost nothing in common, but she pointed out to him the distressing incidence of hedgehogs among the road kill and made him promise to remember the Hedgehog Trust in his will. He was bound to die first as he was thirty years her senior. But he didn't, of course. He saw to that. She had a miserable life with him but she never told him so and he never noticed.

12

FENELLA GOT COLD FEET. That wasn't what she told her mother. It wasn't suitable, she said, for a granddaughter to tell her grandmother such things.

"But it's all right for a daughter to tell her mother?"

"It's a question of age."

"Well, thanks for giving me back my youth."

"You know what I mean, Mum," said Fenella.

At least Judith wouldn't have to look after her grandchildren and maybe she wouldn't tell her mother. Maybe the occasion wouldn't arise. She would have to wait for a suitable moment, some mention for instance, of how happy Alan and Rosemary's marriage had been as against that of people who lived together without marriage, a common subject of conversation. But, no, that wouldn't do. If perhaps her mother were to say that she was worried about her father, suggest he was becoming senile? It would be awkward and perhaps ineffective. She would, she decided, trust to the inspiration of the moment.

Also to be thought of was what Rosemary would do. Have hysterics, cry, or even be silenced and tell Judith to go away, get out of her house, how dare she say such things about her father? It was a long drive from Chiswick to Loughton, and Judith and Maurice had often grumbled about it, but this time it seemed to her short. The pleasant hills and green folds of the forest were upon her within not much more than half an hour, and she was soon driving up the High Road. Many times had she done this since she had first learned to drive at seventeen; everything was familiar to her—for this part of Loughton hadn't changed much—the Lopping Hall and the old police station, and turning off down Station Road, St. Mary's Church ahead. She was suddenly seeing her mission as serious, not the rather awful joke it had at first appeared to her but a matter so serious that even at this late stage it might break up her parents' marriage. Her children's *grandparents?* Was it possible? She drove past her old school, which she had walked to every day in the days when teenagers thought nothing of walking long distances. Her mother had fetched her in the car when it rained. Sometimes, on the mornings her father went to work later than usual, he and she had walked down together and parted at the school gates, he going on alone to the station. She drove on up Alderton Hill, at the top turning left to her parents' road, down to her parents' block of flats that hadn't been there or even thought of in those days. She parked in the designated slot they hadn't used since they got rid of their car and looked up to their windows. Her mother had come out and was waving to her from their balcony.

"Is Fenella all right, darling?" asked Rosemary when she opened the door. "Not that I'm not delighted to see you of course, but I did wonder if Fenella was unwell and was hiding something from me."

"Well, I'm not hiding anything from you, Mum." It was true or soon would be. "Fenella is fine and so are the children."

"They're so sweet and good," said Rosemary incredibly. "I'll make the tea straightaway."

"Mum, would you mind awfully if I had a drink instead? Just one because I'm driving. But if I could have a glass of wine . . . I'll fetch it."

The possibility had only just occurred to Judith, and once it had occurred, as is often the case when an unprecedented alcoholic drink is in prospect, couldn't be resisted.

"Of course, darling. Why on earth not?" Then Rosemary proceeded to say exactly why on earth not. "It's just that you *are* driving and it's better not to drink at all. Anyway, don't you think it's a good idea to restrict one's drinking to certain hours and to stick to it? That old saying about waiting till the sun is over the yardarm isn't a bad principle."

But Judith was already fetching herself a large, full glass of Pinot Grigio. She sat down and gulped down more than a large sip and nearer a swig.

“My goodness, you were thirsty, if that’s the word.” Rosemary began on the wedding, though they had exchanged their individual opinions of it at least twice since the event. Judith’s verdict on the copper-coloured silk suit was again invited, and Judith again said it was lovely and much admired. She was starting to feel sick and drank some more wine, not the best remedy.

“Are you all right, Judy?”

“Mum, I’m fine. Tell me something. Where’s Dad?”

“Why on earth do you ask?”

“I’d just like to know where you think he is. Sorry, I’m being a bit clumsy. Would you mind telling me where he is?”

“Now, Judith, I did try to warn you. I think that wine is going to your head. It’s really affecting you. You’ve drunk half a large glass in two minutes and it can’t be good.”

Judith thought, I could give this up, I could say I’m a bit drunk, I’m sorry, let’s change the subject. But there was no subject as yet.

“Mother, listen to me. I am serious, very serious. Do you know where Dad is now?”

It had reached Rosemary at last. She creased up her eyes, held her mouth open before she finally spoke. “Yes, of course I do. He’s gone to see Michael Winwood up in town somewhere.” Her voice faltered. "You won't know him, he was a childhood friend. One of those we've got to know again over that ghastly hands business."

"No, he hasn't. I'm sure he hasn't. Phone this Winwood man and find out."

"Oh, Judy, I couldn't check up on your father."

Judith decided after another swig of wine that she had better come straight out with it. "Freya and David saw him with a woman in a restaurant in St. John's Wood. It was about a month ago. They were holding hands. When they left, he had his arm round her. I'm sorry to tell you like this, but I don't know how else to do it, and I think you have to be told."

Rosemary sat quite still, then she began shaking her head. The head-shaking went on so long that it became alarming. When she spoke, her voice, quite unlike her usual tone, was high-pitched, almost squeaky.

"It must have been someone else. Not your father, it couldn't be your father."

"Tell me this Winwood man's number."

It was doubtful that her mother would obey but she did. She took the directory out of a drawer, lifted the handset off the rest, and handed it to her daughter, mouthing the number silently as if some spy might be listening. Her hands clenching, then twisting in a wringing gesture, Rosemary sat waiting. For someone to answer or perhaps in hopes that no one would?

"Mr. Winwood? . . . This is Judith Hayland, Norris that was. I believe my father is with you. May I speak to him?"

Judith was as certain as could be that her father wasn't there and he wasn't.

MICHAEL WINWOOD SOUNDED as surprised as she had guessed he would be, but not suspicious. And after she had put the phone down, he still suspected nothing. Infidelity and its deceit and stratagems didn't come within his experience but that of his clients. This was an area of innocence for him, and if he wondered a little, it was only to recall that if Daphne had agreed to his visiting her today, he wouldn't have been at home to receive Judith Hayland's call. But as the day passed, their brief conversation recurred to him, and later he thought it a little odd that Alan Norris, who had never been to his house, to whom he must have given his phone number but certainly not his address, could have told his daughter that she would find him here. They were not friends, they had met only once—that time in George Batchelor's house—since Michael's father threw them out of the tunnels sixty years before. He didn't want to think of his father, that immortal creature who seemed superhuman in his refusal to die. Michael had still not phoned Urban Grange, though the piece of paper on which he had written the number was still in his pocket, crumpled through frequent handling.

• • •

BEFORE SHE BROKE the dire news to her mother, Judith had given some thought to the possibility of her tears, hysterics, stony silence, or rage, but none to what would happen next. Rosemary might want to run away, come home with her, send for Judith's brother, Owen, or send for a doctor (was that possible these days?) or more likely a solicitor. But all she said was "What am I going to do?"

"Well, nothing, Mum. What can you do?"

"I can't really believe it, you know. Not your father. It's going to turn out that this woman is a doctor, some sort of specialist, more women than men are these days. He's been consulting her about something serious, he went to hear the news of some scan or other he's had, and the news was so good he took her out to dinner and they celebrated. That will be it."

Judith had never known her mother to be so inventive. It was plausible, but it wasn't true.

"He didn't tell me because he knew it would worry me," Rosemary said.

Then why didn't he tell you afterwards? Judith wanted to ask, but knew her mother would only have an alternative explanation to put forward. It made Judith speculate as to what her father would have invented to convince her. He had more imagination than she and might even at this moment be sitting in a train elaborating some fiction. It was getting on for seven. Judith would very much have liked another glass of wine, but if she did, she dared not drive home. Wait, leave the car here and take the tube? But to be here when these two confronted each other? No, absolutely not. She looked at her silent, rigid-faced mother and took note of what she generally ignored or never saw at all: how wrinkled her face was, how sunken her eyes and hooded their lids, her jawline drooping, her upper lip clustered with parallel vertical lines. The first thing you noticed about her hands along with the corrugated nails was the overlay of branched purple veins. Veins too pushed out the thin fabric of her stockings. She was old. Things like this didn't happen to old people, but evidently they did.

"When do you expect Dad home?"

Her mother seemed to have forgotten all about the mysterious doctor. "Will it make any difference what time I *expect* him?"

"Oh, Mum, would you like me to stay?" Judith said it because she knew she ought to. The prospect was awful. "I could phone Maurice. I could leave the car here."

Rosemary said suddenly, "What did she look like, this woman?"

"All Freya said was that she was tall and dark and—well, she said 'quite old.' "

"I see." Rosemary looked as if she did see. "Is that supposed to make me feel better, that she's old? It makes it worse. No, I don't want you to stay, darling. I'll see him alone."

In the past few minutes Judith's old mother had not so much grown older, she had grown up. At her age she had at last seen what life was about.

WHILE HIS DAUGHTER was checking up on him, Alan was in bed with Daphne. They had been there since late morning, apart from a break for lunch at Carluccio's, but had returned for more love-making and then sleep. He went downstairs in the evening and fetched a bottle of champagne he had put on ice in the afternoon and cut two large slices from the carrot cake he had bought while they were out. They loved carrot cake—it was one of the many things they had in common—and, both thin, never thought about their weight. Too old for that nonsense, said Daphne. The champagne was drunk, the cake was eaten, and at nine Alan said he'd better go. God knew, he didn't want to but he'd better. Daphne put on a dressing gown and fetched him a key to her front door—three keys rather, as it was always well locked up.

"You may need it," said Daphne. "I've had a premonition."

"Doesn't sound like you."

"Ah, but it is. Remember I used to be a fortune-teller."

He thought of that when he was in the tube,

precisely when the train was passing through Snaresbrook. Up there was his old school, and why he was remembering that he didn't know. What had she foreseen? Nothing. He felt the keys in his pocket as once he had felt her card. It was ten thirty when he got out of the train and he was tired. The walk home to Traps Hill was shorter than any Loughton walk he had taken in the past, but even when they lived in Harwater Drive right at the top of Church Hill, he had never thought of taking a taxi. He was older now and a taxi was waiting. But still he walked, and as he walked, he thought of his past life as drowning men are said to do: the tunnels, schooldays and university, and then Daphne, always Daphne, parting, and then Rosemary and marriage, children and grandchildren and retirement. How we grow away from our children, he thought. He cared little what his children thought of him now. They probably loved him in a remote kind of way. Did he care what Rosemary thought? What he wanted was what most men want, and it came to him as a devastating truth. They didn't want trouble, that was it, they wanted life to be without trouble, to have peace, and that was odd in the far more warlike of the sexes.

Rosemary would be asleep at ten to eleven. She always was. He closed the front door softly as he always did. She was sitting in the living-room with the door to the balcony open. A half-empty glass of red wine was on the table in front of her. Some tremble at moments of anxiety, some feel sick, some flush; Alan turned white.

"I need a drink of water," he said, then went into the kitchen and filled a glass.

Rosemary said nothing. She sat, holding her wine but not drinking.

"You had better say what you have to say," he said.

She set down her glass and looked into it, her hands round the stem. "Why her? That's all I want to know. If it was someone young, I could understand, but why her? Why that old witch?"

He didn't ask how she knew. Maybe she had talked to Robert Flynn. It didn't seem important. "Insults don't help."

"There's another thing I want to know. Have you had relations with her?"

That was exactly what he expected her to ask, the very words. He could have written the script for her. Over the past weeks, months now, he had told so many lies that he was in the habit of it. He was so practised that he could easily tell another. He could easily say no, he had betrayed Rosemary so often; was he now to betray Daphne? "Oh, yes," he said. "Of course."

She lifted her head, stood up, and cried out, "How could you? How could you?"

"There's no answer to that, Rosemary. You know there isn't."

"Are you sorry? Do you want me to forgive you?"

"Can we talk about it tomorrow? I want to go to bed."

He thought she would start crying. She didn't. "Have there been lots of others? Right through our marriage, have there been others?"

"No. No one else. I'm going to bed."

When a crisis of this kind happens in a marriage, the first action that is taken, as against words exchanged, is that one of the partners—spouses they used to be called—moves out of the marital bed, into the spare room or onto a sofa. When Alan went into their bedroom, intending to fetch his night things and go to the spare room, he found that Rosemary had been there before him, her nightdress already on the single bed, her little radio that she called a wireless on the cabinet along with her reading glasses.

NEITHER OF THEM slept much. He thought, We can thrash this out over and over, as people do, or as I've been told people do, and in the end I shall go. She has never lived alone in all her life. What will she do? I won't desert her, I will be there, I will do anything she asks—except stay with her. I am old but I won't tell myself that on those grounds I am entitled to some happiness for the years that remain to me. I'm not, no one is. He slept a little, woke up, and got up at five thirty.

She was already up and not in her dressing gown as she would normally have been at this hour. She wore a floral dress she had made herself. Her hair was carefully arranged in waves and curls as if the night before she had used those rollers she sometimes did for a special occasion next day. He saw, to his horror, that it was not "as if," that was what she had done, and he shivered. It was her way of trying to get him back.

"Alan, if you will promise not to see her again, I will forgive you. I will let bygones be bygones. Just promise me and we can forget all about it."

He said nothing.

"After all, it was very short-lived, wasn't it? You could call it a moment of madness. You're over seventy years old. You don't want this kind of upheaval, do you? Just tell me you won't see her again and let this be the end of it. I won't hold it against you."

He hadn't expected this. She was being reasonable, and that was unusual to say the least. Men want peace and a quiet life. He had had more than half a century of a quiet life and he wanted no more of it. He wanted Daphne, and their ages didn't matter.

He said the things he had thought of in the sleepless night: he would be there when she needed him, he would never desert her. He added other things: she could have the flat, he would give her any income within reason that she asked for, but he was going. He would stay only to pack a case. Then what he had feared happened, what he had been so relieved about when it appeared it was not going to happen. She stood up, clenched her fists, and began to scream. She beat her fists against his chest and screamed into his face. Though much stronger than her, he was still shaken by it. He held her by the arms, enduring the noise, knowing the remedy was to slap her face but unable to bring himself to do this. A horrible change took place. Instead of screaming she began kissing him, clutching his shoulders and covering his face with kisses.

"Rosemary, stop. Please stop."

She threw herself onto the sofa, sobbing now. He went into the bedroom he had shared with her until the previous night, found a suitcase, and threw clothes into it. Most of his stuff would have to be sent, but who would send it? One of his children? He heard Rosemary shouting now. She was standing in the bedroom doorway.

"No one will speak to you, do you know that? Your children won't have anything to do with you. You'll never see your grandchildren again. Have you thought of that?"

He found his mobile phone and the charger, which he dropped into the suitcase. Rosemary came in and snatched the phone out of his hand. Back in the living-room he picked up the landline receiver and called the number of a taxi service he had sometimes used, but never to be driven the distance he wanted now. "Hamilton Terrace, London North West Eight," he said. Rosemary would know the address now but she would have to know it sooner or later.

She had begun shouting that she would like to kill him. Going back into the bedroom, he found her pulling all the clothes he had packed out onto the floor. She had dropped his phone into the washbasin in the bathroom and run both taps onto it. He put the clothes back, a jumble of shirts and odd socks and pyjamas. She watched, waiting, he supposed, for him to leave the room again. He did but with the case, which he put a leather strap round. She was muttering threats, how she hoped he would die, how she would like to kill Daphne. The landline phone rang to tell him his taxi was waiting in the block car park. He said good-bye and she screamed at him again. He closed the front door behind him and walked out into the car park, savouring peace and silence.

Three-quarters of an hour later he put the keys Daphne had given him into her front door locks, the top one, the middle one, and the bottom one, feeling that he had come home.

13

LONG AGO LOUGHTON had really been a village, and right up to the Second World War and beyond its residents still talked about "going down to the village" when they went shopping. Like any village it had its class system, and everyone, including the children, knew that the poor lived in Forest Road and Smarts Lane, the middle class in those streets bounded by Hillcrest Road and Rectory Lane, and the rich ones in Church Lane and Alderton Hill. Everyone knew everyone else or knew of them as is true of villages, so when the cleaner gave up her job at Anderby, on the Hill, on account, she said, of "goings-on," the news spread along Smarts Lane, where she lived, and reached the ears of Clara Moss in Forest Road. She was already working for the Batchelors in Tycehurst Hill, but she could do with a second job. So Clara Moss, a soldier's widow, her husband killed in the first year of the war, came to work for John Winwood and his wife, Anita. As for the "goings-on," she didn't care about that, it wasn't her business. The house next door to Clara's had been sold in the year before the war for two hundred pounds. If hers was worth the same, it made her feel rich.

She never grew rich. She might have done so when she was old and the house would have sold for two hundred thousand pounds. But where would she have lived? She had no children to take her in, and she was afraid of old people's homes. You heard such dreadful things about them. She would have been all right in her house if she hadn't had her knee done, but the pain was so bad she couldn't carry on as she had been. Nor could she work, not at her age. When Fred died in the war after a year of marriage, she had been nineteen, and now she was eighty-eight. She was waiting for the second knee to be done. Clara loved the NHS; it had been good to her when it did her hip and her broken wrist when she fell on the ice, but it did keep you waiting. Months had gone by since they'd said the knee must be done. It had started giving her gip, as Mr. Batchelor put it. Clara loved Mr. Batchelor almost as much as the NHS—not that she would have admitted that even to herself. He had had his hip done on the private and hadn't had to wait, but what was the result? He was still limping about and he still used a stick.

Now she had to have an MRI scan and Mrs. Batchelor was going to take her in the car. Clara liked this Mrs. B much better than the first one, whom she'd worked for when she first went to Carisbrooke, but she wished it was Mr. Batchelor that was taking her. It was for something to do with her heart, this scan. When you got to her age, there was always something wrong with you. She wanted someone to talk to and not just the TV. It was small and the colours faded as if she were sometimes looking at it through fog. The people on it weren't real, and it was real people she wanted, though no one was left now. Her sisters were dead and their husbands. She couldn't expect nephews and nieces to bother with her even if they knew where she lived. Fred's family were long gone. When she was young, it was family you knew, not friends. They *were* your friends.

Since her knee had got so bad, the girl next door had done her shopping for her. Mrs. B said she shouldn't call her a girl, it wasn't politically correct, whatever that meant. It had nothing to do with politics as far as Clara could see. She should say "young woman," Mrs. B said. When Clara remembered, she compromised and said "young lady." The young lady next door was called Samantha, and she had a partner instead of a husband. Clara didn't know what to think about that so she didn't think about it. Samantha went to the supermarket for her, and when she came back and Clara tried to pay her, she often wouldn't take the money. Not that it came to much, tea and bread and Flora margarine and Tiptree jam, half a dozen small eggs, and a bit of ham. In the days when she could make it round the corner to the surgery, the lady doctor had told her she should be eating vegetables and fruit, but Clara had never liked that kind of food, and now that she couldn't walk so far, she didn't have to hear that sort of thing. That was one blessing.

MAUREEN BATCHELOR AND Helen Batchelor were having tea at Carisbrooke. George had graduated from the sofa to a new armchair with a footrest, and Stanley was in the garden, throwing a ball for Spot. Having taken care to eat no more than a ginger biscuit each, Maureen and Helen were exchanging views on their favourite subject, the stubbornness of men, their intractability and tendency to hide their heads in the sand when threatened by anything unpleasant. George, wishing he could be outside with his brother and the dog, had nodded off. Helen was holding forth on men's unwillingness to go to a doctor even when anyone could tell they had all the symptoms of cancer or heart disease, to which Maureen rejoined with a tale of a friend of hers whose husband had now had a stent and a quadruple bypass as a result of refusing to keep a hospital appointment.

George opened his eyes and struggled to his feet. "Need a bit of fresh air," he said. Taking hold of his stick, he took two steps towards the open French window, then one more before crumbling at the knees, the stick slipping from him, and crashing to the floor. Stanley came running across the lawn, followed by Spot. Helen was already on her knees beside George, her arm under his head, lifting him a little to check his face, to see if he could lift an arm and if he could speak.

"Nine nine nine," she said to Maureen. "Now. Ask for an ambulance and tell them he's had a stroke."

The women behaved in exemplary fashion, as Stanley said afterwards, and Maureen said it was funny that they had been talking about that very thing and then this happened. The ambulance came quite quickly and took George away to the stroke unit at St. Margaret's Hospital, Maureen sitting beside him and holding his hand. His mouth was pulled down on one side, but he could speak and he could see. Left behind at Carisbrooke, Helen cleared away the tea things while Stanley poured her a stiff gin and tonic.

"You need it, baby," he said, though she hadn't argued.

She was sitting down, stroking Spot for comfort and sipping the gin, when her phone rang or, rather, began playing "I Walk the Line." It had to be Maureen with news, though it was a bit soon. Instead of her sister-in-law, it was a woman she knew from her bridge club who lived in a flat in Traps Hill.

"I don't believe it," said Helen.

"It's true. They've split up. Alan's left her for someone else, I don't know who. At his age! He's must be seventy-five. But people don't grow old like they used to, do they? I'll let you know if I find out any more."

Stanley, with a small glass of wine because he was driving, said, "What was all that about?"

Helen told him.

"Alan Norris? No, it can't be. Him and Rosemary are the perfect couple. No, no, it must be someone else."

"Well, Suzanne seemed to know all about it. Let's get off home and wait to hear from Maureen. She may know more."

It was hard to say whether Helen meant more about the Norrises or about George.

THANKS TO HELEN'S prompt action, George Batchelor responded to treatment quite quickly. The clot-busting drugs, according to the doctor, were effective. He was made to get up when he longed to stay in bed, walked around his private room holding Maureen's arm, and became surprisingly cheerful. Maureen, however, took it badly. Stanley, who had described the Norrises as the perfect couple, could now have had that term applied to herself and George.

"I realised Dad might die," she said to her daughter. "The funny thing is, I'd never really thought of it before."

"We're all going to die one day, Mum."

"Yes, but not soon. He might have another stroke, he might have one tomorrow. It's left me feeling really depressed."

"Try and put it out of your mind. How about those friends of yours, those two who've split up? At their age? You don't think about them dying, do you?"

Maureen wasn't interested in the Norrises. She wasn't interested in anyone but herself and George. How dreadful, she thought, only to realise how much you love someone when you're about to lose him. George was at home now, preoccupied with his health. He had sent her out to buy a sphygmomanometer and took his own blood pressure several times a day. In spite of the doctor's warning he overdosed on low-dose aspirins, intended to thin his blood. Apart from a quick visit to the pharmacy, Maureen never went out. She was afraid that if she left him alone, he might have another stroke. By night she hardly slept, dreading that if she fell asleep, she might wake to find him dead.

Relatives came to visit George: Stanley and Helen of course, and Norman came over from France, bringing Eliane with him. Maureen didn't want any of them. All she wanted was to stay at home alone with George. The day came when she was due to take Clara Moss for her MRI, but she'd have to miss that. There was no need to go out because they had all their groceries delivered. Helen brought chocolates and a bottle of sherry, though Maureen wouldn't allow George alcohol, she was too frightened. She did worry a bit about not seeing Clara, but Clara had no phone, strange as that was. Maureen had heard that the young woman next door did her shopping for her, so that would be all right. Still her conscience worried her, and she asked Helen if she would go and knock at Clara's door, just to see if she was mobile.

"I couldn't do that," Helen said. "I don't know the woman, it'd be very awkward. I'd be embarrassed and so would she."

Maureen said she sometimes thought she'd never go out again, she'd be too afraid to leave George.

"He won't be stuck here for ever," Norman said. "He'll want to be out and about and you'll be with him."

When she told George that no one had visited Clara Moss, he was disproportionately upset. Well, it seemed disproportionate to her.

"She can get about, George. She's not bedridden. I'd call her quite a tough old bird."

"I can order a car and have it take me to Forest Road. The driver can help me up the path, and once I'm inside Clara's house, I can sit down. I'll be fine."

"I'm not having it, George. You'll kill yourself. I'll take the phone away."

George said all right, he wouldn't do it, but to pass him the two phone books, the one for North West London and the local one. He would find someone else to "look in" on Clara and take her to the hospital.

14

ALAN HADN'T ANTICIPATED the enormous fuss. Perhaps he hadn't because he gave little thought to what would happen after he had walked out of the flat in Traps Hill and come here to Daphne. That it would be lovely with Daphne he had known and it was. No surprise there. Not only the love-making. He might even say not so much the love-making as the pleasure of being able to walk down the street with her, hand in hand if they chose, making a restaurant reservation in both their names, driving out together in Daphne's car and going home together, walking up the path to the front door and letting themselves in—together.

But trouble had begun on their first morning. When he got there in the dark and paid off his taxi, he let himself into the house, rather surprised that he could, that she hadn't bolted the door. She must have thought of that when she gave him the keys, have thought she would never bolt the door again until he did it himself when he lived here with her. He had gone upstairs and found her asleep. He knelt down by the bed and kissed her until she woke and put her arms round him. The phone rang at eight in the morning, the landline. How did Judith get this number?

"From Michael Winwood. I thought of asking him—rather clever of me, wasn't it? He had no idea. He seemed to think I was holding some sort of reunion of oldies."

"What do you want, Judy?"

"For you to come back, of course. Come home now and she'll forgive you, she'll overlook it. It was such a monstrous thing to do, but she wants you back just the same. Does she want you back! My God, Dad, she is in such a state as I've never seen. She can't believe it, she says she's in a nightmare she can't wake up from."

"Other men have left their wives. It's not uncommon."

"Is that all you can say?"

"No, Judith, it's not all I can say. I can say a great many things. But I'm not going to say them to you."

"Owen is absolutely furious. He says it must be Alzheimer's. He says you could be made to come back."

Alan didn't feel like laughing but he did laugh. "Alzheimer's has only been known or only called that for a few years. What did people blame the failings of the old on before that? Senility, I suppose, which is much the same thing. As for Owen, he can't talk. He walked out on his first wife. Yes, but he was young, you're going to say, aren't you? Good-bye, Judy."

Fenella was the next to phone. Alan said it was nothing to do with her and she should mind her own business. He had never spoken to a granddaughter like this before and he rather enjoyed it. That was the second day. With Rosemary it was different, he had to talk to her and for as long as she liked. He was treating her badly, worse than badly, and he knew it. With no excuse and no defence, in a strange way he was set free. Her voice on the phone was so unlike the voice he knew that he would hardly have recognised it.

"What have I done? I'd like to know what I've done. If I've done some awful thing, I'd like you to tell me. I thought I'd been a good wife to you. We've passed our Golden Wedding, Alan, and you've left me and I don't know why."

He didn't know what to say except that it wasn't her, it was him. It was his fault, not hers. Fault, of course, didn't come into it. They had been incompatible for nearly fifty years. Both knew it without even expressing it to each other or, come to that, to themselves. They had made the best of it because when they were young, you dissolved a marriage only because of adultery or violence. He let her talk. He listened because he owed her that. When she had said enough or had exhausted herself, he would leave it to her to say good-bye and put the phone down.

Daphne never commented on these calls or asked what they were about, but after three days of them—Freya and her new husband and his son-in-law Maurice and a cousin Alan hadn't spoken to for years and two neighbours in the block all called—she went out and bought him a new mobile phone.

"No one can get through to me," she said. "You're so popular."

One of the people who had been trying to get through was Michael Winwood. He knew nothing of the Norrises' break-up and wanted to talk to Daphne as if she were a sort of therapist. She of all the people he knew, and he had few friends, might listen to him if he talked to her about his father and Urban Grange and his loss of Zoe. While he was waiting to make another attempt to get hold of her, his phone rang. It was George Batchelor, to ask him if he would come to Loughton and "look in" on Clara Moss.

"Who's Clara Moss?"

"You know who she is, Mike. The charlady who used to char for my family and your mum and dad, lives in Forest Road, old as the hills now. Even older than us as she'd have to be."

"Mrs. Mopp, we called her," said Michael, still

wincing from the diminutive no one else had ever used. "Well, my father did. It was from a character who was a cleaner in a radio comedy. Moss and Mopp, you see. Not very kind, was it?" But his father was never kind, Michael thought, not saying it aloud. "What about her?"

"Look, Mike, I've had a stroke, much better now. I used to pop in and see her, have done for yonks. So would you look in on her? She'll remember you. Come and have a bite to eat with us first. Maureen's found a smashing new sherry, and on your way back you could pop in to Clara's."

After expressing his sympathy about the stroke, Michael said he would and they fixed a day in August. George put the phone down and Maureen came running in to ask what Michael thought about Alan and Rosemary.

"I never told him. I forgot."

"Oh, lovey, when that's all anybody's talking about."

"You can tell him when he comes."

George's call had cheered Michael up, helping him to realise how much he needed a friend to talk to and encouraging him to try Daphne's number once again.

"Why not come over?" said Daphne. "This afternoon or tomorrow. You can be our first visitor."

"Our?"

"Alan Norris is living with me now." She said it

in the same tone she might have used to remark that it was a fine day.

"I'm sorry?"

"Yes, I did say that."

"What, living with you like *living* with you?" Michael the lawyer said. "Cohabiting, you mean?"

She laughed. "Exactly that. Come to supper and all will be explained."

Two pleasant and friendly voices enhanced Michael's feeling of well-being. He did something rare with him. He took the handset of the phone upstairs to Vivien's room and felt her presence near him. Anything he said and anything that was said to him would be bearable, livable with, if he lay on the bed and made his phone call from there. The number of Urban Grange he had by heart.

Big institutions had begun a response system irritating to most people, but especially to the elderly, those who expected a human voice, someone who would listen and answer questions. As he touched the keys—you could no longer call it dialling—he thought of the pressing of one for a booking, two for a cancellation, three for an extension, and so on that would ensue, but, no, he got a human voice, a female one of upper-class distinction. How could she help him?

"My name is Michael Winwood. John Winwood is my father." He felt as if he were in court, in the witness box.

"Mr. Winwood who is a commensal in Urban Grange?"

Michael had never heard the word before. "Well, he lives there."

She must have had recourse to a computer. "Yes, one of our valued inquilines. We have a Mrs. Zoe Nicholson as his next of kin."

"Yes. She is now dead and I am his next of kin. Perhaps you would like to make a note of that and take my details."

He gave them to her; she thanked him and asked if he would be paying Urban Grange a visit in the near future.

"Should I?"

"We do like to see our commensals' loved ones occasionally, and of course Mr. Winwood would appreciate seeing you." Back to the computer, followed by a soft sigh. "Mr. Winwood is a very old gentleman."

Michael said he would call back to give her a day, put the phone down, and rolled over face downwards with closed eyes, imagining Vivien close to him. But she had receded, shrinking away perhaps from that ultraposh voice. Alone again, he went downstairs to look up the two unfamiliar words. *Commensal* meant "resident," and *inquiline* meant a guest in a house not his or her own.

YOU READ ABOUT such things in the papers, Michael thought when he saw them together in

Daphne's living-room. But in those cases the two people had forcibly been parted when young by war or the intervention of others. It looked as if these two had been happy enough with other partners, in Alan's case with a wife, and were brought together by the finding of two hands in a tin box. Yet it was Michael that Daphne had taken home after that reunion. It might have been he and she that the hands brought together, and for a fleeting moment as she gave him a glass of wine, he wished it had been.

That thought passed as he began to tell them—necessarily both of them—about his aunt and the father he had hardly seen since he was a child. "What do you think?" He was looking at Daphne. "Should I go to this Urban Grange and see him? I mean, be the dutiful son? Not that I owe him any duty."

"Isn't there a wife? Your stepmother?"

"She died. She was very rich and left him everything, which is why he can afford to live out the rest of his life at Urban Grange."

"He must be very old," Daphne said. "Do you want to see him? It doesn't sound as if you do."

"He's a few months short of a hundred. Imagine saying that of anyone when we were young. It's the equivalent of saying 'he's over eighty' in our tunnels days—I mean *qanats*." Michael smiled at her. "Do I want to see him? Of course I don't, I dread it. I'm an old man and I ought to have left those kinds of fears far behind me, but I haven't." Michael paused, knowing he should leave it there but unable to stop. "When I look back—and I have to look back because I haven't seen him for so long—when I do, I see him as a sort of monster, an ugly, shrivelled creature like an alien from a horror film."

"Oh, Michael."

"I ask myself, am I going to be shown up to his room or suite or apartment or whatever he has and left there by whoever escorts me, and he comes in, and I—I scream?" He drew a deep breath. The other two said nothing but their hands moved along the sofa and each joined the other. "Sorry. I'm sorry for putting you through this. Sheila, my stepmother, I suppose she was, though I only saw her once, drank a bottle of whisky and took an overdose of pills. The verdict at the inquest was death by misadventure. I think he—well, helped her die. I shouldn't be telling you this, I should be telling the police, but he's my *father.* And he's almost a hundred years old."

Alan said, "You can't tell the police, I see that. Very probably he won't live long. I don't know what Daphne will say, but I think you should see your father, steel yourself, make an enormous effort, and maybe stay no more than half an hour. What do you think, Daphne?"

She hesitated. "I knew him, you know. We lived next door. Perhaps ask him if he wants to see *you.*

Get this Urban Grange place to ask him. He may be as reluctant to see you as you are to see him. We dislike those we have injured, don't you think?"

"They'll say he wants to see me, but I'll ask. I'll do that. I will."

"And now I think we should have our supper."

15

MICHAEL WAS DUE to visit another extremely old person. When first asked by George Batchelor, he had quite looked forward to this. He had thought a good deal about Clara Moss, that small, thin woman whom his father called Mrs. Mopp and scorned behind her back. After Anita had gone, no one else but Michael was there for him to say unpleasant things to about Clara, how stupid she was, how inefficient, what a hopeless cleaner. She always wore plimsolls, as trainers were called then, and a cotton crossover overall, but even John Winwood couldn't call her dirty. Michael liked the hugs she occasionally gave him because she smelled of Wright's coal tar soap. Her hands were scrubbed until they were red and her nails to whiteness. He had noticed that the wedding ring she wore on the third finger of her left hand was loose, slipping up and down, because she had grown so thin after her husband was killed.

One day it was lost. The tale of her losing it stayed in his child's memory for ever. Anita was still there when it happened, and how to deal with it, or not deal with it, was almost the only time he remembered his parents being in accord over anything. Clara told Anita that her wedding ring had slipped off her finger and fallen down the waste pipe in the kitchen sink. Tentatively, for Clara was always shy with Anita, she had said it would be stuck in the S-bend and would Mr. Winwood retrieve it for her? She knew he could because she had once before when the pipe was blocked seen him do whatever was necessary. Michael had heard his parents discuss the matter, and John Winwood, agreeing with Anita, said, "Like hell I'm going to take the sink apart for the char's bloody ring."

A child doesn't know how much a dead husband's ring might mean to his widow, but he knew when he was older. He knew when he was far away with Zoe, when his mother had gone, his father had left the house as far as he knew, and the ring was still down there. It might be still down there now, he thought, when George asked him to visit Clara Moss. For a few days he thought about Clara and the ring. He thought about how he was going to have lunch at George's on Wednesday of next week and call on Clara afterwards, and he thought it likely George would phone to arrange a time. He didn't phone. Michael phoned him and a woman answered. It was Maureen, but he didn't recognise her voice, it was so low and dull and broken.

George was dead. Another stroke had come three nights ago, and he had never wakened again. She had half expected it, but it was still a terrible shock. Michael asked if there was anything he could do, and Maureen in her new, fractured voice said to please come to the funeral. She told him when and where it was and said all his friends would be welcome at the sherry party she would have afterwards. No flowers, please, she said, and sobbed quietly.

HE WOULD GO. Michael decided this not entirely out of altruism and not at all from duty. He had no duty to George. But since his visit to Daphne and Alan, he had reproached himself for having given up nearly all social life after Vivien's death. He had kept up with Zoe, of course he had, but abandoned all his friends. There had been that single visit to George, and that was about it. Zoe would have wanted him to keep an eye on Brenda, but he never had, reasoning that now she was living with her sister she wouldn't need him. A funeral wasn't exactly a social occasion, but he would go to it. It would be a start for getting back into something like the sort of life he used to have. In Vivien's room he lay on the bed with the curtains drawn and told her all this, certain that if she knew, she would approve.

He would go to the funeral, and the day after that he would phone Brenda at her sister's and arrange to . . . what? Take her out to tea? Take her and her sister out to tea? That would be best. Meanwhile he would phone Urban Grange. He got off the bed, ran downstairs, and snatched up the phone. A different woman answered. She had a normal sort of voice but sounded harassed, almost distraught.

"Oh, Mr. Winwood, yes. Of course. I'm terribly sorry but we've had a—well, a disaster here. Terribly upsetting. May I call you back, say tomorrow? I have your number."

He couldn't face waiting for it. "No, I'll call you. . . . It's not my father, is it? This—this disaster?"

"Oh, no, not at all. Good heavens, no. I must go. Please call us tomorrow."

What could it be? If it had been his father's death, Michael would have been relieved.

GEORGE'S FUNERAL WAS at St. Mary's Church in Loughton High Road. Michael got there early and was shown to a pew halfway down by a man in his fifties who said he was Stanley's son. Four rows ahead of him he could see Lewis Newman, and near the front on the other side of the aisle Norman Batchelor was with a woman in a smart black suit and pillbox hat who couldn't be anything but French. Michael hoped Alan and Daphne might be there but realised that they couldn't be because it was far more likely that Rosemary would be. Strange, interesting, he thought, how all sorts of social occasions were forbidden them now, but they wouldn't always be, not when people got used to the set-up, when they were accepted as what his children called an item. If it lasted, if they stayed together. If they lived long enough. That was what you always had to think of at their ages. If they lasted long enough.

A lot of grown-up and even late-middle-age children of George's two marriages came in. One young woman was carrying a baby, which must, Michael guessed, be George's great-grandchild or even great-great. Rosemary wasn't there. Maureen arrived, supported by two women who looked so like her that they must have been her daughters. Everyone rose as the "Dead March" from *Saul* began and George's coffin was carried in.

Michael didn't join in the hymn singing and managed not to listen to the eulogy, delivered by Norman. He was thinking about the tunnels and the things the children did, the games they played, the cards and draughts, and wasn't there back-gammon? The awful wartime food they brought and devoured because they were growing and always hungry. He refused to let himself think of his father coming to the cave-like entrance and shouting at them all to come out and never go there again, his voice loud and rough with its coarse accent. Instead he was remembering Daphne in a black cloak with gold stars, saved from Christmas decorations, pinned on it, Daphne peering into her glass bowl and foretelling long lives. She had been right there. He found himself falling asleep. Nodding off, they called it, one of the penalties of growing old.

Maureen, someone told him, couldn't face the crematorium, and who could blame her? Instead they all made their way up York Hill to Carisbrooke. Michael found himself walking with Lewis Newman.

"Two old widowers, that's us," said Lewis in a cheerful tone. "We're quite a rare breed, you know. I can't remember the statistics, but usually we chaps die first."

Michael remembered Lewis had been a GP. "Yes. People tell me I'm lucky."

"Depends how you look at it. They say we're very sought after by the preponderance of widows, but I can't say I've noticed."

"Nor me." Michael decided that he quite liked Lewis after all.

Some relative left behind at the house had organised a huge spread. Noticing the sherry bottles of every variety, Michael felt greatly touched. Poor old George, he would have enjoyed this. The tears came into his eyes but stayed there as Stanley, retrieving Spot from the laundry room, where he had been shut up during the service, slapped Michael on the back and asked him what he thought of the "lovebirds—Alan and Daphne, I mean."

Michael thought gossip the prerogative of women, though Vivien had never gossiped as far as he knew. "They seem very happy." Refusing to expand, he said he expected Rosemary might have been at the funeral.

"We did ask her. Apparently she goes nowhere. Just stays at home brooding. He'll come back, you know. It's just a matter of time."

"I wonder."

Michael had a glass of Manzanilla and ate a stuffed vine leaf. Here in George's house, Michael's conscience troubled him about Clara Moss. It had begun to seem to him that every minute he spent in Loughton without seeing her was letting George down. He had promised George—well, he hadn't promised, but he had said he would go. After he had tried to talk to Eliane Batchelor and unwisely attempted the French he had acquired from a fortnight in Dijon forty years before, only to be asked in perfect English why he couldn't speak that language, he began to make his escape. Lewis Newman asked him to share the taxi to Loughton he had ordered, and when Michael mentioned Clara Moss, Lewis said the taxi would drop him off. Taking in Forest Road on the way to the station meant a detour along the edge of the forest and passing their old primary school in Staples Road.

"It's a good many years since I've been along here," said Lewis. "My mother insisted on bringing me and fetching me home even after I was far too old for it. The kids next door to us went to Staples Road and they would have brought me, but she wasn't having any."

No one brought me or fetched me. I walked up there on my own when I was five. Michael didn't say it aloud as it would have sounded like self-pity. It *was* self-pity. For something to say, "Let's not lose touch," he said, and gave Lewis his card. That meant the other man might make the first move. If they had been women, he thought, they would have kissed. It's awkward shaking hands in a taxi, so they did nothing but muttered something about its being good to see each other.

Clara's house was the least well-kept on the outside of any in the row. The black paint was peeling from the front door, but the brass knocker and letterbox shone as brightly as gold. A young woman with an enormous mass of bright ginger hair, in jeans and a sleeveless, low-cut top, answered his knock.

"Yes?"

"I've come to see Mrs. Moss. My name is Winwood, Michael Winwood."

"She never has visitors. Does she know you?"

"She did once." Unusually assertive, he walked over the threshold so that the young woman was obliged to step back.

"Wait a minute. I'll have to ask her. She can't walk very far."

He was tired of waiting. He followed her into a tiny room with a single bed in it where a little old woman, a very old woman, sat strapped into a wheelchair. His conductor, seeing him close behind her, shrugged and shook her head as if washing her hands of the whole business. Clara Moss was staring at Michael, and in those dark eyes, half buried in gatherings of wrinkles, he could see she was perfectly intelligent and fitted the lawyer's description "of sound mind."

"I know you," said Clara. "Since I was a girl and you was a little boy. Wait a minute." It was more than sixty years ago. He knew from photographs and looking in the mirror when he shaved that he was unimaginably changed. Who wouldn't be? "I think you're Michael. You couldn't be no one else."

His tendency to weep in times of emotion had affected him earlier when remembering George, and now it was back again. This time a tear fell, and then another.

"Well, I'm off," said the young woman. "See

you on Friday, Clara. You owe me twelve pounds forty-nine, but I can pick it up when I come."

Clara said, "Thank you, Sam. You're a good girl."

The front door closed and Clara smiled at Michael. "She don't like being called a girl but I always forget. It's not PC, whatever that may mean."

"Politically correct. Mrs. Moss, it's very good to see you. Would you like to come out of that chair?"

"I would, but then I can't get to my kitchen or the WC."

He hadn't heard it called that since he was very young. "Water closet," the letters stood for. It was *toilet* to everyone now. "I could make us a cup of tea. Shall I?"

"In a minute," she said. "You tell me what you've been doing all these years."

So he did, but he made the tea first in a spotless kitchen where everything was so neatly and properly arranged that no one could fail to find what they were looking for. He rearranged the wheelchair for her, propping her with pillows from the bed and a big cushion. She had, she told him, a "bit of a dicky heart," and a thrombosis in her right leg had left her what the nurse who came in called "incapacitated." "A cripple, she means, but she's a good girl. Kindness itself."

He told her about Zoe and his law degree,

becoming a solicitor and marrying Babette, then his happy life with Vivien and their children. Hardly knowing why he did, he said, "My father is still alive. He's nearly a hundred now."

"Lives with you, does he?"

"I've only seen him once since I was a boy."

Her face sank into even deeper lines, her forehead corrugated. "They say the good die young. Him and me must have been very wicked, then."

"Not you, Mrs. Moss."

"No one calls me that no more. The young don't know the meaning of Mrs. D'you remember your mum? She was a lovely woman—to look at, I mean. Red hair, really red, I mean, not like that Sam. Hers comes out of a packet. That friend of your mum's that used to come round—I'm not saying there was anything wrong, mind—he had red hair. No one took any notice of it then, it was just ginger hair, but now it's supposed to be okay on a girl but ugly on a man. Funny the way things change."

"It is." Michael thought about what she had just said. "Mrs. Moss, I have to go. May I come back and see you soon? I've enjoyed our talk. It's been wonderful to see you."

The tears came then and streamed down his cheeks. It was too much for him, Clara Moss herself and his mother and maybe the red hair. He wept, scrubbing at his face with a tissue while she watched him with wide eyes. "Come here," she said, and as he bent over to kiss her, she reached up and put her arms round his neck. "Poor little boy," he thought she said, but her voice was too muffled for him to be sure.

IT WASN'T TOMORROW, as he had told the woman at Urban Grange it would be, but the day after. He had thought of little in the intervening time but of Clara Moss and her reminiscences. Was it true that redheaded men were thought ugly? Certainly red hair must be considered beautiful on a woman or so many with perfectly pretty hair wouldn't dye it chestnut or crimson or copper or burgundy or russet or, as people used to say, carrots. Anita's hair was naturally chestnut and her eyes were almost navy blue. He could remember that well. Lewis Newman had red hair, or had once when they were at school. Most of it was gone now and what remained was a pale gingery grey. He couldn't remember Lewis's father's hair. Darkish, he supposed, a sort of dull brown like most people's. He would be long dead now, like everyone else's father except his. He picked up the handset, walked about a bit carrying it, repeating the number to himself, then dialling it.

Posh-voice answered. "Oh, yes, Mr. Winwood. You wanted to know if you should visit your father. I'd say yes, of course. He's perfectly well—well, he's very old, of course, so little ailments are to be expected, but he's really remarkable for his age."

"When should I come?"

"I think we told you when you last spoke to us that we have had a most unfortunate mishap at Urban Grange. One of our inquilines had an accident and we thought we were going to lose her. But thanks to the truly wonderful medical attention our medical staff give, it looks as if all will be well."

"When shall I come?"

"Shall we say next week? Any day that suits you. Shall we say in the afternoon, perhaps the late afternoon for tea?"

16

THE PILLS THE doctor prescribed gave her a night's sleep. You couldn't call it a "good" night's sleep, but it was eight hours of unconsciousness. Rosemary's trouble, among others, was that since her wedding night she had hardly ever slept alone. There had been the three nights when Alan stayed at his mother's when his father died, and the times when the children were born, but that was all. Now she thought she would never sleep again without pills. Although the pills worked, she would wake up, at first to reach for Alan, then, and soon, realise that he wasn't there, that he had left her and she was alone.

Her children and her grandchildren were good to her. All of them took her side unreservedly. All of them thought she had been cruelly treated, and even Owen and the husbands said Alan must have succumbed to senility. This was the onset of Alzheimer's. She was getting tired of that word. This woman, this Daphne whatever she was called, must have seduced him when he was bewildered, unable to understand his sudden loss of memory and his confusion. Owen went to call on him and Daphne, all set to compel his father to pack his bags and leave with him, but instead found himself accepting a glass of wine and only with reluctance refusing to stay for supper. He told Rosemary the pair of them had been recalcitrant, a word he had to define to his puzzled mother, which rather took the force out of it. Fenella was more to be reckoned with and treated Alan and Daphne to a long diatribe on her grandmother's sufferings and told them what they knew already, that Freya was pregnant. Alan's absence would take away all the joy Rosemary would feel in the birth of this new great-grandchild.

Alan settled things for the time being by dismissing her: "Oh, go away, Fenella. You've said your piece and it's not your business anyway."

"Isn't it?" Daphne asked when Fenella had gone.

"No, I don't think it is. It's my children's certainly, but not my grandchildren's. That's too far removed."

Fenella walked up the road to Freya's flat. "I've seen Granddad. It's a funny thing to say at his age, but he's *grown.* I mean in strength. It's not long since he never stood up for himself. He really couldn't stand having Callum and Sybilla around, you know. I could tell, I'm not a psychologist for nothing, but he never said, he just put up with it. He wouldn't now. He's grown strong. Must be her doing. I shan't tell Grandma, of course. She's in a bad enough way as it is."

"Did you tell him about the baby?"

"Well, I did, Frey, but I can't say it made much impression. Sorry but he hardly seemed to notice."

"That's the Alzheimer's," said Freya.

It would be a good idea, Judith said to Rosemary, to come and stay with her for a week or two. For longer, if she wanted to. She shouldn't be alone. Rosemary refused. She had to be in the Traps Hill flat, she said, in case Alan came back.

She had done no dressmaking since he went. She cooked nothing unless it was a scrambled egg or to heat up some ready meal in the microwave. The long walks she had taken with Alan were a thing of the past; she missed her weekly visits to the hairdresser and gave up the bridge club. In the old days, as she saw her long marriage, she wouldn't have thought twice about writing a condolence letter to Maureen Batchelor, but no letter had been written and no visit to Carisbrooke had been paid. She stayed at home, deeply miserable. Alan occasionally phoned, mostly to ask if she was all right. Was there anything she needed? Was she all right for money? He seemed to understand that as she had never paid a bill since her marriage or filled in a form or questionnaire from the council, she might need help. She said Owen or Judith saw to all that, and then, invariably, she began to cry.

"You can't go on like this," said Judith. "You'll be ill."

"If I'm ill, I might die and that would all be for the best."

"I would never have advised this," said Judith, who could be pompous, "but I think it might be a good idea if you were to go there and see him. Talk to him. I'll come with you if you like. I know exactly where it is. We could have lunch with Freya and walk down to Hamilton Terrace."

"Don't be ridiculous," Rosemary snapped, jolted out of her despair and unusually sarcastic. "Make a party of it, why don't you, and invite the neighbours. This is my life, Judith. This is my life, and your father has wrecked it."

"Shall we go then?"

"Yes, all right, why not? Things can't be worse than they are."

Unlike her daughter and her brother, Judith announced her projected visit in advance. She wrote her father a letter, which arrived on a Saturday morning along with flyers, communications from the City of Westminster, mail-order catalogues, and pleas for charitable donations. When the post came, Alan and Daphne were sitting up in bed eating the breakfast Alan had just prepared and brought upstairs. They had passed the muesli stage and were beginning on the egg-and-bacon course when the bell rang. Alan went down again in his dressing gown. It was the postman, hoping to deliver a package from a friend for Daphne's birthday. Recognising his daughter's handwriting on an envelope, Alan wanted to ignore it but knew he would have to open it sometime. He took it and the package upstairs, where his egg was getting cold. Daphne took the package from him and began opening it.

"Look, a very pretty scarf. Isn't that kind? Alan, what's wrong? You're wearing a bad-news look."

"Rosemary wants to come here next Tuesday or Wednesday. Up to us. Judith will bring her."

ON HER WAY HOME from visiting Freya, an even more frequent happening since her daughter's pregnancy was known, Judith drove down the road and round the corner into Hamilton Terrace.

If anyone came out of the house or just looked out of the window, they wouldn't recognise her car. Her father might know the make and the colour, but silver was the most popular shade for a Prius and thousands of them were about. Nice house, she thought, must be worth a fortune. Had it occurred to her mother that her father might have left her because Daphne was a wealthy woman? That he might prefer to live here than in a suburban flat? Judith dismissed the thought, though it would certainly be pleasant sharing such a palace, with its covered way leading up to the front porch, its front garden with its pair of lawns and tubs that overflowed with trailing Thalia fuchsias.

Driving across London was not pleasant. Roadworks clogged the streets, and bad-tempered motorists swore and screamed. Her nerves were shattered by the time she was back in Chiswick. If they kept to the plan she had made, they would go on the tube. Rosemary said Judith would have to organise it as she hadn't the faintest idea how to get to St. John's Wood. She had only once been there and that was "ages ago" when the children were small and they went to the zoo. Alan had been told on the phone to expect them at about three.

Not the kind of woman who bakes cakes or even serves tea as a meal and not as a cup of the stuff, Daphne walked up to the High Street, where she bought a box of meringues and another of petits fours. It seemed ridiculous, as she told herself, but not as ridiculous as dressing up in a special dress and special shoes would be. She put the cakes on two plates and some milk in a jug.

"I can do that," said Alan.

"Okay." She was not usually so laconic.

Upstairs, at two thirty, she looked at herself in the mirror, in one of her everyday garments of black skirt, light beige jumper, and string of black beads. She took off the beads and put on a leather jacket she had bought years ago but never worn. With its embossed and panelled front, its studs, it was too young for her. It was, she decided, vulgar, *common* was the word no longer used but somehow appropriate. Shock waves would be aroused in Alan's wife and daughter. As for him, he wouldn't even notice. He had laid the table with what she always called "the worst china." No fuss must be made. If Judith and Rosemary liked to think he and Daphne ate tea like this every day, let them.

"If Rosemary tries to persuade you to go back to her, will you be persuaded?"

"I will not," he said like someone taking a serious vow.

"I won't speak about it. I mean not about us, unless she asks me, and then I'll have to. I can talk about cakes and clothes and this house but not about us."

He took her in his arms, and to his surprise she clung to him in a way she had never quite done before, while the stiff and shiny leather jacket made an unwelcome barrier between them. "Do you realise that you and I are together because of those hands? We met again because of those hands in a biscuit box?"

"I do now. I never thought I'd be glad of something like that."

The doorbell rang. It was two minutes to three.

THEY KNEW EACH OTHER, of course. You could say they had known each other all their lives. Daphne said, "Rosemary." That was all, just the given name.

Rosemary said, "Good afternoon."

Judith introduced herself. Neither she nor her mother spoke to Alan, but they sat down side by side on the sofa when Daphne asked them to. That was all anyone said for perhaps two minutes, a very long time. Judith, the intermediary, broke the silence and said, "I think my mother would like you, Dad, and Mrs. Furness to tell us what you intend to do." Judith tried to smile but it turned into a grimace. "If anything." Rosemary was fidgeting with her handbag, lifting it from one side of her and transferring it to the other, shoving it between her left arm and the arm of the sofa. She held tightly to it by its strap and the zip which held it closed. "Or what you intend to do, Mother."

Another silence, during which Judith wondered why her mother had brought with her what was probably the largest handbag she possessed, and then Rosemary said, "I don't intend to do anything. I'm alone, my husband has been taken from me, and I want him back." She said to Alan, not for the first time, "You've broken my heart. It can be mended if you do what you ought to do and come back to me. Leave that woman and come back."

"I don't much care to have this conversation in front of my daughter," said Alan.

"Too bad. I'm not leaving." Judith looked at Daphne for the first time. "Can I have a cup of tea? Can we *all* have tea?"

Without replying, Daphne stood up and poured tea into Judith's cup and Alan's and her own, Rosemary having covered hers with her hand, like someone preventing the refilling of a wineglass. The milk jug was passed silently between Alan and his daughter. Daphne passed them the meringues.

"Haven't you anything to say to me?"

Alan looked at his wife. "I'm not coming back, Rosemary. I've told you many times. I've no fault to find with you—sorry, that's a horrible way to put it. I expect you have faults to find with me. We no longer get on. I want to live with someone I get on with."

"And that applies to her?"

"You know it does."

Rosemary moved the bag onto her lap. "And all those years you spent with me mean nothing?"

"They mean a lot. They meant a lot. We have shared our home, we have two children. It's over now. It's over for a lot of couples as we've seen among our friends. They break up, earlier than it is for us, but eventually we are doing it too. I will make it as easy for you as I can, I will help you to get used to it, even one day to think it's for the best."

"If that's all you've got to say, I'll ask her." Rosemary swung round and fixed her eyes on Daphne. "One good thing, everyone that knows us, all his friends, side with me. More than that, they've come to hate him. Their sympathy is all for me, they've shown me what friends are. But just the same, they want him to come back and then they'll return to him. We'll be as we used to be. Do you understand?" Daphne said nothing, she gave a small nod. "I don't know what he sees in you. You were never specially good-looking and you haven't improved. Who has? You've apparently got a lot of money." Rosemary waved a hand round the room. "But he's not badly off himself. When he retired, he got a big golden handshake and he's got a huge pension. You're no chicken, you're older than him and me. I suppose he wanted a change. Was that it? So will you give him up, send him back to me? Will you let him come home with me? Come back with me now, back to his *home?* Will you?"

Rosemary had seemed perfectly calm, but as she spoke the last two words, she snatched up a cup from the table and hurled it across the room. It struck a painting on the wall and shattered. Another followed it.

"Stop that, Rosemary," said Alan.

"I'll break the place up until she answers me. Will you give my husband back to me, Daphne whatever your name is? You've changed it often enough."

"No," said Daphne in a voice of ice. "I don't want him to go, but he must do as he chooses, go or stay." If she had left it there, all might have been more or less well, but she didn't. "I love him. I love him and want to keep him here with me."

Rosemary stood up. She unzipped her handbag, and at once Judith knew why Rosemary had brought such a big one. From its depths she took a long knife, the carving kind that has a thin blade and a point on its end. She held it like a dagger, blade pointing down. People think they know about such events, they see them happening day after day on film and television, on computer screens and mobile phones. Reality is different. No one moved, but Daphne, who took a step backwards, and then Alan. He tried to seize Rosemary by the shoulders but she spun round, slashing at him and cutting the palm of his hand. Blood splashed, more than could be expected from a cut palm. Rosemary spun round and stabbed at Daphne, stabbing vainly at the air, at her hair, and grazing her neck. Rosemary pulled the knife back and plunged it at Daphne's chest just where her heart must be. The vulgar jacket, armoured with studs, deflected the blade before it could penetrate. Alan seized Daphne, pulling her back, forcing her behind him. The knife, still in Rosemary's hand, slipped from her fingers and fell to the floor.

ALAN WAS HURT the most. Judith called 999 for an ambulance. She picked up the knife and wiped the trace of her father's blood off the blade. With great presence of mind she fetched a fruit-and-nut loaf from Daphne's kitchen, with butter and a pot of jam. When the paramedics came, they encountered a happy family gathering, and if their smiles were strained and Rosemary was shivering, no one seemed to notice. Judith explained that her father had been cutting bread. No one remarked on the unsuitability of the knife for this, and Alan's request not to be taken to hospital but have his wound dressed on the spot was reluctantly agreed to. Alan agreed to go to the hospital and have the wound checked the following day, but he had no intention of doing so.

• • •

"EVEN IF I'D driven you here," said Judith, "I wouldn't feel up to driving back. Do you have a taxi number?"

Daphne gave her a number to call. Daphne didn't speak. She had picked up the broken pieces of the cups and removed the life-saving jacket. Because it was turning cold, she wrapped a shawl round herself and put on the central heating. Judith said to her father, "Have you got any drink? I could use a brandy, and come to that, so could Mum."

"I suppose so."

It was fetched. Daphne fetched herself and Alan a glass of wine each, a gesture of possession not lost on Rosemary. She began to cry, mopping up her tears with a couple of the paper table napkins, put out with the tea things.

"I'll stay the night with you, Mum."

"Do as you like," said Rosemary. "Nothing matters anymore."

The taxi came and took them away. Alan and Daphne, who hadn't stirred from their seats since Daphne fetched their wine, now rose simultaneously, threw their arms round each other, and sank onto the sofa.

17

ONE MORE VISIT was paid to Clara Moss before Michael went to Urban Grange. This time he was admitted to the house in Forest Road not by the red-haired Sam but by a much older woman, who introduced herself as "Mrs. Next-Door." Clara was in bed. She hadn't felt like getting up, she said. He had heard this phrase before, used by old people coming to the end of their lives. Zoe had said it before she was taken to the hospital, and he remembered hearing it from Vivien's mother in her last days.

"I don't know why, dear," said Clara, "but I just didn't feel like getting up." He had brought her a box of chocolates and they seemed to bring her inordinate pleasure. "I'll have just one a day, make them last."

"I'll bring you some more. I'll come over and see Mrs. Batchelor in a week or two and bring you a bigger box. Then they'll last longer."

"How's your dad?"

"Going strong. I'm going to see him next week." Now he would have to, there would be no escape. Her eyes had closed and her head turned a little away, but she put out her hand as if feeling for his. He took the hand and held it lightly, sensing that she would prefer this to a firmer clasp. After a minute or two her hand slackened and her breathing grew regular. She was asleep.

"Sam and me," said Mrs. Next-Door, "we'll be in every day, take it in turns. She isn't long for this world."

"Ring me. I'll give you my phone number."

It wouldn't be a week or two, he thought, recalling his words, but not so long. Then he thought, I'd never have met Clara Moss again but for those hands. Finding those hands brought me to her and her to me.

ABSURD FOR A man of his age to be so nervous. No, worse than that: so *frightened.* The train took him to Ipswich. He had never been there before, and he found the town—city?—unprepossessing. But the country around, seen from a station taxi, was beautiful. Years ago he and Vivien had spent a weekend at a hotel in Southwold, a long way up the coast. Here it was all green fields and woods, each village they passed through with its own pretty church and in some cases a big Georgian house that these days newspapers called mansions. The biggest, at the end of a long avenue of trees Michael didn't know the name of, the taxi driver introduced him to as Urban Grange. The day was bright but with a cold wind blowing, and the old man being wheeled across the lawn that the drive bisected was wrapped in blankets and swathed in a duvet. Michael thought with a sinking heart, Maybe that's him. How can I tell? The driver enlightened him.

"See that old guy as looks as if he's still in bed? He's been here since it started twenty years ago. Like the oldest inhabitant, aged ninety-eight."

Not the oldest, thought Michael, but he didn't say so. The receptionist he recognised by her voice. Next time, if there was a next time, he would recognise her by her looks. She was a beauty with waist-length, blond hair, in a white dress as unlike a nurse's uniform as could be imagined. Her name, it said, above the left breast, was Imogen. He felt like asking how her inquilines were, but thought he had better not.

"Mr. Winwood expects you, Mr. Winwood." She picked up the phone. "Darren will take you along to the principal garden apartment."

"I expect I can find it."

"Oh, no, Mr. Winwood. We never expect our visitors to go unescorted."

Darren, whom she made sound a boy of sixteen, was a middle-aged man dressed like a butler and wearing some kind of insignia round his neck. Following him along a corridor whose windows showed lavish gardens, Michael had lost his fear. It had been the same when he was young. You were afraid, and often badly afraid, two or three weeks ahead of the looming event, but when the time was at hand, the fear receded until what remained was only curiosity.

John Winwood looked old. He looked about as old as a human being could ever get to be, like bones in a bag of skin. No hair remained on his head but a white wisp above each ear. It was warm in Urban Grange and, it seemed to Michael, even warmer in this room, and his father was wearing—of all things at his age—a short-sleeved tee-shirt, which showed forearms where the skin looked more pleated than wrinkled. He sat in a luxurious velvet armchair of a rich coral colour with a matching footrest on which his feet, in espadrilles, stretched out. But the tee-shirt was what shocked Michael. Everything else was more or less what he expected: the jeans that were casual wear for everyone of any age, the tiny gold nodule under his ear that was a deaf aid, the yellow claws that were his fingernails, the pallor of his face, usual in the very old. Any young person would have accepted the tee-shirt as within a present-day trend, commonly seen. On John Winwood, Michael felt it as an affront, a horror, as, walking up to his father, he took in the white, grinning skull painted on the black cotton.

It was worn, he supposed, as defiance, but Darren appeared to accept it, perhaps to be used to it. On him, after all, it would be an acceptable, even favoured, weekend garment.

"I'll leave you," he said. "Please ring if there's

anything you need or when you and Mr. Winwood senior are ready to say good-bye."

"Long time no see," said the old man—the older of the two old men. Michael hadn't heard the phrase uttered for many years. Perhaps the last time was when his father had brought Sheila to the house in Lewes.

"How are you?" Michael didn't know how to address his father. As a child he had called him Dad. "How are you, Father?"

"That's what you call me now, is it? Why have you come?"

"To see you. Because you're my father."

"That's true. I am. No question about that. The problems in that area came later." His father's eyes were clear and surprisingly young-looking. No doubt he had had his cataracts removed, just as he possessed that tiny jewel of a hearing aid and implanted porcelain teeth. "You look older than your age. How's your wife?"

"She died," Michael said, terrified some insult would follow.

There was none. "They do. All mine did. You going to marry again?"

Through almost closed lips, "No," Michael said.

"Nor me."

They stared at each other without speaking. John Winwood's gaze was the first to fall but he broke the silence. "We've nothing to say to each other, have we? Nothing much. I never liked you. I never liked your mother either. I don't know why I married her. In those days you had to marry someone, it was the done thing, and it might as well be a looker. I don't like people, it's as simple as that. Did you inherit that?"

"No."

"I thought it might be in the genes. I'm going to stay alive till January the fourteenth. That's my birthday. You may not know that but it is. I shall be a hundred and I'm going to live till then, and then I'll die. I won't pass away or 'give up the ghost'—that comes from the Bible, did you know?—I shall die."

"I'll come again before that."

His father would tell him not to bother. He waited for it.

"All right. You do as you please. Make an appointment. I pay a fortune for this place so that I can make choices and tell folks what to do. Another bit from the Bible. I was brought up on it and made to go to church, that's why I sing hymns, as you may not know. I'm like that chap who was a centurion and said to one, 'Come and he cometh, to another go and he goeth, and to a third do this and he doeth it.' That's all I want someone for, to do this and he doeth it."

His father's laughter, a shrill cackle, made Michael jump. He rang the bell and asked Darren to come and escort him to the exit. He was suddenly thinking of the train and the platform at Lewes, the lady with the little dog, and the tears came into his eyes. His father wasn't looking at him.

"Why do you wear that tee-shirt?" Had he ever asked his father a question before? Certainly not a question that might be construed as rude.

"I like it." His father closed his eyes.

Darren escorted Michael to reception, where he asked Imogen to call him a taxi. If she noticed his drying tears, she made no comment on them. They seemed to irritate his eyes and swell his face. In the guests' cloakroom he sat on one of the velvet settees—velvet was the fabric of choice in Urban Grange—and gave himself up to weeping. Anyone who came in would take this as a sign of understandable emotion, quite naturally brought on by visiting his dying father. But he was crying for the lady with the little dog who would be dead long since and the dog too of course. I wish I believed in an afterlife, he thought, so that she could be there but far away from that man's centurions and ghosts.

Imogen came in and told him his taxi had arrived.

MAURICE COULD BE TOLD, but not the girls. Fenella would want to have Rosemary sectioned, and Freya would advise telling the police. Her husband, on the other hand, told Judith that she had done the right thing—which meant doing nothing—and it would all blow over.

"I wish I'd killed her," said Rosemary. "She's no fool, she guessed I'd attack her and that's why she wore that ridiculous, vulgar garment that's about fifty years too young for her. Next time I try it, I'll succeed."

"There mustn't be a next time, Mother."

"Why do you keep calling me Mother?"

Because you don't call a would-be murderess Mum, Judith wanted to say. She said nothing. Some sort of awe attached to a woman who would do what Rosemary had attempted to do.

"I've wasted my whole life on him. After we were married, a friend of mine called Melanie told me that your father had been going out with Daphne Jones before he met me. Well, not before he met me, because we met in the tunnels, but when we were grown-up and met for the second time. D'you know what else she told me? That he slept with her. No, I don't suppose that shocks you, it wouldn't. But people didn't then. Or the people I knew didn't."

"But why did you mind if it was before he met you?"

"He had met me. When we were children. He met her then too. He forgot me for years but remembered her, couldn't wait to get his hands on her."

"Does all that matter now?"

"Of course it matters. How do I know he hasn't been sleeping with her all these years? People behave like that, I've read about it. They meet and then they don't see each other for a few years, and they meet again and it all starts again. That's how it was with your father and that woman."

"You don't know that," said Judith.

"It's an intelligent guess. And you've got to remember that she's very well-off. That house! You think that didn't weigh with him? Of course it did. He's got money, but people always want more. D'you know what he asked me the other day? Did I think we'd led a dull life? Always living in the same place, not being adventurous, never been further abroad than France and Spain. Well, he's abroad now, isn't he? He's in the finest residential street in London. That's what the papers call it and I think—"

This diatribe was interrupted by the front doorbell. At the same time Judith's mobile rang. She had never been so glad to hear her husband's voice: "I thought I might as well come, darling."

Maurice's arrival brought less pleasure to Rosemary. She had always been a little in awe of her son-in-law, but now she seemed to have forgotten all about that. "Judith's told you, I suppose. She didn't waste any time. I tried to kill my husband's floozy." The word was so outdated, so archaic even, that it had fallen out of use before Rosemary was born, but she used it with a flourish. "I meant to do it. I took a carving knife with me in my bag, and when she said she loved him and wouldn't give him up, I stabbed her. That is, I tried to stab her, but she was wearing *armour.*"

This was not the way they had conducted themselves in the embassies of Cairo and Caracas. However, the denizens of these sanctuaries had recognised one kind of solace. "I think we all need a drink," said Maurice.

Another remedy was to go out to dinner somewhere. He suggested it, not tentatively but firmly.

"If you like. I don't care. It's all the same to me. You go if you like. I shall stay here."

"The point is to take you out, Mum." Having raised her mother to a level of dignity, Judith was now demoting her again. "Of course you must come."

"I will never go out to dinner again. I may never go out anywhere again. You don't seem to understand my position. I have tried to kill my husband's mistress and I will try again until I succeed. Then they will put me in prison for the rest of my life, which won't be long." Rosemary's voice rose to a high note on that last word, a note that became a scream. Then the sobs began. Scream, sob, sob, scream. She tore at her hair, clutched at her clothes, fell facedown into the sofa cushions, sat up again, and emitted staccato screams.

The other two stared at her, aghast. Both knew they were supposed to slap her face, but neither dared. Judith crept over to her mother and tried to take her in her arms. Rosemary fought her off, but suddenly sat up straight and shuddering, twitching from side to side, heaved a great sigh, and was silent.

"I'll stay here with you," Maurice said to his wife.

"Thank you, darling."

Rosemary spoke. In a voice unlike her normal one, she said hoarsely, "What did you do with my knife?"

"Left it there, Mum."

"Pity. Still, I've got other knives."

IF ALAN AND DAPHNE, particularly Daphne, had seemed to Judith and her mother to be largely unaffected by the attack on her, their calmness was the result of an iron control both were capable of. They hadn't previously had much need of it, but now they had. Both, simultaneously, realised that to seem indifferent or to seem perhaps disbelieving that Rosemary's attempt was seriously meant was their best course. But when it was all over and Alan's wife and daughter had gone, they succumbed to shock, held each other and lay side by side, aware that the other was shaking.

After a long time Alan said, "I'm sorry. It's all my fault."

"No, it's not. It's mine."

"I didn't know she was capable of that. I wouldn't have dreamt of it. I can hardly believe it now."

"Everyone we know, everyone we've ever known, all the people down this street, the children we knew in the tunnels that are still alive, all of them would be on Rosemary's side. Do you realise that? They would sympathise with her and condemn us. Would they be right?"

"I don't know. D'you know what I keep thinking? This started because of us all meeting in the qanats and Mr. Winwood turning us out of them."

IN THE SPARE-ROOM BED, a narrow double, Judith and Maurice lay stretched out side by side like a medieval couple on a funerary slab. Maurice was a tall man and not thin.

"This was the first bed Mum and Dad ever had," whispered Judith. "Owen and I were conceived in it."

"With difficulty, I should think."

"They didn't get a bigger one till we were quite old. What are we going to do about Mum, darling?"

"Take her back with us tomorrow?"

"If she'll come," said Judith.

"I find it hard to believe what she did. I mean, I know what she did, but it remains incredible. Would she try it again? If she comes back with us, we can keep an eye on her."

"Oh God. Do you think we have to? I must go

to sleep, I'm exhausted. Turn over, darling, and let me put my arm round your waist."

"I haven't got a waist," said Maurice.

Rosemary, in the bigger bed in the bigger bedroom, lay awake wondering where she would now be if her attempt on Daphne's life had succeeded. In a cell at Paddington Green police station, probably. She had seen that place on television; it was quite famous and couldn't be far from Hamilton Terrace. Tomorrow morning, *this* morning now, she would be due to appear in a magistrates' court, possibly one in Marylebone, she thought. It was amazing how much she knew about this sort of thing. She wasn't the ignorant little housewife her children and evidently her husband thought her.

Stabbing Daphne, trying to kill Daphne, had done her good. She felt younger and more alive. She could remember perfectly what it had felt like to grasp that knife in her fist—not the way she had ever held a knife before—and drive it into Daphne's heart. Or what it would have felt like but for that armour the woman was wearing, a breastplate put on deliberately because she feared Rosemary's just vengeance. Under the duvet, in her peach silk nightdress Alan had once admired and said suited her, she clenched her fist around an absent knife and thrust it up and down against an imagined ribcage, an imagined breast and heart. She would try again. Next time she would succeed. No Judith would be there and no Alan. The rivals for Alan's love would engage in combat, and she would be the victor because she had right on her side. Rosemary turned on to her side as sleep began to come. She was happier than she had been since Alan left her.

NO, SHE WOULDN'T go back with Judith and Maurice. She was perfectly all right on her own, she said. In fact, she thought she might spring-clean the flat. It had never had a thorough clean since they'd moved in.

"I'll come back and see you on Wednesday. I might bring Freya if she can take the afternoon off. I don't think I'll say anything to her about what happened yesterday."

"Say what you like," said Rosemary. "I'm not ashamed of it. Rather the reverse."

They left. She was alone, but instead of sitting and brooding, she wrapped herself in an apron and, fetching the requisite brushes, cloths, and cleaning fluids, began the spring-cleaning she had promised Judith she would do. While she worked, she thought about Alan and Daphne, thought about them together, though not exactly as a couple. She and Alan were the couple. The newspapers and the television were full of sex these days. Sex—or, as she preferred to call it, intercourse—was everywhere. It had happened, and not all that gradually, over half a century, yet it was only now that it seemed to have exploded in her face. It was painful and enraging too to think of Alan and Daphne having intercourse. But did they? It was a long time since she and Alan had.

All this had happened—all of it—because of those tunnels and old Mr. Winwood turning some children out of them. She backed away from scrubbing the en suite bathroom tiles and pictured it. It couldn't be, it mustn't be. The only person who could stop it was herself. This time she must go there on her own, giving them no warning. Why had this spring-cleaning seemed a good idea? It was hateful, the sort of chore no young woman would dream of doing, if the women's magazines and the women's pages in newspapers were to be believed. She knew from the distant past that once it was completed, the only thing she would get out of it was to sit down in the lounge and look with admiration at her handiwork. And how long would that last? Ten minutes? There would be no real satisfaction, no triumph, just the acceptance that she had done it, and "it" was what she had been brought up to do for the rest of her life.

What had Daphne done for a living? Before all this began, Maureen Batchelor had told her Daphne had been a lawyer. A lawyer who worked as an adviser to a big company, not a solicitor. That would be useful, thought Rosemary, when she tried to make Alan get divorced. It mustn't happen, it mustn't get that far. Don't even think about it. What she must think of was how to get in that house in Hamilton Terrace without one of them opening the front door to her. And no one must know, not her daughter or her son or either of her granddaughters. They must see her—on the coming Wednesday, for instance—as her calm old self, perhaps seated at the sewing machine when they arrived, embarking on some new garment for one of them. Her watchword must be that Alan would come back. She would say it to them to reassure them.

"He'll come back."

No one would ask if she would take him back. They would be too relieved for that. Her love for them, not long ago the mainspring of her existence, had turned to resentment. She wanted to see no one. All she wanted was to think about the situation from every angle and plan how to get into that house. She wouldn't be in a hurry. She would take her time. After all, it was her time now, not Alan's, hers alone to do as she liked with.

18

VISITING THE OLD as a duty, caring for the old, should normally come to an end when one is old oneself. Perhaps when one is between fifty and sixty. But no longer, Michael thought. Not when people expected to live into their eighties and nineties. The young visitor, such as himself, was around seventy. He went upstairs and into Vivien's room, saying aloud as he stood at the end of the bed, "When half the world lives to be eighty-eight, why did you have to die at fifty? When I cared for you so much, why did you leave me to care for people I don't give a damn about?"

His father and Clara Moss. He preferred Clara over his father, but that was true of anyone he knew. He had dreamt the night before of his father in that tee-shirt with the skull on it, and out food shopping this morning, he seemed to see skulls everywhere. It was a fashionable adornment. He saw a woman with skulls on the black moccasins she wore, another with skull earrings, and of course a tee-shirt like his father's. It puzzled him because the woman in the moccasins was elderly, if not as old as his father—who was?—and while it seemed fairly reasonable for a thirty-year-old to dress in such macabre gear, why would an old man or woman want to be so grimly reminded of his or her mortality?

Clara Moss was due for another visit. Last time Lewis Newman had been with him or at least taken him to her door. He had been to lunch with Stanley and Helen Batchelor. Whatever happened, no one would come with Michael this time, so he was surprised by a phone call from Maureen Batchelor to ask him if he would "look in on" Clara again. It would only be once or twice as she would be able to take it on herself once she was feeling "more up to it." He asked if she hadn't been well.

"I miss George. Of course I do, I'm bound to. Why not come and see me before you go to Clara's? Come and have a sherry." Her voice broke on that last word. "Oh, dear, I'm not back to normal yet."

Carisbrooke looked just the same but the atmosphere was different. Big George and his big personality had filled it, his loud voice audible all over the bungalow. In his absence, his absence for ever now, Michael found himself subduing his tone so that he had to stop himself from whispering. They drank some sherry, dry oloroso for both this time, dark brown and sharp. Maureen in the black that most new widows avoided these days. She was thinner and paler. It seemed to him that once or twice she looked round the room in a sort of bewilderment, as if trying to find or conjure up George.

But the sherry put some life into her. He told her about his father and Urban Grange, leaving out a lot, including the skull tee-shirt and his aim to live until he was a hundred. Maureen, unlike her brothers-in-law, had never known Michael as a child or the father they all thought of as an ogre, and she changed the subject as soon and as politely as she could.

"I ran into Rosemary Norris the other day. You remember her?"

"Of course."

"Well, I think she's lost her mind. Does getting senile take you that way? I mean, make you have crazy fantasies?"

"I don't know," said Michael. "How would I know?"

"She's having one. Rosemary, I mean. We were in Tesco, lining up at the cheese counter. The queues are worse than at the post office in there. You wouldn't think they would be now everyone's got the Internet, would you? What was I saying? Oh, yes, Rosemary. Mind you, I didn't believe what she told me. I *don't* believe it. That's what I mean about the Alzheimer's. She said she went to Daphne Jones's house—Furness, I mean—and stabbed her with a kitchen knife. How about that?"

"You mean really stabbed her? Was Alan there?"

"She said she tried to stab her with a knife she took with her, but Daphne was wearing something she called a 'breastplate' and the knife wouldn't go in. The only one that was hurt was Alan. She cut his hand and he wouldn't go to hospital and she says he's got blood poisoning as a result."

"As you said, it's some sort of fantasy, Maureen."

"Him leaving her has turned her brain. If you're going to Clara's now, Michael, I think I'll come with you. To get my hand in, if you see what I mean. Would you mind?"

"I'd love it," he said sincerely.

No one appeared to be at home in the little house in Forest Road. If he had been alone, Michael might have given up, but Maureen knew Clara's ways and called through the letterbox.

Clara's feeble voice just reached them: "In the flowerpot by the camellia."

She belonged in a generation who knew the names of flowers. Maureen fished out the key from among the camellia's roots and they let themselves in. Most of the ground floors in houses along here, Maureen told him later, had been converted to incorporate hall and living-room into one, but Clara's had always been that way so that the front door led straight into the single big room.

It smelt of overcooked cabbage and a cheap, lemony room freshener. Clara was half lying, half sitting up in bed, propped up on pillows. She was thinner and paler, as pale as Michael's father had been, the skin on her neck and her forearms pleated as fine silk can be. Michael kissed her cheek. She put up her creased arms and fumbled to touch his shoulders. He gave her the chocolates he had bought on the way there—the same kind as those he had given her last time and which she seemed to like—while Maureen filled the only vase she could find with water and arranged in it the flowers she had brought.

He could tell at once that since he had last been here, Clara had deteriorated not only in body, in thinness and weakness, but in her mind too. She began talking now about her youth before the Second World War, when the only possible career for a working-class girl was in a factory or going out cleaning. She had done both, in the first years of the war working in munitions and later when she met and married her husband as a "charlady" to families in Tycehurst Hill and for Michael's parents. The Winwoods were her only employers on the Hill. It was farther away than she wanted to go, almost twice as far from Forest Road as the bottom of Tycehurst Hill was.

She knew about George's death and asked how Maureen was getting on. "At least you had him beside you all those years, dear. I'm glad of that. Not like me, losing mine after not quite two. I've sometimes wondered if he'd come back, would we have had kids? Maybe. My sisters had seven between them." To be sociable, to be polite, Michael thought, she left the subject and asked him about his father. He answered her as best he could, though he would rather have talked about anyone else they both knew.

"Did he ever marry again, dear?"

"Yes, he did. Twice. I never met the second one and I only met the third one once. She was called Sheila, a woman called Sheila something."

"That wasn't the name," Clara said. "I'd know it if I heard it. Very young she was. Used to come there sometimes, had long, black pigtails. It was after your poor mum passed over and you'd gone down to live with your auntie."

"Would you like to get up and let me help you into your chair?" said Maureen.

Clara said not this time. She was tired. She didn't know what had come over her but maybe it was old age. "I asked you about your dad getting married again because he said to me once or twice that when she was a bit older, he was going to marry her. But she wasn't called Sheila, I know that. 'A bit older?' I said to him. 'She's never going to be as old as you, is she?' Maybe I spoke out of turn, but he never said nothing."

"Mrs. Moss, is there anything I can do for you? Anything I can bring you? I'd like to do something."

"There's nothing I want, dear. What you want

gets less and less when you're as old as what I am. Your dad, he used to call me Mrs. Mopp. After that character in *ITMA* it was. I never liked it but I couldn't say, could I? She used to say, 'Can I do you now?' I'd never have talked like that."

When they were out in a High Road café having tea, Michael asked Maureen what *ITMA* was.

"Before your time and mine. George remembered it. It was a radio programme, a comedy show. *I-T-M-A*, the initials of *It's That Man Again*. A comedian called Tommy Handley was in it. Clara often talked about it. Understandably, she didn't like being called Mrs. Mopp."

"Resentment dies hard," said Michael. "It outlives good memories." Yet the lady with the little dog lived on in his. "Let me know, won't you, if anything happens to her?" He mildly despised himself for the euphemism and marvelled that he could talk with such care about the future demise of his father's cleaning woman while speaking brutally of death and dying in connection with his father.

On his way home in the tube, he thought not of Clara Moss but of the Norrises. Perhaps Rosemary did have Alzheimer's, perhaps that would make her fantasise about killing Daphne. He knew nothing about the disorder, eschewing all thoughts on the subject because at his age he might be a candidate for it. Strangely, because Alan and Rosemary had never been friends of his, he wanted to know what had really happened if anything. It wasn't his business, but when did that ever stop one's trying to find out what the business that wasn't one's own, in fact, was?

A breastplate? It sounded like one of those television serials set in the Dark Ages where men with swords bounded about on horseback and women wore nothing but scraps of armour just to cover their erogenous zones. Having some knowledge of Daphne's house, he tried to imagine the scene, but the picture that appeared was of the kind of women in the serial fighting each other with knives, not a rare event. When he had changed onto the Jubilee Line he thought of getting off at St. John's Wood and walking down to Hamilton Terrace. But to what purpose? At first he had had some idea of being that confidant, that someone to talk to they might need, of being, as the current jargon had it, *there* for them. But it wasn't in his nature to do that. In all his life the only person to wish to confide in him was Vivien. He had listened and comforted because she was his wife and he loved her. The train stopped at St. John's Wood, the doors opened, closed, and he went on to Swiss Cottage, where he got out.

19

PRIDING THEMSELVES ON their stoicism, Alan and Daphne pretended to each other that they were unaffected by what had happened. Rosemary had made a feeble attempt to hurt Daphne, no more than that. It was a gesture more than a life-threatening onslaught. She hadn't intended serious harm.

That was at first. That was how they were in the hours following Rosemary and Judith's departure. Shock came twenty-four hours later, manifesting itself in a shivering on Daphne's part, a trembling of her whole body that she couldn't control. For Alan, his wounded hand was a constant reminder, but thanks to the immediate treatment he had had, it would soon be healed.

But he was aware of it all the time, conscious of who had cut him, his wife of more than half a century, and that many would say she had right on her side.

He wasn't afflicted with tremors as Daphne was but with repeated visions of that knife in Rosemary's grip and of his own hand ineffectually attempting to reach it and stop its progress. All that had come of that was the damage to his hand.

Daphne's leather jacket had saved her. Had she worn it because she had a premonition of what Rosemary would do? He and Daphne had got into the habit of telling each other everything. Everything about their past, their present, their cares, their fears. He had never achieved this with Rosemary in all their years together. He had often tried, but she had been too ready to be shocked, disgusted, or disbelieving, and when he had told her she could tell him anything she chose, she only said there was nothing to tell, she didn't have those sorts of secrets even if others might. But Daphne had no such inhibitions, had told him all about her past—or so he believed—and listened to his confessions of his own, mild and irreproachable as it was, with a smile.

So her trembling, her shaking hand when she lifted a cup or a pen, alarmed him. It was unlike her. He feared it as a symptom of a pathological loss of control.

"I don't want to go to a doctor," she said when he suggested it. "He or she will ask me if I've had any sort of shock, and it's no good going at all if I don't tell the truth. Now if we knew a doctor, if we had a friend who was a doctor, I'd go to him, but we don't."

"We do. Lewis Newman."

"We did once. We hardly know him now."

"I'm worried about you. I'm going to phone him."

"I rather like him," said Daphne, the hand that touched his arm trembling.

TELLING PEOPLE WHAT she had done was for Rosemary a way of showing them the gravity of her case. Everyone would understand and would sympathise. There could be no opposing view. Right was on her side. She was a good, virtuous woman, married for fifty-five years, the mother of her husband's children, one who had never looked at another man and one who had devoted herself to him. The first to be told of her attempt to stab—to kill?—Daphne Jones (as she always thought of her) had been Maureen. She thought it likely Maureen would tell other people, at any rate the Batchelor family, Stanley and Helen in Theydon Bois, Norman in France, and they would no doubt tell their children. The more who knew the better. She thought a little about Alan. She had cut his hand, but that was his fault; he shouldn't even have been in Daphne Jones's house. He was Rosemary's husband and she wanted him back, in spite of what he had done. What was all this about except an effort to get him back?

Though she had taken it for granted all those Batchelors would tell their friends and their children, she had somehow assumed that Judith and Maurice wouldn't tell theirs. It was the kind of thing they would want to keep in the dark. So it was a surprise when Fenella appeared at the front door with Callum and Sybilla and greeted her with "Oh, Gran, what have you done? How could you?"

Rosemary instinctively said, "Not in front of the children."

They all came in, Fenella replying that they wouldn't understand and her son and daughter rushing to that usually forbidden place, the balcony, in pursuit of the neighbour's cat. Not expecting them, Rosemary had left the French windows open. The windows were now closed, the screams silenced by stuffing mouths with chocolate truffles from the box on the coffee table.

"I would never have imagined you could do such a thing," said Fenella, referring to the knife incident.

"I couldn't imagine it myself till I did it."

"Thank God you didn't succeed."

"That's your opinion, dear. I wish I had succeeded. They wouldn't put me in prison at my age." Rosemary laughed. "They'd give me a few weeks' community service. Or maybe just a caution. I'll make us some tea."

"No, you stay there, Gran. I'll make the tea."

She spoke as if Rosemary were an invalid, but of the psychiatric rather than the physical order, Fenella's tone of the sort generally known as humouring. Rosemary left her to it, wishing she could be alone to make her plans. Her job now was to find a way of getting into that house or luring Daphne out of it, preferably unaccompanied by Alan. One way might be to appear changed in her attitude, to convince Alan that she had relented towards him, that she forgave him and wanted to be friends with both of them. She might even tell him that having thought it over carefully, she could be persuaded to a divorce. She'd like to keep the flat, but he'd agree to that—wouldn't he?—living as he did in Daphne Jones's beautiful house. . . . Callum had rolled himself in one of the rugs, and Sybilla was kicking his head. Rosemary told them in an abstracted tone not to be so naughty and returned to her thoughts.

When their mother came back, Sybilla had got the French windows open and Callum was climbing over the balcony rail.

They were both dragged back into the living-room, loudly rejecting the grapefruit juice that was the only alternative to tea. Rosemary sat with her eyes shut, wondering how to get hold of Daphne Jones's phone number. Perhaps instead she could do what Judith had done on that previous occasion and write a letter.

No decision had been reached by the time Fenella and the children left. Many attempts had been made to convince Rosemary that she should depend more on her family, confide in Fenella herself, in Freya and their husbands, be alone less and come to stay with one or the other of them whenever she felt like it, spend some time with Owen and his wife, or why not go away on holiday with her sister? Surely Maureen Batchelor would go with her. Rosemary agreed to nothing. She had never liked Owen's wife; she might as well be honest about it now. As for Maureen, the woman would probably be afraid to be alone with Rosemary in case she got herself stabbed. Having always disagreed with Alan about Fenella's children, she was now being honest with herself. They were badly behaved, very much so, and she was glad to see the back of them. As they departed, she said to Fenella, "Phone me before you come again, won't you?" Rosemary left off the almost requisite *dear* or *darling*.

Alan always used to say that when you have a decision to make, things always get better when you make up your mind to what you're going to do. Make up your mind, settle it, and you have gone a long way to lifting the load that is weighing on you. Well, she had made up her mind. She would write her letter tomorrow morning and write it to Alan—or should it be to Daphne Jones? He would recognise her handwriting, whereas if Daphne picked up their correspondence first, she might not. But she would still open it, wouldn't she? She would take it for some sort of apology as it would indeed be. Anyway, Rosemary would write it, and perhaps to both of them, however much she loathed the idea of coupling their names together on the envelope.

TO BE A DOCTOR of medicine means that a fairly large proportion of the people you meet will tell you of their ailments and ask you what should be done. Most of them know they shouldn't do this, but still they do it, accompanying their request with an apology. Lewis Newman had a friend who had a PhD and who had been unwise enough to call himself "doctor." For a little while, that is. He soon learned better. But everyone knew Lewis was a doctor of medicine and a member of the Royal College of Physicians, and there was no hiding it. So he wasn't surprised when Alan Norris phoned to ask for his advice. It was his own fault, he thought, for giving the man his card. Still, he didn't much mind. He rather liked Alan and this woman he had run off with. They were his childhood friends, a long, long time ago but still fresh in his memory. Besides, he was only human and wanted to see where they lived and what they were like together and even to make some estimate as to whether their relationship, as it was called today, would last.

Daphne Furness must have a GP, an NHS one, or a doctor she saw privately, so why wasn't she seeing her or him? Possibly because she didn't want her doctor to know that Alan Norris (or any male person) had moved in with her.

"I could pop over tomorrow afternoon," he said. "Just have a look at her."

"She shakes," said Alan. "But come and have supper with us. It'll be nice to see you."

Daphne shook even more when she saw Rosemary's letter. It was addressed to her and Alan, but she opened it with him beside her, her hand shaking. " 'Dear Alan and Daphne,' " she read aloud, though Alan could see the letter as well as she could, " 'This is an apology. I want to say I am sorry for what happened last week. I don't know why I made that attack on you, Daphne. Violence is always unnecessary and useless. I deeply regret it now. If you can forgive me, I would very much like to see you both. The only way to get through this trouble is to talk, and that is what I would like to do. It may be that you would think a divorce the best way forward and that it is time to move on. I firmly believe that we should discuss it and for that we must meet. Would you let me come to your house again but in a spirit of friendship? You could come here if you prefer it.

" 'Please do not ignore this letter. I am very anxious to talk to you both. Rosemary.'

"I don't know what to say," said Daphne. "What do you think?"

"Could you bear it? I think she's sincere. My granddaughter Fenella would say her attempt on your life sort of cleansed her of those murderous feelings."

"Why Fenella?"

"She's a psychologist."

"And the letter has sort of cleansed me of shaking. It's stopped."

Alan kissed her. "I'm so glad. We'll still have Lewis over, shall we?"

ROSEMARY WAS BACK at her sewing machine. She possessed a dress pattern she had never used because she considered it too ambitious for her. In the sewing room was a dress length, several metres of flowered silk, also never used. On the crest of a wave, as she put it to herself, resulting from that letter and imagining its reception in Hamilton Terrace, she had pinned the pattern to the silk, tacked it up, and was now machining a side seam. If she could finish it in time, she would wear the new dress when she paid her visit to Daphne and Alan, or when they came to her. Fantasising, she pictured herself in the dress when the police came and arrested her, charging her in Daphne's drawing-room with wilful murder—did they still say *wilful* or was that American? Her photograph would appear in the papers, which would describe her as a "pretty elderly woman, elegantly dressed" and would inevitably give her age. Daphne Jones was older, she thought, maybe by three years. Rosemary completed the seam, removed the tacking stitches, and was about to start on the next one when the phone rang.

Daphne? Alan? It was neither of them. Robert Flynn said how sorry he was to hear that she and Alan were separated. It was sad, she said, but she hoped it wouldn't be permanent. Robert talked about his long friendship with Alan, grown rather distant in recent years. Rage, which had been in abeyance since her return to the sewing machine, suddenly surged up in her.

"Don't you dare tell me you knew nothing about it!" she shouted down the phone. "You were his alibi. All the time he was with her, he told me he was meeting you. He told you the whole thing and you were prepared to lie for him. Lies, lies, lies, that's what I had to put up with. And I was his wife for more than fifty years."

Robert Flynn stammered that he was sorry, it was nothing to do with him, he knew nothing about it.

Rosemary screamed, "Liar!"—and crashed the phone down.

Her breath was still coming in rapid gasps when it rang again. Alan's voice said, "Are you all right? You sound ill."

"I'm not ill. Your friend Robert Flynn phoned and—well, he made me cross. I'm all right now. Did you get my letter?"

"That's what I'm calling about."

"I thought *she* would."

He made no reply to that. "You want to talk to

both of us, you said. When would you like to come?"

Both of us had once meant her and Alan. "Would Friday suit?"

He said it would. Maybe in the morning. That would give her time to decide. Not to kill Daphne, that was already decided on, but how to do it and how too to make the maximum show of it. Make a show that everyone passing and everyone in the gardens of Hamilton Terrace might know how Rosemary had been wronged and what she had done.

"Give my regards to Daphne."

It was absurd. The only regard she had for Daphne Jones was hatred. Returning to the sewing machine, she tried to adjust the needle to the point in the sleeve seam she had reached, but it ran crookedly. The stitches would have to be unpicked. She pulled the beginnings of a dress out, rolled it up, and stuffed the material into the table drawer where she kept scissors and cotton reels and a box of pins. How much she would like to seize Daphne Jones's hand, thrust it under the needle, and start the machine. Daphne had thin hands with long fingers. The needle would try to enter the back of that hand, would plough up skin and veins and bones even if it failed, as it would, to penetrate to the palm. Rosemary savoured it. In the past she had always hated torture, stories about it in the papers, books with torture in them.

She could easily and happily contemplate it carried out on Daphne: the rack, electric shocks, St. Catherine's wheel. She had never known but always wondered what the wheel did to you. Come to that, what did the rack do? Whatever it was, she would like to see it done to Daphne Jones.

She had till Friday to decide how she would do it. Characters in books often tried to make their killing look like an accident. Some tried to make a death look like suicide. She went into the room Alan had called his study, though he never studied anything in there. One wall was covered in bookshelves that were full of books. Green-and-white Penguins of the 1940s filled two shelves, books by writers once famous: Margery Allingham, Ngaio Marsh, Agatha Christie. There was one by A. E. W. Mason called *The House of the Arrow*. She had read that when they were first married. It was about the arrow poison South American tribes used, something like strychnine called curare. She knew she wouldn't be able to get hold of it. Imagining dropping poison in Daphne's drink was no more than fantasy. Far more practical was to push her downstairs or in front of, say, a bus. St. John's Wood was full of buses, coming and going. But that too was impossible. Suggest to Daphne that they go out for a walk and push her under that little bus, the single-decker that ran past the tube station? It again was no more than fantasy.

Besides, the bus had a driver. In her previous life (as Rosemary thought of the time when Alan was with her) she had cared for people, what happened to them, and sometimes how she could help. If she pushed Daphne in front of the number 46 or 187, wouldn't she be involving the driver in something he would never forget? Wouldn't he remember for ever how he had been guilty, if involuntarily, of causing a woman's violent death? She had seen something like that on television, a train driver who had ploughed through a car on a level crossing and saw the dead couple and their children his train had slaughtered in nightly dreams. It wouldn't just be Daphne Jones who suffered. . . .

She had arranged to go to Hamilton Terrace on Friday, so she had better make up her mind.

IN THE DAYS when he practised, Lewis had had a private paying patient in Hamilton Terrace, a man with nothing wrong with him but who liked to have a tame physician on call. The calls came pretty often and in the night. Eventually Lewis left him, but he retained a memory of the street, particularly of what it looked like at midnight, silent, empty, and faintly lit. The patient, who was anything but patient, lived a long way up, almost on the corner with Carlton Hill, but the number of his house gave Lewis a good idea of where Daphne's must be.

After he had been in the place five minutes and already been given a large gin and tonic, he had begun wondering if Daphne's illness, rather like that of the other resident of Hamilton Terrace, was no more than a ploy or excuse to see him. Then she said she had had "the shakes," which had started the previous week after she had had a "shock." She hesitated, looked at Alan, whose hand she was holding, thereby inexpertly concealing the plaster that covered the palm, and said in a low voice not much above a whisper, "Someone pulled a knife on me."

"You mean stabbed you?"

"It was a kitchen knife," Alan said, "but it didn't break the skin."

"This happened out in the street? Some young villain tried to mug you?"

"I suppose so."

"Of course you called the police?"

"Neither one of us was carrying a mobile. By the time we got home, we said to each other that as nothing had happened, Daphne wasn't hurt, there didn't seem any point in calling them." Lewis knew Alan was lying and lying badly with the clumsiness of someone who habitually tells the truth. "Everything seemed all right, and then Daphne started shaking."

Lewis looked at her. "She isn't shaking now." He wished he hadn't accepted that drink. What had really happened? Not that trumped-up mugging, he was sure. It was on the tip of his tongue to ask, but he wasn't a policeman. "It's the result of shock. It often happens. Gone now, it appears. You don't need me."

Daphne made an appeal to him. Sitting next to him on the sofa, she laid her hands on his arms, said, "I think you were going to leave, but please don't. Please stay. It wasn't true about the mugging or it being outdoors. It happened in here, in this room, but I can't tell you who it was, I can't. I wasn't hurt. As you say, it was the shock of it made me shake. Don't bother about it but please stay to supper."

So Lewis did. It gave him the opportunity to watch the two of them together. They seemed very lovey-dovey, as his mother would have said, though nothing in their behaviour was indecorous. After thanking them for supper and drinks, he said rather grudgingly that when they needed a doctor, he would come to them privately, "but not in the night, and I'd still recommend the National Health Service."

It was too late to phone anyone by the time he got home. Not too late for the young, but people of his age had been brought up to believe that it was a breach of good manners to make a phone call after 9:00 p.m. at the latest. He called Stanley Batchelor next morning.

"You went to Daphne's place, did you? You actually saw the two of them together?"

"That's right." Lewis's doctor's code forbade his telling Stanley about Daphne's tremor, but not of the attack that apparently caused it. He began hesitantly, skirting around what he knew of the stabbing, but Stanley interrupted him.

"Rosemary turned up there out of the blue and ran at Daphne with a carving knife. She brought it with her in her bag. Daphne must have expected it because she was wearing some sort of armour. Chain mail, I think it was, or it may have been a bulletproof vest."

"Wow. Good heavens."

"You may well say so. It's absolutely true. Rosemary told Maureen herself, and Maureen told Helen. Alan was wounded and an ambulance came. They dressed the wound but Alan wouldn't be taken to A and E. I don't blame him, the hours you hang about in those places. No one called the police; you wouldn't, would you, if no one was really hurt? You'd be too ashamed."

This had come about, thought Lewis, because of a builder finding two hands in a biscuit box buried underneath a house. Well, as far as he was concerned, it need go no further.

20

MICHAEL WAS IN Vivien's room lying on the bed and talking to her as he often did, when the phone rang. He let it ring. There was no one he wanted to talk to. It was probably a wrong number. Five minutes later it rang again, and this time he went down to the floor below to answer it. Of course he wished he hadn't.

Imogen's always-recognisable voice said it was Urban Grange and he must prepare himself for a shock. Michael hoped and didn't attempt to stop himself hoping that his father was dead. But, no. Mr. Winwood, said Imogen, had had "a minor heart attack."

"I expect you'd like to see him. If you'd care to come in this afternoon, our resident physician, Dr. Stefani, will be here to talk to you. There is no immediate cause for concern, but of course, as you are aware, your father has reached a very great age."

How could he not be aware? Never mind. "I'll be with you about three."

They must wonder at Urban Grange why he had never been near his father until Zoe died. Perhaps they didn't wonder about things like that. In there they must see all sorts, all sorts that made a world. He had long ago stopped believing in God. Any belief he may have had, had died on that platform at Victoria when his father confessed with no apparent regret to having forgotten to bring Michael's lunch. His first wife revived his belief for a few years. Babette, of all people, used to go to church and, ridiculously dressed like a Barbie doll, sang hymns about the house as she made perfunctory efforts at cooking and cleaning: "O God, Our Help in Ages Past" and "Guide Me, O Thou Great Redeemer." When she left, he also left her faith. It was gone many years before he married Vivien, too late for him to question why this deity had let her die in the prime of life and kept his father alive up till his century.

He was sitting up in an armchair, wrapped in a dressing gown embroidered not with hands but with dragons, gold dragons on red silk. Once they used to keep people in bed, but not now. Get them up as soon as reasonably or, come to that, unreasonably possible. His father's calloused, old feet were concealed by argyle socks, the kind you knew were expensive without knowing how you knew.

Michael sat down in the other velvet armchair. Age had not withered his father's eyes or his voice. The eyes were fixed on him and Michael noticed for the first time how seldom the old man blinked. Once or twice in Michael's life, an optician testing his sight had asked him not to blink while she operated some machine. He knew how difficult this was, but his father seemed to pass whole minutes without the flicker of an eye.

"How are you feeling?" Michael said because that was always what you said to people in hospital.

"Much the same. Chap called Stefani, an Eyetie of course, wants to see you. That'll be a relief, get away from me. I can tell you what he'll say. That I'm stable, that's their new word. Stable. Nothing to do with horses. The next step will be critical, but I'm not there yet." His father sneezed, an enormous sneeze, unimpeded by any handkerchief or tissue.

Michael suppressed a desire to say, *Bless you.*

The old man blew his nose on a beautifully laundered snow-white handkerchief he pulled out of his pocket. "I suppose you think that by coming to see me I'll leave you something in my will. When I go, that is, which won't be till January."

Michael said nothing, though he hadn't thought about it. What would be the use when his father wouldn't believe him?

"There's plenty left. I'm not leaving it to you but to the Hedgehog Trust. I promised Sheila I would, and it's one of the few promises I've made I'm going to stick to."

Now Michael could no longer control himself. "The what?"

"I thought that would get you. You heard. I've always liked hedgehogs. We had one used to come into the garden at Anderby. I put bread and milk out for it. It upset me, hedgehogs always getting themselves killed on the roads."

So there was something that upset him. The Batchelor brothers embraced when they met, hugged each other without embarrassment. Michael hadn't seen it but Maureen had told him, wonderingly, yet with approval. What must that be like, to put your arms round a family member and hold him? Of course he had kissed and hugged Zoe, but no one else when he was small. He never recalled his mother kissing him and as for his father . . .

"Well, good-bye," Michael said. "I'll keep in touch."

His father's laugh was almost frightening to hear. It had been really frightening when Michael was a child. Something about it was Gothic, something belonging in one of those horror films when with a similar cackle a scaly beast slinks out of the mouth of a cave or rears up from a dark lake.

"Suit yourself. When you come in here—I mean me, when I came in here—they don't search you, you pay too much for that. If they had, they'd have found the pills I was carrying. Cyanide. Half a dozen in a bottle. For use if I don't die soon enough. You don't believe me? Suit yourself."

Downstairs, Michael was shown into a spacious room, carpeted in fashionable grey and furnished with pale hardwoods. Dr. Stefani was tall, suave, and good-looking in a characterless way.

"Inevitably, there must be concern for a gentleman of your father's age."

Gentleman was a strange sort of usage, Michael thought, and even stranger when Stefani said, "The old ticker is slowing down. Like the clock it is, telling its owner the time. It will soon stop. The time left we cannot count in years or even months. Weeks perhaps."

Should he tell this man who seemed to him like an impostor or charlatan? Why bother when he didn't believe it himself? "He wants to live till January the fourteenth. That's when he'll be a hundred."

"Just what I would have estimated. Would he like to see a priest, do you think? Some like the last rites."

"Ask him on January the thirteenth," said Michael, fighting an urge to scream with laughter. "Ask him, not me. Good-bye."

All trains apart from tubes brought back to him that train journey from Victoria to Lewes, that first one, not his subsequent visits to Zoe. They seemed different, though the same route was followed and the same station reached. The Suffolk countryside was subtly unlike that of Sussex, flatter, bleaker, but still he might have been nine again, stroking and fondling the lady's little dog. He put his head back against the not very comfortable seat and, though it was the last thing he expected, fell asleep. The dream he had wasn't of dogs or the lady or—thank God—his father, but of the qanats, where Alan and two of the Batchelors sat on upturned boxes playing cards, and on a pile of old pillows covered in striped ticking sat Daphne, watching them, her long, black hair cloaking her shoulders.

A voice announcing the train's arrival at Liverpool Street woke him. For a second or two he was a frightened child again, rubbing his eyes, afraid he might have drawn attention to himself by whimpering. But no one stared at him. He got out and went to find a taxi.

21

A LETTER WAS ON his doorstep, such a rarity that he stepped on it entering the house. It had an enclosure, wrapped in adhesive tape. More interesting and suddenly painful was the sender's address: Anderby, The Hill, Loughton, Essex, and the postcode. Michael sat down at the kitchen table with a small whisky in a tumbler. The sender, Daniel Thompson, wrote that he had recently moved into Michael's old home, and in the remodelling of the kitchen, the first carried out for over fifty years, the plumber had discovered the contents of the package. Daniel Thompson supposed it might belong to a member of Mr. Winwood's family. He said nothing about how he had discovered Michael's whereabouts. But all things were now possible online. Michael unwrapped the tiny package and laid Clara's wedding ring on the palm of his left hand.

ROSEMARY HADN'T DRIVEN a car for years but she still had a licence, having renewed it when she was seventy. If she could hire a car and drive it to Hamilton Terrace, if she could take Daphne out in it, killing her would be easy. Didn't they call the place where the passenger sat the suicide seat? It was impossible. No car-hire company would rent a car to her at her age, licence or no licence. Daphne would never get into a car that Rosemary was driving. Would Daphne go out for a walk with her? And walk where? According to Freya, St. John's Wood had a nice High Street with clothes shops, but why would anyone choose to go shopping there if they came up from the suburbs? They would go to the West End or Knightsbridge. No, on Friday she must go to the house in Hamilton Terrace as she had arranged. It would be lunchtime or close on, and they would serve her a drink while they talked. They would talk, that was what they believed to be the purpose of the visit. Talk about divorce, financial arrangements, where to live, all the things a couple who were separating discussed. It wasn't anything she had thought she would ever come to, her marriage was so happy, or that was what she believed. If they had separated, wouldn't it have been in their forties or fifties, the age, she had read, for people breaking off the old and starting anew? It was an outrage, making that change at the end of their lives.

How much bleach would be a lethal dose? She looked inside the cupboard under the kitchen sink, took out the bottle, and poured a little of the viscous liquid onto a saucer. The smell was so strong it made her gasp. That was no good then. How about the morphine? That had no smell. When her mother was dying of cancer and no more could be done for her, she had moved in with them to the house in Church Lane. It was so big she could have a large bedroom on the ground floor. Rosemary had nursed her mother devotedly (even though she said it herself), and only when she was no more than a week from the end did they move her into the hospice. The doctor, visiting her, had prescribed morphine when the pain got bad and, when her mother died, told Rosemary she must destroy what was left in the bottle—quite a lot because she hadn't lived long. He would leave it to her to dispose of it safely. "I know I can trust you," he had said.

Trust her not to do what she intended. She put the bottle in her handbag, a bag too small to hold a knife. There need be no disguising what she had done. No refusal to admit her guilt or saying she had made a mistake—what mistake was possible? She would even tell Alan to call the police and she would meekly await their arrival. What symptoms Daphne would exhibit Rosemary didn't know. Choking? Gasping? Rosemary thought she could watch Daphne's struggles without a qualm, watch them with interest. She had read a newspaper story of a young girl's swallowing bath cleanser because her boyfriend had left her and dying from it, but the results which led up to her death were not detailed.

Judith had come to see her on Wednesday afternoon, and on Thursday evening Fenella was with her, mercifully leaving the children with their father. Her family never left her alone for long. They brought presents, as if a box of chocolates or a vial of perfume could comfort you for the loss of a husband. Judith wanted to arrange a holiday for her, a boat trip up the Danube with Maurice's sister, whom Rosemary had met only once and taken a dislike to. Fenella suggested Rosemary come to stay with her and Giles, "just for a week or two." The children would be company for Rosemary, prevent her getting depressed. Rosemary said she would think about both offers. Of course there was nothing to think about as by the time either could take place, she would be in prison or possibly in a mental hospital.

IT OUGHT TO make him feel young, Michael reasoned, visiting all these old people, years older than himself. It didn't. Rather, he looked at his father and now at Clara Moss and thought that this was how he might be in ten or fifteen years' time. If he lived so long. Better if he didn't, if he could have a stroke that killed at a blow or a heart attack. This time he would creep into Loughton—that was how he put it to himself—not alerting any of the Batchelors but making his way from the station to Forest Road, a walk of ten minutes at most. But before he could put this into practice, a phone call from Maureen told him that her brother-in-law Norman was ill in hospital in France and not expected to live. She thought Michael would wish to know as he was one of the tunnels people. Would he pass it on to Lewis Newman?

Recalling how Norman always told everyone that he had been born on the kitchen table, lately comparing his birth circumstances to those of the Duke of Edinburgh, who had also been born on a table, but in Corfu, not Loughton, Michael phoned Lewis with his news. Lewis naturally was not particularly interested. He hardly remembered Norman Batchelor. Michael called Maureen back and, this time, much against his original plan, asked if he could see her and would she come with him to visit Clara Moss.

After lunch—of course Maureen asked him to lunch—they went together to Forest Road. She was in low spirits. It seemed to her, she said, that everyone was "going." First her George, now Norman, and Stanley had had pains, which might be the forerunner of a heart attack.

"Well, we're old," said Michael. "Recently a prevailing belief has been that we shall live for ever, thanks to modern medicine. Stanley will probably be saved for another dozen years. I hope so."

Winter had come early, and in leafy Loughton all the trees had lost their leaves. It was cold and grey but dry. Oaks kept their leaves longer than any other tree, brown, dried up, and shivering in the wind. Maureen remarked that when leaves turned in England, with a few exceptions they changed to yellow, not copper or red. You had to go to America or Canada for that, where maples abounded, a visit she and George had paid a few years before. Memories silenced her and no more was said until they reached Clara's door. It was opened by Samantha, in the young woman's dress of jeans, stripy tee-shirt, and, so common as to seem like part of a uniform, the almost inevitable long, straight hair, its red tinted blond for a change.

"She's asleep. She sleeps a lot these days."

"Should we come back another day?"

Michael could tell by Maureen's tone, though probably Sam couldn't, that Maureen was hoping to be allowed to leave before seeing Clara. "No, you stay," Sam said. "She'd want me to wake her up. She'd be mad if she missed you."

This appeared to be true. Clara woke slowly, struggled to sit up, helped by Sam. Michael hesitated, then kissed her cheek. "You was always a good boy," Clara said. "God knows why. You had everything to make you bad." She had a word for Maureen. "Sorry about your George. There was another good man. But they all go, there's no help for it."

Michael sat on a chair by the bed. Maureen stood for a moment or two, then went into the kitchen to talk to Sam.

Clara said, "I was thinking about your mum. Well, having a dream about her. I dream a lot these days. That pal of hers, the chap with the ginger hair, I remembered his name." She drew a long sigh, then seemed to change the subject. " 'The body is more than raiment.' D'you know where that comes from?"

Michael shook his head. "Should I?"

"My mum and dad would have said you should. Not nowadays, I reckon. It's the Bible. We had it in Sunday school. I was there every Sunday for years and years at St. Mary's. You want to know why I thought of it? On account of it was his name, that chap with the ginger hair. Raiment was his name. She called him Jimmy."

Her words were making him uncomfortable. This, after all, was his mother, and a man's mother, however indifferent she had been as a parent, had something sacred about her. Clara seemed to sense his unease. "She had a lot of friends, gentlemen more than ladies, but there was nothing wrong. You can be sure of that."

"Of course."

Having, as she thought, reassured him, Clara went on, "Like there was the soldier as was Mr. Johnson's brother, used to come to the Johnsons on his leave. You remember the Johnsons?" Michael vaguely did. The son had been in the tunnels with them, was now an ambassador somewhere. "Mr. Clifford Johnson—well, captain he was. He used to admire your mum, as a lot of fellows did, she was as pretty as a picture." Clara was growing tired, he could tell, her voice flagging. "Maybe I shouldn't be saying this, but your dad, he didn't like visitors, ladies or gentlemen, he didn't like it. Wanted his wife to himself and I don't blame him." She laid her head on the pillows once more. "My husband was long gone by then. And that Captain Johnson died on a beach in France. Or so they said. . . ."

She was asleep. Maureen came in with tea for him and Clara, but he wouldn't wake her.

“She’s been quite chatty,” said Sam.

“Talking nineteen to the dozen.” Maureen adjusted Clara’s eiderdown, pulling it up to cover her. “We could hear her from the kitchen, couldn’t we, Sam?”

“Does the doctor come?” Michael asked.

“The lady next door says she was here last week. Looks about sixteen, but I will say this for her, she knows her stuff. Took her blood pressure and listened to her heart, all what they always do. Her heart’s in a bad way, but what can you expect at her age?”

“I’ll come again next week,” said Michael on an impulse.

A SCENT BOTTLE was what she decided on. An ornate object, with a glass stopper and gold bands—real gold, she had been assured by Fenella, the donor—decorating its emerald-coloured surface. No perfume was in it; you were supposed to pour that in yourself from the Armani or Guerlain you bought at what the young called a pharmacy but she the chemist. Of course Rosemary had never done this—who would bother?—but put the bottle on the mantelpiece, where it made a pretty ornament along with the china dog and various framed photographs. She doubted that the stopper had ever before been taken out. The neck of the bottle was quite large enough to pour the morphine into it without difficulty.

She did all this on Thursday evening, even putting the bottle in her handbag, unwilling to leave anything till the morning. Judith phoned her at nine thirty, later than Rosemary had brought her up to think calls should ever be considered, but Rosemary didn't reproach her.

"Yes, I'm going to Hamilton Terrace. We're going to talk."

"What, Daphne as well?"

"It's going to be very different from last time," said Rosemary with absolute truth. "I've given the situation a lot of thought and I shan't do anything rash."

"I'm very glad to hear it, Mother. Let me know how you get on."

"Oh, you'll hear all about it." Rosemary was determined not to lie and had skilfully avoided it.

Her mind was made up and her preparations were in place; even her recently-made-but-never-worn dress was on a hanger outside the wardrobe, her shoes neatly placed together. Not knowing why, she brought the handbag with its lethal contents into the bedroom with her. She didn't want to let it out of her sight. With everything settled and nothing left to do except drink the hot milk she had drunk before bed on almost every night of her life, she expected to sleep well. She hardly slept at all. At every hour she saw the numbers on the bedside digital clock, and when it said 5:30, she got up. It was dark, the season far enough advanced for dawn not to come before seven. She hadn't yet turned on the central heating and the flat felt cold. It was rare for her to get up so early, and it reminded her, though in a different house and long, long ago, of when her babies had awakened her. Grizzling Owen and placid Judith. Did Alan ever think of those days? Did he think of her as bearing his children and nurturing them, of caring for them and looking after them, while he was off to the city to remain there for hours, working, of course, but enjoying himself as well with his friends he called colleagues, eating and drinking, until always later home than he had promised? She had never been a feminist, but she thought she would be if she could have her life over again.

In the tube, clutching the fatal bag, she thought of him again using this train or its forerunner, sitting there reading his newspaper, maybe doing the crossword, while she was changing nappies, mopping up sick, spooning slop into kids' mouths only to see it spit out. She had wasted her life, and all he could say was that it was dull! The stations flowed past. Forty years ago the men who got in would have glanced at her surreptitiously, admiringly, because she had been pretty then, a desirable woman, lovely to look at. All gone now.

Two changes on the tube lay ahead of her, the first onto the Circle Line, the second to the Bakerloo. It surprised her that she could do it alone. She never had before, these changes or others. Alan or one of her children had always been with her. In a way it was easier on her own, no one with her to fuss or hurry her or caution her to hold on or keep away from the platform edge. She should have tried it before, when she was younger, it might have transformed her life.

I am cleverer than I thought, she told herself as she came out of the tube station at Warwick Avenue, pleased to have emerged from the Clifton Gardens exit and not the one for Clifton Villas. She had remembered and remembered correctly. Glancing at her watch, she saw that she was early, she would be ten minutes early, so she took a long way round, walking up the hill and just before the bridge turning down Blomfield Road. On a seat she sat down and looked at the canal without really seeing it, busy with her thoughts, which had taken her back to the last time she was here, to her attempt on Daphne's life. Seeing the scene with her mind's eye, she pictured Daphne, tall and graceful, wearing that life-saving leather jacket, intended for a young woman. Fenella and Freya could have worn it and looked suitably dressed.

Rosemary remembered noticing it long before she reached in her bag for the knife, and now she remembered thinking Daphne was well protected against any attack. No ordinary and rather blunt kitchen knife could penetrate that. She had tried it just the same, but *had she tried it because she knew it wouldn't succeed?* Perhaps. Not perhaps; certainly. Of course she couldn't kill or even hurt someone with a knife. These teenagers in London could, they did it all the time, but they were young and their lives had been anything but sheltered. This time would be different. They called poison the woman's method of murder—call it *killing* instead, it didn't sound so bad. Morphine wasn't poison, but a pain-killing, not person-killing, remedy.

Again she looked at her watch and was surprised to see how much time had passed. She might even be a few minutes late. In an estate agent's window she caught sight of her reflection and stopped to look at herself in the new dress, worn for the first time. It fitted well, it made her look younger. No one would take her for a day over sixty. As she turned away towards the traffic lights where she would cross Maida Vale, she thought in a rare moment of honest self-revelation, When I was thirty, how I would have laughed at someone's being pleased to be taken for *sixty.*

Alan opened the door to her. They had probably arranged it that way, Daphne telling him it would be better if he was the first person Rosemary saw, not her supplanter. He asked her how she was, then hesitated, and she knew he was wondering whether he should kiss her. On the cheek only, of course. They went into the lounge that Daphne called a drawing-room. The way her own grandmother might have, thought Rosemary. Daphne was there, standing up, looking out of the window that gave onto the street. She must have watched for me to come. Are we going to shake hands? No, do nothing but say hallo, awkwardly on both their parts. She thinks I tried to kill her but I didn't.

Alan began. She had thought he would. "This isn't going to be easy. I'd better say first of all that last time is forgotten. I know you didn't mean it. Daphne knows that. But that's over and, as I say, forgotten." Rosemary said nothing. She wanted him to have a hard time. "These things happen in many marriages, only the people are usually younger than us. It's hard for us all. I'd like to make it easier, especially for you, Rosemary, but there's no easy way. It's a tragedy that can't be avoided."

He was waiting for her to speak and she did, though not in the way he expected. "You pompous ass."

Daphne started. She jumped so hard Rosemary could see her move. Alan said, "I'm sorry you take that attitude."

"What did you expect me to say? Be happy, my children, is that what?" Rosemary touched her handbag, the bag that was not big enough to hold a knife, but was the right size for a small bottle. She felt its outlines.

"I think it might help if we all had a drink," said Daphne. "I know it's a bit early but these are special circumstances."

Rosemary nodded. "The sun is over the yardarm, as my father used to say. I never knew what it meant."

Neither of the others enlightened her. Alan said, "Good idea," and left the room. Daphne said, "Sorry to leave you alone. I won't be a minute."

The sauvignon was evidently to be poured elsewhere and into rather tall glasses. A memory came to Rosemary of one of the rare occasions she had been to the opera, to see *Lucrezia Borgia*. She had never heard of it before Alan was given the tickets by a client arranging a musical party. Lucrezia was administering poison much as she planned to do to Daphne, but at a dinner where her son was a guest and her lover who was to drink the poisoned wine. The glasses got switched somehow, and to her grief and agony her son drank the poison and not the intended victim. This wouldn't happen now.

The three full glasses were set down on the coffee table in front of the three chairs, Daphne's nearest the window. The opera came back into Rosemary's mind, and as Alan brought in a bowl of nuts, she thought, What if the glasses get changed round and he gets the one with the morphine? But, no, she would stop that even if at the last moment. The glasses were only half-filled, the way Rosemary had read was the fashionable trend. That would help her. She felt the bottle through the thin suede of the bag and undid the clasp. Holding the bag upright but leaving the bottle where it was, she loosened its top. Maybe she wouldn't get the chance to do it, maybe they wouldn't be out of the room together. It seemed that that was what would happen. When she had set a dish of olives on the table, Daphne sat down in the chair that had its back towards the window and turned to Rosemary with a polite smile.

But Alan was on his feet and looking into the garden as if he could see something interesting. "Come here a minute."

Daphne turned, got up when he said, "The fox is here again. The first time I've seen him for weeks."

Now they both had their backs to Rosemary and were peering through the glass. She reached across the table and poured half the contents of the full bottle into Daphne's glass.

"You want to see this, Rosemary," he said. "A big dog fox. We never saw any in Loughton."

His use of the past tense enraged her, as if when he left, her life was over. "Don't be ridiculous. We're here to talk about our future, not the bloody wildlife."

Wondering if she had ever used the word *bloody* aloud before, she could see he wondered too. She should have said *fucking,* but that would have been too much for her. Even now. Daphne sat down again. Reluctantly, Alan came to join them, his eyes still on the garden. Rosemary thought, I have done it, this is it, I have killed someone. I have killed Daphne Jones. As she said it to herself, something seemed to clutch at her chest, making her heart beat with heavy thuds like a piece of machinery about to go wrong. Alan lifted his glass, hesitated, about to say "Cheers" or "Your health," but stopping himself because it was so inappropriate. He said nothing, took a sip. I can't kill her, Rosemary thought. Not me, not murder, not kill anyone.

Saying aloud, "I can't. No, I can't," she reached across the table and half fell across the dish of olives, sweeping with an outstretched arm Daphne's untouched wineglass to the floor.

Wine flew across Daphne's legs and skirt. She jumped to her feet. "Please don't worry. White wine doesn't stain. I'll get a cloth."

She went off to the kitchen, the wine and morphine mixture dripping off her skirt hem. Alan was perfectly still, silent, staring at Rosemary. He knew. She could tell he knew. She could tell by his face, tell because she had lived with him for half a century, read his face the way Daphne never would. Daphne came back, mopped up the floor, picked up the fragments of glass, and dropped them into a large envelope. Rosemary, ostentatiously, lifted her own glass to her lips, drank the contents, and said to Alan, "I'd like a refill, please."

He left it to Daphne, the innocent one, who knew nothing. Rosemary immediately drank half of what she had been given, thought, The shock of what I have done and not done will come later, and I don't know what form it will take. The wine would go to her head, but it hadn't yet. She swallowed the rest of what Daphne had brought her, got to her feet, still steady, and said, still lucid, "I might as well go. I don't care what you do. Suit yourselves."

Daphne started to say she was "sorry about all this," but Rosemary's face silenced her.

"I'll walk you to the station," said Alan, "or would you like me to call you a cab?"

"Neither. I don't want anything from you."

Alan opened the front door, took a step outside behind her. "What did you put in her drink?"

"Hatred. I will never speak to you again."

He went back into the house, leaving her on the front path. He had already made up his mind to say nothing to Daphne. Poisons came into his mind: arsenic, strychnine, curare, all gathered from detective stories. Which of them had she brought with her and used?

"Let's go away somewhere," he said to Daphne. "Let's go to Italy. I've never been there. Let's go to Florence or Rome."

"Why not? I'd love to."

22

THE DRINK HIT HER or it might have been pain, passion, rage, and shame, all combined. She found a seat near the junction of Hamilton Terrace with the St. John's Wood Road—there were a lot of seats round here—and sank onto it. I am too old for this, she said to herself, this is for a young woman who still has all her physical strength. I should never have gone. Why did I think that I, who have never done a violent act, who never gave one of my children a tiny slap, never smacked a pet dog, who rescued a trapped wasp rather than squash it, why did I think I could kill a woman? No, much as I hated her, I should have known killing was impossible for me. She put her head against the wooden bars of the seat back, felt her eyes close and her mouth fall open. That jerked her awake and she struggled to get up but made it. Freya lived near here, in a block of flats opposite Lord's.

Few people were about. She thought she could get to Freya's, and she remembered that her granddaughter had given up work prior to the birth of her baby. She would probably be at home. Rosemary remembered too that when

Judith had told her the date the child was due, she had remarked censoriously that it must have been conceived long before Freya's marriage. Attempted murder was morally worse than sex outside marriage, even contemplated murder must be worse. Her guilt was greater than poor Freya's. She was standing up, holding on to a wall on the corner of the major road, and now, still reaching for the wall at every step, she made her way, hesitating and stumbling, to cross the road carefully, on a pedestrian crossing, to scramble into the lift and just manage to ring her granddaughter's bell.

ROSEMARY FELL INTO Freya's arms. Freya could smell the wine on her breath. Gran was certainly drunk, but this wasn't just drunkenness, this was worse than that. She took her into the spare room, a second bedroom which as yet had had no guest, and helped her to lie down on the bed. Having fetched her a jug of water, a glass, and a packet of paracetamol, she phoned her mother and sister.

"She must have been at Daphne's," said Judith. "Something horrible has happened and she's come to you straight from Daphne's. I'm on my way."

Fenella also arrived, bringing Sybilla, having picked up Callum from school. Not herself a resident, she had left the car parked on residents' parking and stood staring down into the street watching for a traffic warden, while her children made mayhem.

"They were trying to break into the fridge," said Freya. "Can't you control them?"

"You wait till you've got one of your own, and it won't be long."

Rosemary slept. Just as Judith was getting worried, fearing stroke or heart attack, her mother woke up, sat up, and asked her daughter to pour her a glass of water.

When she had drunk it and drunk a second one, she said, "I have done something terrible. I nearly killed someone."

"Mother, you haven't been driving a car!"

This, then, was the conclusion anyone would jump to. "Never mind what it was. I didn't do it." Rosemary got up, pulling down and smoothing her crumpled dress. "Do you know where my handbag is?"

Freya came in with it. Rosemary retrieved the half-empty bottle, made her way into the bathroom, and poured the contents into the basin. "They call it a sink now," she said to Judith, who had followed her. "In my day a sink was something you only had in the kitchen." Then, returning to the bed, she handed the empty bottle to Freya. "Would you put that into your bin, dear? And, Freya, could I stay here? I need to sleep. I need a long sleep. I don't think I can go home, so would you let me stay here?"

Freya, who didn't want her, who had a lot to do before the birth of her baby and was herself feeling tired, said, "Of course, Gran. You must stay as long as you like."

"Shall I find a doctor for her?" Judith whispered.

"I don't know."

Rosemary went back to bed, fully clothed, and fell immediately asleep. When she had been asleep for five hours, Fenella had had two parking tickets, and Judith wanted to go home, she phoned her father.

She got his voicemail: "We are on our way to Italy. Possibly back on the fifteenth."

ALSO TRYING TO get in touch with Alan was Michael Winwood, and he too got the Italy message. Rosemary simply wasn't at home, he concluded, but it was hard to tell as she apparently had no mobile phone and no email address. Stanley Batchelor was another possibility. But the voice that answered his call he would never have recognised, it was so feeble and high-pitched.

"Not at my best, Mike," Stanley whispered. "Had a bad turn. Still in bed actually, though I'll get up later. I've got Spot with me and he's a great comfort, I can tell you."

That kind of voice made you want to clear your throat because the speaker needed to do so. Poor Stanley was ill. He couldn't remember Lewis

Newman's number. He couldn't even remember where he had written it down. Helen was fetched and she quickly found it in Stanley's directory, the proper place. But now Michael had it, he wondered if he even needed to call Lewis on this rather delicate matter. Going directly to Colin Quell might be best.

But when he tried it, a young woman who said she was Quell's PA answered. It was a revelation to Michael that police officers, even senior police officers, had PAs. Calling him Michael, she told him that Detective Inspector Quell was no longer on the case. Would he like the extension number for Inspector Inshaw? Noticing that she didn't use this Inshaw's given name, he said he would like to speak to Mr. Inshaw and was told, in rather an admonitory tone, that it was Ms. Inshaw. At the extension was a pleasant-sounding, friendly woman. Yes, the "hands in the buried box" case was now in her hands. The pun wasn't remarked on, and Michael's wincing was invisible.

Would he come to her or would he like her to come to him? He chose the second option. Caroline Inshaw, as she introduced herself, was quite unlike how he had pictured her. Not that he had pictured her much, it wasn't something he did, but he had expected a tall, thickset woman with cropped hair, in her late thirties and dressed in a dark suit. Instead, she was tiny, slender, and though her hair was black, very long. If anyone had told him she was a ballerina, he would have had no difficulty in accepting it. She arrived at six in the evening, and sure she would say she didn't drink on duty, he nevertheless asked if she would like a glass of wine. Somehow her saying yes endeared her to him.

With their glasses of Chablis on the table before them, he told her about Clara Moss and what she had said to him about a man called "Raiment," and because she was old with a Sunday-school childhood and was probably a churchgoer, aligned the word with "clothing." Caroline Inshaw—she had asked him to call her Caroline—had never heard the term before. She frankly told him so.

He talked about his parents. "It wasn't a happy marriage. I never heard them speak a fond word to each other or even a polite word, come to that. At a later date they would have separated or got divorced, but not then, not in the 1940s. My mother had a lot of friends—I mean men friends." He was hesitating now. Perhaps she could see how much it cost him to talk like this about his mother. She hadn't wanted him; if she had never been cruel to him, she had been indifferent. But she was his mother. To speak of her sexual life, of her possible adultery, seized hold of his chest and bowed him over. He made himself straighten up. "There were several men she saw and went out with. I don't know if my father cared, perhaps he did. According to Clara Moss—she cleaned for us, was often in the house—one of them was James Rayment. He was the uncle of a man—well, a boy then, of course—called Lewis Newman. You do know about the tunnels?"

Caroline Inshaw said she didn't, which made Michael wonder how much of the case Quell had been interested in, let alone cared about, and how much he had passed on to her. Michael described the tunnels as briefly as he could and told her about the children who had been there. She showed more interest than Quell ever had. "I must tell you that even after so long I find it pretty hard—worse than that really—to talk about my mother like that." Michael bit his lip, stared down at the hands in his lap—the hands!—and made himself go on. "She was very lovely to look at, my mother. I expect the temptations were great—all those men in uniform, you see." He saw as he finished speaking the lady with the little dog who hadn't been lovely to look at except to a lonely child. She was talking to him again in the railway carriage and he was stroking the dog. Again he pulled himself away from the familiar dream. "It's not for me to tell you how to do your job. I don't mean to do that, but if you were to do a DNA test on me and on Lewis Newman, wouldn't that show if the hands belonged to James Rayment and . . . and . . ." It astounded him that he couldn't go on, that the two words that in the past, on the rare occasions when he'd uttered them, had left him unaffected now refused to be spoken.

“And your mother?” Caroline Inshaw spoke so gently and kindly that he was touched by an enormous gratitude.

He nodded, silent because all his effort at control was going into preventing the tears from coming.

“I think we could do that. You and I could go together to speak to Mr. Newman and do a test on him. I can do one on you today. It’s only a matter of testing saliva.”

“It’s Dr. Newman. I don’t mean to correct you. It’s just that he’ll know more about this sort of stuff than I do.”

She produced a tablet in a green leather cover. “I’ve a note here that your father is still alive. Is that so? Sorry to put it like that, but when one is a hundred, or nearly that, it’s a reasonable enquiry to make.”

“He’s still alive.” Michael felt that these were ominous and in some ways terrible words. He said nothing about the cyanide.

IF LEWIS NEWMAN hadn’t entirely forgotten about the hands in the box, the subject had drifted to the back of his mind. It was all so long ago. It wasn’t as long as it would appear to a young or middle-aged person, but still the box of skeletal hands had half hidden itself in that mental compartment where unexplained but not very interesting mysteries of one's early life lived. Such as what had happened to Uncle James, and what a strange thing it was that Lewis's mother, who had been what in those days they called an infants' teacher, was the daughter-in-law of a man who couldn't read or write. Uncle James was still present in Lewis's memory and quite active there. He thought how different James's disappearance would have been today, essentially because he would hardly have been allowed to disappear. James would have had a mobile phone, very possibly an email address, credit cards, be registered with a doctor like one of Lewis's own patients. Probably the police would no more have searched for him today than they would have then. Lewis recalled walking across the fields with his young uncle and, though there was a war on, the peace and silence of those fields. At home, although there was radio, there was no television, no music you could choose to accompany you wherever you went, no Internet, no antibiotics in general use though they had been discovered, no DNA.

He was thinking about the discovery of DNA, about the double helix, while he went about his daily chores, washing dishes—he saved them up until he ran out—putting clothes in a plastic bag to take to the launderette, a little basic dusting, thinking about DNA's use in medicine and police work, when the phone rang. Such an amazing coincidence, almost uncanny, as if this detective inspector woman were reading his thoughts, that for a moment he could hardly speak. DNA? Yes, of course, though he couldn't imagine why. She told him.

MICHAEL HAD ALSO received an unexpected phone call. That was the reason for his sitting beside Clara Moss's bed, holding her hand. The call had come from "her next-door," whose name he learned at last. "It's Mrs. Beecham as lived next to Mrs. Moss, sir."

He was taken aback by that "sir." Perhaps she had discovered from Clara that he was a lawyer. He would have liked to tell Mrs. Beecham not to "sir" him, but he didn't know how. She might be offended or, worse, upset.

"The social come in," she said. "They've poked their noses in a lot since you was last here, sir." There it was again! "They want her in one of them hospices, she's got the Big C, you see, and she's not got long. Clara wouldn't budge from here and she's asking for you. I told the social, sir, that if she stayed here, I'd take care of her, me and Sam, we'll look after her."

"I'll come now," said Michael, thinking, How good these people are, how endlessly kind. "Tell her I'll be there in a couple of hours."

"Thank you, sir, that's very good of you," she said, echoing his accolade of herself.

Now his tears fell, those ever-present tears that flowed not so much from grief as from admiration of the goodness of others. Was it because he had seen so little goodness in his early years and because he'd first encountered it with a woman and a dog in a train? He went up to Vivien's room, lay down beside where she had lain, and cried all the tears he had.

So now in the afternoon he was with Clara Moss. The first thing he did was give her the wedding ring, wondering if she would recognise it after all these years. But she knew it at once. She smiled and nodded. He needed no medical knowledge to tell she was dying. The doctor, Sam said, came in and gave her morphine, that was the only thing to keep the pain away. Proudly, Sam said the doctor trusted her and left liquid morphine with her to give Clara the prescribed dose. Clara gave Michael a small smile and squeezed his hand. He would come back again tomorrow, he said, and he wondered what was wrong with him that he had made such a fuss about visiting her at Maureen Batchelor's request. It was easy, almost a pleasure. Not too long on the tube and then a short walk. The following day he found a bed-and-breakfast in Lower Park Road and stayed the night, returning to Clara in the morning.

23

THE HANDS IN the box had from the first been a plague to Colin Quell. "A pain in the neck," he referred to it. To use his detective skills on investigating the possible provenance of ancient body parts that may have lain where they were found for six or seven decades was beneath his dignity. Such an investigation had no urgency. The hands had been there for sixty years or more and wouldn't go away. Moreover, the owners, if that was the word, might not even have been dead, still less murdered, the hands removed from living bodies. True, no half-hearted enquiries on his part had uncovered any evidence that local hospitals were missing amputated hands at the relevant time. His own solution to the mystery was that the hands had been taken from bodies found on bomb sites in the East End of London. Taken by perverts, of which there was no shortage in his experience. Whoever they might be they were long dead by now.

Because the police boast that they never give up on an investigation and Detective Inspector Quell feared this one would be with him for life, he was overjoyed when his chief superintendent told him the case would be handed over to Caroline Inshaw.

"I've no objection," Lewis said. "You can have my DNA if you want. But why?"

"I believe you had an uncle who went missing in 1944 and was never found. A Mr. James Rayment?"

"That's so. But a lot of people went missing in 1944. The war was on."

"You never found what happened to your uncle?"

"I was a child. Children aren't much concerned about things like that. The ways of adults are strange to them, why they behave the way they do, why they care. My parents were worried, I remember that. They made enquiries, I believe, but the police wouldn't look for a missing young man."

"No, perhaps not. Do you know if your uncle knew Mrs. Winwood? Anita Winwood?"

"Michael's mother? I don't know. Possibly. Uncle James stayed with us, you know. He stayed with us on and off during that summer and he used to go out in the evenings till very late. My mother gave up the search in the end. She decided he'd been called up and joined the forces, though the army had never heard of him."

"And you? You didn't think about it?"

"I told you. I was a child. Maybe I wondered why he'd never said good-bye to me, told me he was going away. But that's all."

• • •

PAYING A VISIT to Rosemary Norris was a way of passing the time and perhaps a duty. He was in Loughton and had woken early as people often do when in unfamiliar surroundings. The sun was shining, though the day had a cold look to it. Michael decided he would walk down to Traps Hill before he went to Clara's. He could tell Rosemary about Clara and perhaps even enlist her help to visit her. He had never been to her flat but he knew the address. Was it too early for a call? Half past nine seemed all right. A man who was retired might have a lie-in but not a woman, he thought. Women always had household tasks that they liked to get through early. But though he rang the bell and clattered the letterbox, there was no answer. Away somewhere or ill? He tried again and then he left it, encountering on his way out a woman with a large, stripy cat in her arms.

"Mrs. Norris is staying with her granddaughter. She phoned to tell me. Very considerate, I thought, but she always is thoughtful." The woman paused, looked doubtfully at him. "Imagine that man leaving her. At his age. You can't understand it, can you?"

Michael said nothing but managed a wry smile. He walked down to Forest Road. Samantha was in Clara's front garden, putting a rubbish bag into a bin.

"Lilian's with her." That would be Mrs. Beecham

from next door. "She'll be glad to see you. She's a bit brighter this morning." The front door was pushed open for him. "Which is funny really considering they're coming to take her to the hospice any minute."

"She wanted to stay at home," Michael said.

"Not allowed. Shame, isn't it? It's not as if she'd no carers."

Clara was in bed but fully dressed, her hair brushed, her shoes placed side by side on the floor next to the chair where Lilian sat. The wedding ring was on the thin third finger of her thin left hand. Michael went up to the bed and, meeting Clara's eyes, evoking a small smile, bent over and kissed her.

"I'll lay down now, Lil. Take my pillows away, would you. Let me lay down. They're taking me away, Michael."

"Sam told me. I believe it's a nice place." He had no knowledge of it, had only heard that hospices usually were nice.

Her voice was faint now but at least there was a voice. "The pain's all gone, Michael. Is it all right calling you Michael? I did when you was little."

"Of course it is, of course."

"You was just a kid, and they was at the kitchen table holding hands like you wasn't there and like I wasn't there, his hand holding hers across the table, and your dad walked in." Clara sighed, closed her eyes, and her hands moved across the coverlet, plucking and picking, reversing the action and then repeating the movements. "Walked in," she whispered, "and saw. He never said a word. I remember it like it was yesterday."

Michael felt sick. He would never hold anyone's hand again. Never, never. He couldn't bring himself to ask her if the man was James Rayment, though he knew it must have been. The room had become quiet. Clara breathed silently. Lilian Beecham said to him, "Get you a cup of tea, shall I?"

He shrugged, moved his hands from side to side in a gesture that might have meant anything. The tea came, and to his surprise he was glad of it. A vehicle had drawn up outside with AMBULANCE printed on its side. He half rose and turned to check that this was what it was. The moving hands that wandered across the coverlet were still now. He had only ever seen death happen once, and that was when Vivien had slipped, silent and still, from life to insensibility to death.

He knew it when he saw it. "Tell them they won't be needed," he said to Sam. "She's gone."

ROSEMARY TOO LAY IN BED. She did nothing. Although Freya's spare room had a small television, Rosemary didn't watch it. Nor did she read or listen to radio programmes. Usually considerate, as her neighbour put it, she forgot all that and in the flat in St. John's Wood Road behaved as if she were in a hotel. Freya or David, home on paternity leave, brought her breakfast, and Judith, who called in every day, told her it would do her good to get up and move around, maybe go out for a walk. Only Fenella, arriving with Sybilla, had the nerve to tell Rosemary she wasn't ill and should pull herself together. Sybilla bounced up and down on the sofa until her great-grandmother shouted at her to stop and threatened her—the ultimate in child abuse—with a "good hard smack."

Rosemary sat at the dining table, silent and patient. "Like a dog," said David, "waiting for its dinner."

"Well, she is waiting for her dinner or her lunch," said poor Freya, back in the kitchen. "What are we going to do?"

"She'll go when the baby's born. You'll see."

"I won't be here to see."

Unlike Norman Batchelor's mother and Princess Andrew of Greece, Freya wasn't preparing to give birth on a table. Her due date was past and the hospital had started making ominous noises. That afternoon, after Rosemary had been given her tea, a scone, and a piece of carrot cake, Freya doubled up and winced. "I'm having a pain."

"Shall I drive you to the hospital?"

"Not yet. Much too soon."

While refusing to watch television in her

bedroom, Rosemary enjoyed it on her host's much larger set. Everything they watched she deemed immoral or called a disgrace and asked for the channel to be changed or changed it herself. She preferred programmes about birdlife or handicrafts in Cumbria or clothes for the elderly. Freya sat down and watched TV with her, getting up from time to time to walk about the flat, secretly timing her pains. At 6:00 p.m. she said to her grandmother, "We're leaving for the hospital now, Gran. Will you be all right on your own?"

"Why the hospital? Are you ill?"

"I'm in labour. I'm about to have a baby."

"Are you?" Rosemary looked at her, mystified. "Nobody tells me anything."

"Will you be all right on your own? Or shall I fetch Mum?"

Rosemary didn't reply. She went into her bedroom, heard Freya and David call out, "Bye, Gran. See you later," and sat on the bed, thinking. She had of course brought nothing with her, had borrowed a nightdress from Judith and a blouse and skirt. These she left in a neat pile on the bedside table. Next she stripped the bed. She dressed in the clothes she had come in, checked she had her front-door key, and returned to the living-room, where the phone was ringing. Like two earlier calls, she ignored this one too. It would be Judith, whom Freya must have called in the car on one of those mobiles people had.

Out in the street, Rosemary would have taken a cab home but doubted the driver would take her all the way to Loughton. She had taken the tube here, so why not take it back again? I have changed, she thought, I am a different person from the woman who came here ten days ago. I no longer care. Caring has departed. All my life I have cared for other people, husband, children, grandchildren, friends, relatives, neighbours. Now I don't, I only care for me. She walked along Hamilton Terrace and crossed Maida Vale, rather pleased with herself for not having a heavy bag to carry. Since her marriage, and rarely before that, she had never been into a café or restaurant on her own, not even for a cup of coffee or a sandwich. Alan had always been with her or one of her children or a friend. Outside the Café Laville she hesitated, then pushed open the door and went in.

The place would be full later, she guessed, but now only a few people were sitting at tables, all couples of course. A man came up and asked her what she wanted, and she said a cup of black coffee. He asked if she meant an Americano, and not having the faintest idea what that was, she agreed. It was easier that way. In future, she thought, she would always opt for the easy option. The coffee was quite nice. She didn't want anything to eat. A bill came—ridiculous for a drop of coffee—but she found the precise sum in her purse, laid it on the table, and added a five-pence piece.

The tube took her to Baker Street, where she changed, as she remembered doing in reverse, for Liverpool Street. A lot of people were in the train for Loughton, commuters, and she was rather pleased for using the word appropriately. She had never been one and wouldn't have cared to have joined their number and made this tedious trip every day. No taxis were waiting outside Loughton station. She didn't feel like waiting for one to come, so she walked, tired by the time she reached Traps Hill.

The stripy cat was sitting outside her front door. The large, long-haired cat had a pleasant, even kindly expression. She had never before invited it in but did now. There would be no one else to welcome her home.

She was in her teens before her parents had a dog, but a cat was always in the house, never allowed to sit on armchairs or on the settee. Defiant now, even of the long dead, Rosemary lifted up the purring bundle and laid it on the sofa.

She slept better that night than she had ever done at Freya's. Having forgotten all about Freya and her imminent delivery, in the morning she remembered without much enthusiasm or anxiety. No doubt someone would call and tell her. Someone did, at 9:00 a.m.

"Everyone's been in a state about you," said David. "Not me, I knew you'd be all right. Judith's phoned all the rellies. Fenella wanted to call the police, but I don't think she did. Incidentally, I'm a dad. Freya had a baby boy at one a.m. Three and a half kilos."

Apart from knowing it was a measurement of weight, Rosemary hadn't the faintest idea of what it was in pounds. She sent her love to Freya, thought about phoning Judith and decided against it, decided against phoning anyone. The stripy cat had got out of a window and was sitting on the balcony. Putting him out the front door to find his way home, she told him she had nothing for him but would buy cat food when she was out. There were no bathtubs at Freya's, so she had a bath, luxuriating in it, then dressed in one of what Fenella had been heard to name as "Gran's own creations" and got out her winter coat from the mothproof bag it had been in since March.

When she was in her teens and the war was over but clothing coupons were still in use, her mother didn't take her "up to town" to buy clothes, but to Leytonstone and Bowman's department store on the tube or to Ilford's shops on the bus. Instead of clothes, the raw materials were what they went there for, dress lengths as they were called, or remnants, just enough fabric to make a skirt or blouse. No tee-shirts and scarcely any trousers in those days. They bought wool too, but more often, while the war was on, unpicked old garments to knit up again. Her mother had taught her to sew and, according to the teenage Judith, behaving like a typical teenager, hadn't been much of a teacher.

Rosemary had been undeterred and was undeterred now. She went into the shop that was run by an Asian family but had once been Penistans—the teenage schoolboys who were her contemporaries had made much of that name—and went on a shopping spree. A length of green silk, the same sort of fabric as the copper-coloured silk she had made into the dress and jacket for Freya's wedding, was her first purchase; then came a few yards of fine wool; next a few metres of tweed; and lastly some expensive blue velvet. Mumtaz, as the shop was now called, thought it was Christmas and were all smiles. Rosemary had spent a fortune. There was too much stuff, in both senses of the word, for her to carry home, and Mumtaz said they would depart from their rule and bring it to her in the van.

Back at home she was hunting through her large stack of patterns when the van arrived. Another rule was broken when Mr. Ashok carried the baskets of materials into the flat for her. Her phone was ringing and she saw that several messages had been left. Let the phone ring and let the messages sit where they were. She would sit on the floor, pin the pattern she had chosen to the blue velvet, and cut it out. While she was machining, there would be no interruptions from Alan wanting her to go out for a walk or watch

TV with him or give up her work and buy a designer frock. The phone rang again. She lifted the receiver and shouted into it, "Go away."

The blue velvet was the same colour as the cloak her mother had made her, aged seven, to wear over her dress when she went to parties. She thought about it as she cut, thought too about meeting Alan three years later. Daphne Jones, Rosemary could see now as Daphne had been then, a young witch with her crystal ball and her cards. When Alan first went off with her or went off *to* her, Rosemary had been shattered, *devastated* was the word everyone used, but that feeling hadn't lasted. Her pride was hurt, she decided, and now she remembered what her grandmother had told her when she was little, told the whole family who were there.

"When you get old," she had said on the occasion of her brother Tom's dying, "you don't have much emotion. It goes. At about seventy, I'd say. All those things and people you were passionate about, angry or adoring or longing, they all go, and a kind of dull calm takes over. I used to worship Tom. Now he's dead I don't much care. That's how it is with me."

Now Alan's gone, said Rosemary to herself, I don't much care. I did at first but now I don't. That's how it is with me. Calm, at peace, thinking ahead to all the clothes she would be able to make uninterruptedly, she began to pin the velvet pieces together. Tomorrow she would go to the shop which had reopened when knitting became fashionable again two or three years ago and buy enough wool to make herself a twinset. Something for the new baby too? I don't think so. Freya wouldn't appreciate it, so why bother?

Why do anything at all I don't enjoy? I won't. That's how it is for me now.

SEVERAL PHONE CALLS were made to Daphne and Alan before Michael got an answer that wasn't a recorded message to say they were in Italy. When he said he had given a DNA sample to the police and that Lewis had been asked for one also, Daphne said, "Come round."

"Shall I? You're only just back from your holiday."

"Never mind that. We'd love to see you."

Putting on his coat, Michael thought how she talked as if she and Alan had been together for a dozen years or more. It was cold and Daphne had lit a fire in the beautiful room—not a real fire, that wouldn't have been permitted, but something gas-fired that looked real. Another first time for him was the kiss she gave him when he arrived. They had sherry and blini. Michael could tell the caviar was real. The sherry was in honour of George, Alan said.

"Tell all about the DNA," said Daphne when they had raised their glasses in George's memory.

"I told you on the phone." Michael was diffident now he had come to the purpose of his visit. It was going to be a monstrous thing to say, so he began with Lewis. "This woman didn't say, but I could tell she thinks the man's hand might have belonged to Lewis's uncle James Rayment." He couldn't go on without prompting.

Alan did the prompting. "And the woman's?" He realised too late what he was asking. "No, perhaps I shouldn't ask that."

"You should if I'm to tell you." Michael wanted to say that it wasn't easy for him, then despised himself for being self-pitying. "Because the woman's hand might be my mother's."

"Michael!" Daphne seemed to shrink, clasping her hands. "How terrible for you."

"Well, yes." The ready tears were there, waiting to fall. He swallowed hard, which sometimes helped. "That's why my DNA. They haven't got the results yet. Clara Moss saw them together, my mother and Rayment, I mean." That his father had seen them was more than he could bear to say. But thinking it made the tears fall. If Daphne put her arms round him it would be too much for him and he might collapse. She didn't. Alan passed him a beautifully laundered handkerchief, and Michael wondered incongruously if Daphne had washed and ironed it. "I'm sorry. I'm inclined to cry."

"Is it a relief?"

"I suppose it is. I even cry when I realise they

think my father put the hands there and buried them. That means my father killed them both."

Neither Alan nor Daphne spoke.

"I may have told you, I don't remember, but he'll be a hundred years old in January. He's absolutely compos mentis, the same as ever. I don't know if either of you knew him."

Alan shook his head, but Daphne said, "I did."

"Of course. You lived next door."

Alan was looking at her strangely. It seemed she had turned rather pale, but she was always pale. Michael wanted to say that his father wanted to live until his hundredth birthday, but if the police came to the conclusion Michael had already reached, wouldn't it be better for him to die sooner? Michael wanted to say it but knew he would only cry again, so he made himself ask them about their holiday, mostly spent in Florence and Rome. That was safe, tearless territory as he had never been there. Daphne and Alan were not the kind of tourists who inflict their travel experiences on their friends, accompanied often by slides, postcards, and photographs on their mobile phones. They simply said they had had a wonderful time, mentioned a church or two, the Pyramid of Cestius, and the marvellous food. Alan said Michael should stay to supper, but Daphne said nothing, her expression suddenly shut-in and—could it be *frightened?*

Michael went. Daphne saw him to the front

door, and if he had feared he had in some way offended her, when she kissed him again and briefly put her arms around him, he knew he was mistaken. The evening he spent in Vivien's room, lying on the bed with his arm round his imagined wife, longing for her and for a while forgetting his father.

"WHAT'S THE MATTER?"

As soon as he had said it, Alan thought how old-fashioned that was, that no one said it anymore, or no one under sixty. They said, *What's wrong?*

"What's wrong?"

"Nothing." Daphne tried a smile and more or less failed. "The classic reply. No, of course there's something wrong. You can tell, can't you?"

He nodded.

"I don't need to confess anything to you. I never confessed anything to my husbands. They didn't ask so I didn't tell."

"I don't ask." He thought, She's going to tell me she had an affair with Michael or even with Lewis Newman. "You don't have to tell me anything." After that, he only wanted to say one thing: "I love you."

"I know and I love you." She had been sitting next to him on the sofa. Their sherry glasses were empty. "Would you get me a small brandy, Alan?" She stood up and moved into one of the armchairs, not far away, just not touching him.

"I've never known you to drink spirits."

"Only when it's medicinal." She smiled. "Michael reminded you that I lived next door to them. My parents disapproved. I mean of both of them, John and Anita. Not that we called them that. They were Mr. and Mrs. Winwood." She took a sip of the brandy and gave a small gasp. "I knew him. He knew me. We talked over the garden fence. I was twelve, going on twenty-five."

Instead of his turning pale, a dark flush had spread across Alan's face. "What are you saying, Daphne?"

"He was very good-looking. That was the age of the film star, much more then than ever since. He looked like Errol Flynn. They say Errol Flynn was stupid. I don't know. John Winwood wasn't stupid, just insensitive, and he wasn't charming or kind or gentle—well, he wasn't unkind to me. He was just amazingly good-looking. You wouldn't think a twelve-year-old could feel like I did, but I did. I wasn't in love with him but I was madly attracted. Madly, Alan."

His mouth was dry. "What happened?"

"We met. Quite often. Anita was out with some man. I never knew who, but it might have been with Lewis's uncle or this soldier she knew or—well, anyone. I think she must have been quite promiscuous, though I didn't even know the word then. We met in John's house. It was easy, just next door. I suppose my parents thought I was out with the crowd of you, you and Rosemary and Bill Johnson and the Batchelors and Lewis and Michael. I was sometimes, but often I was with John."

"You mean you slept with him?"

"Not exactly. Not what the expression means. No, I didn't. We did everything except the thing people mean when they say 'slept with.' We didn't do that because though I was twelve, I could have had a baby. You know what I mean. But do you know how terrified girls were then, even very, very young girls like me, of getting pregnant? Never mind, we were, I was. I think John was aware of that and he didn't mind. He was afraid as well, of me, of my parents."

"Why did it stop?"

"John turned us—well, you all—out of the qanats so that we could go there, he and I, use the place, I mean, instead of his house. I don't know why not his house. Anita had gone or had died, later he said she had died. I was frightened and I said I wouldn't see him again. I didn't threaten him, I mean like saying I'd tell my parents, I never did that. I just stopped seeing him except in the street sometimes or over the garden fence. Alan, I knew something horrible had happened in that house." Daphne raised the brandy glass to her lips and took a sip. "I missed John, I didn't even like him, I was afraid of him, but he was afraid of me too." She hesitated. "There's more. Shall I go on?"

"Yes, of course. Go on."

"That's a particularly ghastly situation. Two people in a relationship that's founded on mutual fear. We were enormously attracted to each other and afraid to be alone together. I did go to his house once. I went to the back door and he wouldn't let me in. He was afraid to let me in, Alan. 'Don't set foot in this house,' he said, and I ran home.

"It was a few weeks later he started a fire in the garden. I was home from school early and I saw him pour petrol on the wood he'd piled up. But it wasn't only wood. There were two shapes in sacks—no plastic in those days. Two long shapes in sacks tied at the tops with string. I watched him out of my bedroom window. The fire burnt down and John poured paraffin on more logs and the two things in the sacks. He fetched another can of petrol. I remember thinking he must be desperate to burn whatever that was because petrol was rationed and very hard to come by. It was after that that the fire got out of hand and spread to the shed and trees and someone called the firemen, probably several people did."

Alan said, "You never told your mother about Winwood? I mean, what Winwood had done to you?"

"I never did. You see, it wasn't what he had

done to me, it was what we did with each other. I know you'll say I was only twelve, but I've explained that. I was old for my age, years older."

"And now you are young for your age."

She smiled. "Well, perhaps. You've seen what was in the papers and on television about those celebs raping young girls and assaulting them. Some of them told their parents and they weren't believed. I knew I wouldn't be believed, and what would I have said? That I'd had sex—well, sort of sex—with the man next door? And say as well that I enjoyed it? I don't think so."

Daphne emptied her glass. "I needed that. I've never told anyone about John Winwood before." She put out a hand and took Alan's. "You don't mind, do you? About me doing that, I mean."

"Of course not. Why would I?"

"Some men would. I never spoke to John again. After the fire, I mean. I never saw him again except in the distance. He moved away somewhere and eventually he sold the house. I've told the police. About the fire, I mean, nothing about my—my relationship with John Winwood."

ALAN MADE SUPPER, scrambled eggs and smoked salmon. Daphne drank water. He had a glass of wine and then another, hoping to deaden his feelings. "Drown your sorrows," people used to say. He hadn't any sorrow or shock. The emotion he felt he couldn't define. He had told a lie and he minded about that. Daphne sat close to him and held his hand. She turned on the television, which he didn't want, but he thought silence would be worse. And more explanations from her, more details, would be worse than silence.

The programme, which was the next instalment of a serial, came to an end. Daphne began to talk about their recent holiday, about walking along the broad top of the city wall of Lucca and about the Roman Forum. They hadn't taken many photographs, and those they had, they still had to print out from their mobile phones.

"We're neither of us great photographers, are we? Prefer to keep pictures of what we've seen in our memories, I suppose."

"That's right," he said.

"Something else we have in common, if you can have a negative something in common."

"Why not?"

They went to bed early. As he held her, one arm round her waist, he thought of her at twelve, a little girl in love with a film star lookalike. Waking three hours later, he murmured to himself in the dark, "My world has changed. Everything is changed."

24

GIVING A SAMPLE of his DNA was almost the last thing Lewis Newman did before going off on his boat trip up the Danube. He and Jo had always intended to do the cruise, then Jo fell ill, was ill for months before her death, and that kind of holiday was impossible. He missed Jo, but not as much as he told himself he ought to. Many a bereaved husband would have hesitated to take a trip which could only have reminded him that his wife should have been with him, but for Lewis that couldn't be and he wasn't going to let it spoil his cruise.

The trip was luxurious. He had a lovely cabin with en suite bathroom that the company called a stateroom, and on his second evening at dinner time when he approached his table as the ship was moving away from Bucharest, the organiser of the party came up to him and asked him if he would share his table with a lady passenger. She was travelling alone as was he. Lewis didn't much care for the idea, envisaging a plump, brightly painted blonde in a low-cut, red dress. He had a rooted objection, almost a phobia, to the sight of cleavage on an elderly woman. He sat at his table and got to his feet almost immediately when a pretty sixty-year-old came up to him a little shyly. She was slender and nearly as tall as he, and the dress she wore, quite high-necked, pink wool, showed off a neat figure.

They shook hands.

"Melissa," she said.

"Lewis."

"I hope you don't mind, but I saw your name in the paper when they dug up that ghastly box with the hands. There was a piece in the *Standard* about the people who were children in Loughton when the box was put there. I grew up in Loughton myself, though I was—well, a bit younger. So I thought it would be nice to meet an old Loughton person—oh, I'm sorry, I didn't mean you were old."

He laughed. "I'm delighted."

Six days later, going ashore in Budapest, they were not only eating together but walking together when the party went sightseeing. Instead of returning to the ship for dinner, they dined at a restaurant in Vienna on their last evening. They had discovered that they lived not far from each other in London, he in Ealing and she in Chiswick. There was no end to the coincidences. Both were widowed, her dead husband had been a GP as Lewis had been. As a child she had lived with her parents in Tycehurst Hill. Phone numbers were exchanged and an arrangement made to have lunch and pay a late-autumn visit to Kew Gardens, where Melissa had never been. Lewis felt positively happy when he let himself into his house and picked up the heap of correspondence from the front doormat.

He hadn't thought about the DNA sample all the time he was away, and now, remembering, he saw nothing from Caroline Inshaw. His head full of Melissa Landon, he wasn't much interested in the hands in the box and what had happened sixty years ago, except that those hands had brought Melissa and him together. The letters were mostly bills, but one had an Australian stamp. He set it aside, paid one of the bills, and marvelled at another printed in scarlet and threatening him with the steps which would be taken if he kept them waiting any longer for their payment. The money was only three days overdue. Let them wait a little longer.

He had never been one to study the appearance of a letter and the mysterious handwriting of the sender before opening it, but then he seldom heard from previously unknown people. Studying this one told him nothing. He sat down in an armchair and opened it. The address was Perth, and Noreen Leopold, in the first line, introduced herself as his cousin. Lewis immediately thought this must be nonsense as he had no cousins, but he read on, at first disbelieving, then astonished:

I am coming to Britain in the spring, March, I

think, and hope to meet you as you are the only cousin I have. You may possibly remember my dad, Jimmy Rayment, who died twenty years ago. He came here and settled at the end of the 1939–1945 war, married my mum, Betty, and later became the father of five children with her. I am one of them. My dad was always going to get in touch with you but never got around to it.

Here, Lewis laid down the letter, put it aside, and marvelled some more. James, Uncle James, had been living in a distant part of the world, as Lewis's mother always thought he might have. He had lived all those years in Perth and had all those children. Lewis picked up the letter again and read to the end: *Let me have a line from you. My email address is Noreenl@periwinkle.com. I would really like us to meet and have a chat about your parents and mine. Your cousin, Noreen.*

He would have to tell people. The police perhaps. Those others he had been in the tunnels with. He would think about it and decide what to do next. He read the letter again, went into the kitchen to make himself tea, thought better of it, and poured himself quite a stiff whisky instead. What he really wanted was someone to tell about this and ask his or her advice. There was no one. His life had been quite solitary since Jo died. Well, there was one. He would sleep on it, wait till morning, and then he would phone Melissa.

• • •

ROSEMARY BOUGHT SOME pink wool and began knitting a jumper. It wasn't for Sybilla or Callum or the new baby but for herself. The dress she had started once she got back from Freya's she had finished and was wearing it when she went up to London in the tube. She had made few shopping trips to Oxford Street or Knightsbridge because Alan disliked shopping, like most men, and, while she tried on clothes, would sit on a chair—provided by the assistant—apparently stunned by boredom and half-asleep. Or else he waited outside, standing in the doorway or finding a seat to sit on while he dozed. This first trip since his departure she made alone, walking along Oxford Street to Selfridges and buying herself a pair of shoes and a handbag. She had all the time in the world and shopped slowly, choosing what she wanted as she had never done since she was a young girl. Then, vaguely remembering where most theatres were, she walked carefully to Regent Street and asked a taxi driver to drive her to the Queen's Theatre, where *Les Misérables* was showing. She had always wanted to see it but Alan never would.

The theatre was open for a matinee. She walked in, felt suddenly shy and frightened, but made herself walk up to the window inside which a girl sat and asked, wondering if she was making a fool of herself, for a seat in the stalls for the evening performance on Friday. Not a fool apparently. It all went without a hitch and she had her ticket. Back now to the shops, but perhaps a walk round Trafalgar Square first. She found a place to eat lunch, and again she wasn't making a fool of herself. With her food she had a glass of wine and afterwards thought, Why not take a taxi up to Holborn and go home from there? So she did and reached home in triumph. It had been good, it had been *fun*. And the shoes and bag were lovely. She sat down by the phone and phoned her daughter, her son, and both her grandchildren, telling them all about her lovely day and learning that her new grandson's name was Clement.

I have grown, she told herself, and I am still growing.

"WHY NOT COME TO ME," said Melissa, "and I'll cook something. I'd like to."

So he went. Her house in a street off Chiswick High Street was nothing to look at outside but charming inside, with large, elegant rooms and a pretty garden. She had made a salad and a rich, hot paella. Lewis told her about the hands in the box and the group of people who had been in the tunnels, Michael Winwood and his mother and father, and the letter from Noreen Leopold.

"What do you want to do?" Melissa asked.

"I don't know. Nothing, I suppose. But I have to

answer her letter, and when I answer it, I have to tell her about all of it. Or do I?"

"Not necessarily. But I think you have to tell the others and the police. You and all of you thought the hands were Michael Winwood's mother's and your uncle's, but they obviously weren't. Hers maybe, but not your uncle's. Whose was the other hand?"

"I don't know. No one can know."

"Surely Michael's father knows and he's still alive, isn't he?"

"I believe so," said Lewis. "Should I tell Michael first, do you think?"

She said he should. And quickly, perhaps as soon as he got home. "People who live to a hundred are always more or less at death's door, aren't they?"

Before making that phone call, Lewis sent Noreen Leopold an email. He told her to get in touch with him in March and that he would like to see her when she was here. The hands were not mentioned. They could go there, if necessary, when she came. He sat at his desk for quite a long time before dialling Michael's number, even thinking that he need do nothing before Noreen came. But it was too late for that, now that he had consulted Melissa. He must phone and it would be best to get it over with.

THE ROOM WAS WARM. Michael had come because Urban Grange had asked him to, telling him that his father had been unwell the evening before. They had hesitated and nearly sent for him at 7:00 p.m. but the old man had rallied, had got up and shifted himself into an armchair. Some weeks before, John Winwood had asked Darren to buy him a print of "some famous picture" and have it framed. This had been done, and its being brought to his room and shown to him had led to the fast improvement in his health. This morning, Imogen said, Mr. Winwood was a lot better, but they still thought Michael might wish to come, as his father was so very old and it was impossible to tell how long he might last.

So Michael was there, disliking his father rather more than he had since his visits began after his aunt's death. This feeling was exacerbated by the sight of the "famous picture," a print of Dürer's *Praying Hands*. The nursing-home staff might, in their innocence, believe that John Winwood had bought it just because he liked the picture, but Michael knew well that it was there, hanging up on the wall, because of the hands in the biscuit tin and what his father had done.

First thing after their tea had been brought, John Winwood asked, "Like it?"

Michael didn't answer.

"You always were sulky, a very sullen child."

His father picked up the plate of biscuits but, in trying to pass it to Michael, dropped it, scattering biscuits, bits of biscuits, and crumbs on the floor.

"Leave it," John said when Michael knelt down and tried to restore the fragments to the plate. "Let them pick it up. That's what they're paid for."

Michael had meant to ask his father about the hands in the box, but since reaching that decision, he'd realised he didn't know whom they belonged to. One was his mother's? He didn't know that. Now that he had been told that James Rayment had died only about twenty years before, he didn't know whose the man's hand was either. Coming to Urban Grange had been pointless. He sat on, drinking his tea, then refilling their cups. His father left his standing there. He had leant his head back, closed his eyes, and appeared to be fast asleep. Michael looked at the crumbs and the broken biscuits and left them there. He too closed his eyes, thought for a while about his children, so remote from him as if they were not his at all, then about Vivien, so good, so loving, his treasure.

He still had his eyes shut when someone came in to take the tray. He heard her click her tongue, exasperated no doubt by the mess. Once she had gone, he sat up and looked at his father across the empty table. The older eyes opened. John Winwood said, "I'm not long for this world."

Michael thought of saying to not say that or to cheer up and be more hopeful. He didn't. "I'll be back," he said instead. "It won't be long."

25

SEVERAL ATTEMPTS BY Michael to speak to Alan received no reply. As is sometimes the case when a discussion seems the only course but efforts to secure that meeting repeatedly fail, the need for it grows less and less until it no longer looks important. Michael made one last attempt, and this time Alan answered. He had seemed a pleasant and thoughtful man to Michael since they had met at George Batchelor's house after so many years, but his tone this time, if not exactly gloomy, was detached and preoccupied. Yes, they could meet, Alan said, but not in Hamilton Terrace, as he described Daphne's house without using her name. He named a pub in Hampstead within walking distance of Michael's house.

That tone in Alan's voice was such as to make Michael wonder if he was speaking to the same man. Of course he was. But hadn't he wondered something like that when he'd encountered Alan in Daphne's house a couple of months after the meeting at Batchelor's? This happy man who looked years younger? No longer, Michael felt, without seeing him. Michael walked across by one of the turnings leading out of the Finchley

Road. A clear, fine evening, rather cold under that sky, it was still early, so that few people were in the pub. Michael watched Alan come in. He looked no older, but a tired man, a disappointed man. The thought came to Michael that if you couldn't be with the person you loved and who loved you, to be alone was the best. He asked Alan what he would like and fetched him beer and himself a glass of white wine.

They asked after each other's health. Both were well, though Alan didn't look it. "You must have wondered who put the hands in the box," Michael said. "When we were children, I mean. Or perhaps you always thought you knew."

"I didn't know. How could I have? Does anyone?"

"I think the police know, but they haven't told me. I also know and I haven't told them. I know whose the hands were, or rather I know whose they were not. You remember Lewis Newman?" Alan nodded. "He phoned me and told me the man's hand wasn't that of a man called James Rayment, who was his mother's brother."

"Did you think he was?"

"I had no reason to think so." Michael winced a little, wrinkling his nose and widening his mouth. "The other hand was that of my mother, you see." He spread his left hand on the tabletop. "One doesn't like thinking of things of that sort of one's mother."

"I imagine not."

"You see, she was my mother. Once before I was born, for nine months I was carried inside her body. I don't like to think of it."

What Michael had said seemed to have affected Alan heavily. Or something else had. Instead of pale, he had gone red, a flush colouring his face. Momentarily, he closed his eyes. "Tell me something," he said, leaning forward. "What did you think when I went off with Daphne?"

The question surprised Michael. Why should the man care? "I'd rather not say."

Michael's preference was ignored. "Did you think I was crazy or she was? Were you—well, astounded?"

"I don't know. I expect you'd be offended or hurt or something if I said I didn't think much about it."

The old Alan would have laughed. The new one said, "Think about it now."

"All right. I'll tell you. I hadn't seen Rosemary since she was—what was she, ten, eleven? When I saw her at George's, she reminded me of my wife. Vivien, my wife, has been dead for years but she reminded me of her."

"I've nothing more to say. That's it. Thanks for coming here."

They both got up. Neither had any idea of shaking hands. Michael went off across Belsize Park Avenue to Swiss Cottage and Alan to Carlton

Hill. They might have walked part of the way together but they chose to go separately. It wasn't often that Michael felt happy to be in his own home, but he did that evening, or almost happy. It occurred to him that apart from a couple of comments, Alan had talked mainly about Daphne. Michael went upstairs, lay on his solitary but comfortable bed, and told Vivien about his evening. He told her how Rosemary had reminded him of her but not all that much, how it was just one pleasant woman bringing to mind another. Not that he needed anything to bring Vivien to mind. It seemed to him that when he said that about Rosemary, Alan winced, but maybe he imagined it.

Alan walked down Greville Road to Hamilton Terrace and took the road where Daphne lived slowly, delaying his arrival at her house.

IF SHE HAD been asked, Rosemary wouldn't have admitted to being happy. How can you be happy when your husband has left you for another woman? When he has left you without a cause, when everything between you has been as it always was, pleasant, loving, a peaceful, quiet relationship. Or had it been? She asked herself that quite often and finally answered that it hadn't. Alan had spoken to her only to ask for something or to tell her it was time for their walk, had kissed her when he did so, but on the cheek, had eaten his meals behind a newspaper. It would have been behind a book except that she protested against that, a ban he seemed to disproportionately resent. Hours passed when he said nothing, but once when she told him she disliked being totally ignored, he said simply that at their ages nothing was left to say. As for sex, or making love as she called it, that had stopped years before. He had sex with Daphne, didn't he?

"He'll come back," Judith said on one of her teatime visits.

Neutrally her mother said, "I don't know. Perhaps he will."

The woman upstairs who had the cat said, "One of these days he'll come back."

Freya, appearing one afternoon with her baby, quoted her own mother without knowing she did so. "He'll come back, Gran."

"Why do you say that?"

"They always do."

Did she think her grandmother would start crying? Would say, no, he never will, and keep on crying? "What about all those divorces then? Those husbands didn't come back."

Freya had nothing to say. She talked about the baby instead.

Rosemary had never before lived alone. At first it had been with her parents, then with Alan. If her home had been a detached house, as it had once been, she might have been uneasy, even frightened, especially at night, but aware here of living in a flat with others above, below her, and on either side of her, she wasn't even apprehensive.

She had started going to bed later. Ever since Alan had said that their lives had been dull, she had often told herself that he was right, but it was painful to admit. This was her whole life gone by. She thought how the friends she had had, the people she knew, that she'd invited to Traps Hill and to whose houses she went, were Alan's, met at the golf or tennis club; one or two with their wives had been at school with Alan. Where were those who had been at school with her? Today was Friday, and she was going to the theatre, going alone. She didn't have to go. She could tear up the ticket and stay at home. Her inner voice told her that if she did that, she would never go to the theatre again, never to the cinema. She phoned her granddaughter Fenella and said that if she bought a computer, would Fenella teach her how to use it? Fenella asked, could Rosemary type at all?

"I'm a good typist. Very good."

Her granddaughter was surprised. As Rosemary put the phone down, she thought how none of the family had ever heard of her prowess or, if any of them had been told, they hadn't listened. She walked to the shops, bought some food for lunch, put a new coat on over her dress, and set off for London. She was early and had nothing to do and nowhere to go for several hours. She could call on Freya or Judith. Sitting down on a seat in the park—which park? Hyde, Regent's, St. James's?—she leafed through her little address book and found a phone number that once had an exchange called Ambassador. It belonged or *had* belonged to an old school friend called Emma. Rosemary went into a call box and got a sharp buzzing tone. Probably all the numbers she had were like that. She found two others, one exchange called Primrose, the other Acorn; similarly, the numbers were of corporations or firms.

It was growing cold. She would buy a mobile phone tomorrow and teach herself to use it. She was sure she would never hear from Fenella on the subject of a computer again. Now what? She walked into a cinema, where the woman behind a window sold her—without even asking—a senior person's ticket. When Rosemary saw what it was, a Japanese film, she nearly walked out. She started to sit it out, but it was rather good, it was *very* good. She enjoyed it. Maybe she would try another of these. To her surprise she saw it was six thirty.

A leisurely walk to the theatre seemed a good idea. She had nearly reached Shaftesbury Avenue when she realised she hadn't eaten since her early lunch. Too late now. She would eat when she got home. Not everything could be achieved the first time of trying. The theatre was full, but there was her empty, inviting, well-organised seat. Halfway through the play, she fell asleep and woke up only when the curtain was coming down for the last time.

CAROLINE INSHAW ASKED Michael if they could meet, at his home or in her London office. It must be somewhere private, a venue where they must not be open to interruption as this was "a matter of the utmost seriousness." She had read the papers he had sent her; by now she knew all the facts and could gradually see her way to confronting Mr. John Winwood. In her words, this needed "an in-depth discussion" between them on the subject. Would he have an objection to this?

They agreed on the phone to meet at his home. DI Inshaw was to come at six. Michael had never undertaken anything in his whole life that brought him such dread, such stress, and such shrinking pain. The night before she was due to come, he slept not at all. It was all he could do to stop himself from pacing the rooms, then up the stairs and down again, until at last he lay in the dark, seeing lights flashing and hearing a slow, dull movement like a train passing through the world's longest tunnel. When morning came—late as it must in December—he sank into a sleep that was all dreams and, finally getting up, swore like poor Clarence that he "would never pass another such a night, though it should buy a world of happy days, so full of dismal terror was the time."

Arriving two minutes early, Caroline Inshaw told him he didn't look well.

"It's nothing," Michael said. "A virus maybe. Isn't that what everyone says?"

He was going to make her tea, but she said no, she'd like a drink, and maybe he should have one too. It would do him good. He thought how pretty she looked with her long, curly hair, her jeans, and her white wool jacket over a blue sweater. When he was young, women police officers never dressed like this as far as he could remember, but then hardly any of them were women. She took off her jacket and he felt pleased that the place was warm and comfortable for her.

She drank some of her wine, began talking about the hands in the box, said she supposed he knew the woman's hand was his mother's, immediately asking him if this brought him pain. He said yes but he was used to it by now. She had spoken to someone who had suggested that the other hand might have been that of a man called Johnson.

"I knew a Johnson," Michael said. "Slightly. When we were children. He was one of the boys who was in the tunnels with us. But it's a common name. He was William Johnson, called Bill."

"This one was Clifford. An army captain, some relation of the Johnsons who lived on the Hill, maybe William's uncle. Your William is a diplomat now, an ambassador."

Michael digested this. He remembered Clara telling him about a Clifford Johnson, that he'd been an admirer of his mother's. "One of the hands is his?"

"It looks like it. We have a DNA match."

"A wonderful substance is DNA—is it a substance?—it's like magic. A hundred years ago—well, less than a hundred—people would have seen it like that. Witchcraft."

She wasn't interested in any of that. Her eyes glazed over as people's eyes did when growing bored. "Now I need to see your father. In a care home, is he?" Michael nodded. It was simpler, easier, not to go into details. "I need to put a great many questions to him. Will he talk to me?"

"I think he may."

She took another sip of her wine. "He should have someone with him, not just me."

"I will come," Michael said, feeling that sad and heavy sinking of the heart. "When do you want to go?"

26

PERHAPS OTHER PEOPLE behaved like this. Alan didn't know. This was what he did: he walked round the rooms and thought, when he saw the bookcase where Michael had stood reading the titles of the books, That's where Michael was when we were so happy. Over there was where Rosemary threw that wineglass and we watched, loving each other. Out in the garden, standing side by side, holding hands, we watched the big dog fox come through the fence. Outside the front door, I went to pick up the parcel the postman shouldn't have left there but did, and when I went back into the hall, Daphne came to me and put her arms round me.

Now I can't go on. At first I thought it was the shock affecting me. What she told me passed through my mind and passed again and again. I told myself to think of something else, expel it, find a book to read, something compelling, interesting. Daphne's house is full of books, but I couldn't read. Not anymore. I saw the young girl in love with a man three or four times her age. She was a child. Depraved, surely? Absolutely corrupt. She kept on asking me what was wrong.

What had she done? I couldn't tell her. I kept on saying to myself that this would pass away, I loved Daphne. All our lives we had been made for each other, destined one day to be together. A voice in my mind said, You fool. You wanted some excitement, you wanted the thrill of Daphne's glamour. You're old but so is she, a rich, old woman, and now you've found out that her life has just been a saga of corruption. All those marriages, for instance, and how many lovers were there? You were too innocent and ignorant for her. She thought you would listen to her and smile, laugh; maybe she would tell you that you were the one of all of them that she truly loved.

The mistake was yours. You should have gone from George's house and left that card of hers lying on the floor.

THEY HADN'T ALL the time in the world. If Lewis had been twenty years younger and Melissa, say, ten years younger—not that he wanted her younger, she was perfect as she was—they could have let everything go slowly. She had been a widow only for months. If he had let the weeks go by, waited a fortnight and then phoned her, someone else might have snapped her up. She had been so kind to him, so helpful: ask Noreen to come earlier—you'd like to meet her, wouldn't you?—and surely you want to talk to her about your uncle. So Lewis had phoned Noreen and been gratified to find himself speaking to a warm, expansive woman. She couldn't come earlier, her flight had been booked, and, no, it wouldn't do to come straight to him, but she would phone him as soon as she was in England. Of course he had thanked Melissa for her help, they had gone out again, and now they were going out on Thursday.

But the next step? What would that be? He thought, We forget these things. We're in a restaurant and I say something about how wonderful it's been to have met her, and she says how lucky she is to have met me, or something like that. We go home in a taxi and I go into her house, and after we've had a drink or something I give her a kiss on the cheek and say I'll call her tomorrow, and then I leave. But I haven't all the time in the world.

He didn't know how to behave, he didn't know what to do. He had been married for years and years, decade upon decade, and if he ever knew, he had now forgotten. He didn't know the words to use. He didn't know how to tell her how much he liked her and, more than that, how he missed her. How could he tell her how it hurt him when she went into her house and closed the front door behind her? When he was young, he used to read a lot. He always had a book, a novel, and it was full of love and pain and words, words, words. Where were those books now? Lost, parted with, disposed of to secondhand bookshops—all except

The Count of Monte Cristo, and he'd read that too often. Except for that, he hadn't read anything except the evening paper and the *Spectator* and the *Sunday Times* for years. He thought he would never learn how to ask her. And what would he ask her? Would he ever recognise the opportunity when it came? Might it not be better for him not to phone her again, just to keep away from the phone, not to answer it if it rang? He would only do something that made him feel a fool.

He tried keeping away from the phone, and he could manage not phoning her. It was less easy when it rang and, when he didn't answer, rang again. Of course it was Melissa. She said, "Please come round. I feel I've done something to hurt you or offend you. Please come round and tell me what it was."

"You haven't done anything," he said, and he went round. She let him in, and when she had closed the door, she put her arms round him and held him in a close hug.

ALAN HAD DISCOVERED something about himself. Love-making was only possible for him if he loved the woman he was with. That wasn't quite correct. *Admired* might be a better word. If he admired her, honoured her, respected her. Those feelings he had had for Daphne, and now as he looked back over the years, he saw that whenever he'd thought of her, which he did quite often, it was with consistent admiration, thinking how beautiful she was, how clever and how accomplished, a strange word but somehow true. All that was gone. He could even ask himself now after so many years what a young girl of nineteen or so was doing having sex with a young man in the back of a car in Epping Forest. How could she? Perhaps the answer was that she had that experience seven years before and it had coloured her whole life. Now he felt he couldn't touch her again, and when they were in bed and she moved close to him, he shrank away. All the time he thought that maybe his old feeling would come back, but it didn't. Rather, he grew more revolted until he knew he would have to leave. He even thought of leaving in the night. Going to bed with her, waiting for her to fall asleep, then getting up and picking up the case he had packed and sneaking out the front door. He couldn't do it. He knew she would soon say something and she did.

"What is happening to us, Alan?"

Even then the temptation to deny it, to say he wasn't well, he was "under the weather," was great. "It isn't working," he said. "I suppose we know each other better. Maybe we should have waited before living together."

"It's what I told you about me and John Winwood, isn't it?"

Something about her compelled him to be truthful. You couldn't look into her eyes and deny that everything that was going to split them up had come about because she, a child, had encouraged a man of forty and more to make love to her, had enjoyed it. "It is. I can't help it, Daphne. I can't do anything to change it. I have tried. You don't know how often I have tried to get it out of my mind, but I can't."

"I would go back and undo it if I could. When I'd finished telling you—no, before I'd finished—I realised how I'd shocked you. I'd horrified you. I knew it was too late. I thought, 'Maybe it'll be all right, he will sleep on it, he'll forget.' But you didn't, did you."

"We're completely different people. I was brought up by quiet, conservative people who wanted everything to stay the same. You were ahead of your time. I don't know why. I thought it was wonderful when we made love in your dad's car. Every time it was a marvellous thrill. Would it have lasted?"

"For a little while."

He packed a bag. He had bought clothes since he'd come to live with her and one bag wasn't enough. Daphne said she would send them on. "You'll be home for Christmas. That will be nice, with the family."

"I suppose so."

The suitcase felt heavy, much heavier than when he had arrived in the summer. He had bought another case and would take that with him.

It must be his age. Not months but years had been added on over the past two or three weeks. He seldom looked at himself in the mirror, but now he did and saw a very old man, a man who looked too old to look after himself.

He wondered how he should say good-bye to Daphne. A kiss on the cheek seemed to insult her, so he did nothing. He stood there and said, "Good-bye, Daphne."

She nodded. "Good-bye."

Her farewell had a more permanent ring than if she had used his name. She stood in the doorway while he went down the steps, walked to the gate, and turned round to face her. He thought he had never seen so sad a face, but he said nothing, only raised his left hand and walked on, through the gate and down the street. Giving up the struggle, he hailed the first taxi that came and asked the driver to take him to Marble Arch and the Central Line.

THE SHORTEST DAY had come and gone. Sitting in the train, Alan thought about that day when Rosemary had come to Daphne's house. Rosemary had fallen half across the table and knocked over a glass of wine. Then she had said she hated him, but he knew she loved him. That was why she had come, to try—and had failed—to get him back. Now, once he was at home, he would make a great effort at being a good husband. It was a long time since he had told her he loved her, and women of all ages wanted to hear that. It was a long time since he had bought her anything or taken her anywhere except to one of those cheap restaurants in the High Road. Well, he could remedy that, it was hardly a difficult task. You could control what passed through your mind, especially when you were old. He didn't want to think of Daphne, yet he remembered how not long ago he could think of nothing and no one else. This was a young man's behaviour, but he was old, old as the hills.

Seven thirty. Dark as pitch, but a moon had appeared and a taxi was waiting outside the station. The driver got out, picked up Alan's case, and put it in the back. Loughton was a nice place. It had always surprised Alan that though it was on the edge of Epping Forest, had some beautiful old buildings, was richly endowed with ancient trees, and had a tube station and a bus route passing along its High Road, it had never taken its place in the limited category of lovely London suburbs: Hampstead, Highgate, Chigwell, Dulwich. The block of flats where he lived—*had* lived and would again—was a beautiful building, built half a dozen years ago when architecture was restored to its former glory. He gave the driver a large tip and got his suitcase carried into the entrance hall.

Lights were on in the flat. He saw that before he stepped out of the lift onto the first-floor hallway. The suitcase dropped onto the floor and his finger touched the bell. He had to ring it again, and then she answered.

"Rosemary. Rosy."

She looked at the case. She looked up at him. "Why are you here?"

"Oh, come on, Rosy. I do live here."

"You did. Not any longer. I'm going to have my supper. Good night."

She closed the door in his face. He rang the bell again and again. The light in the hall was turned off. He picked up the case and went down in the lift. Outside again, he looked up and saw that the lights in the flat were all off. What had he done with the key to his house? Put it in one of the pockets of his suitcase and never touched it since. On a wooden seat in Traps Hill he set the case down, opened it, and looked for the key. Nothing there. He was putting clothes and shoes back when he remembered this was the new case he had bought, while he had left the key in a pocket of the old case he had brought with him to Daphne's.

It was cold and a white frost was showing on the tops of garden walls. He sat down on the seat where he had put the case and tried to think what to do. Find a hotel? Go to a friend's?

If he could find a friend, perhaps he and the friend could go to Rosemary in the morning and explain that he had come back, that this was permanent, their separation was over. He got out his phone, called Maureen, and was told not warmly that he could come to Carisbrooke if he liked, but only for the one night. The suitcase was heavy. He trudged across the High Road and began the climb up York Hill. Loughton, at only ten minutes to eight, was empty. The only people who were ever about on a weekday evening were teenagers in hoods, loafing about in doorways smoking and carrying drinks cans. "Lost your way, granddad?" one of them called out to him. Alan wondered why he had ever thought Loughton a desirable place to live.

27

EVERYTHING STOPS FOR Christmas. Daphne flew to Seville on December 22 and stayed at the Alfonso XIII Hotel, accepting a friend's invitation to Christmas dinner. Melissa's daughters came home (as they called it, though they hadn't lived there for years) and Lewis stayed, living in a dream, appreciating how nice everyone was to him and going out on the day before Christmas Eve to buy presents for all. Michael took a call from Urban Grange that told him his father had had another bad turn and perhaps he would feel like coming. He went, found his father up, eating a large meal, and went home to phone Caroline Inshaw and say that if she wanted to talk to John Winwood, they should not delay it much longer.

IT SEEMED ABSURD. John Winwood was close on a hundred years old. He could die not any day but any minute. If only he would, thought Michael. It would be best for him, best for everyone, and for peace and quiet. Michael's children came home for Christmas as they always did. Jane began phoning him a week before, promising him a turkey, "all the veg you could possibly want, Dad," some presents that were "way out." Richard also phoned. He would stay just Christmas Day and the night and then be off to Seattle to attend a conference that would begin next day. Michael went out and bought each of them an iPod because it was easy and quick. He dialled Daphne's number on Christmas evening and got a message: "Alan and I are no longer together. I am in Spain until January second."

Christmas is often mild and damp in London. A sluggish rain fell. Richard left for Seattle, having spent the previous afternoon loading all the music he could find in his father's house onto the new iPod. He seemed enraptured by it. Jane, on the other hand, repeatedly said she would never learn how to work hers. She loved it, Dad was so clever to think of it, but she was so hopeless she would never even get it out of its box, let alone make it play music. Michael thought there must be something wrong with him that he was relieved when his children left.

His father didn't die. On the morning of January 10, Michael asked himself if he should buy his father a birthday present and immediately castigated himself for being so stupid. He had last given him a present at Christmas 1943. His mother had bought it and he could no longer remember what it had been. She had thrust it in his hands and left him to do the impossible, wrap it up.

He was due to meet Caroline Inshaw at Urban Grange at 10:00 a.m. He got there at twenty to, and as he noted the time, it occurred to him that no one said that anymore, no one had said it for years; people said nine forty instead. Caroline walked in at five to ten—there, he was doing it again—and they went along the passage to John Winwood's room. Michael had arranged this visit with his father, so they were expected. He knocked at the door, he didn't know why, he never had before, and immediately thought himself stupid. There was no response, so he walked in, feeling sick.

Dürer's hands were up on the wall, but they had been moved to the prime place for showing off anything in that room. Sitting up in bed, sitting in the best armchair, walking to the bathroom, John Winwood could see that picture and, for all Michael knew, be amused by it. At present, his father sat in that best armchair, dressed in obviously new clothes. He must have had some member of Urban Grange staff go out and buy them for him. Michael wondered what Darren or one of the other carers (would you call them that?) had thought about being requested to find and purchase dark blue trousers and a tunic top, patterned in scarlet and white, with a high collar to enclose his neck. Red, yellow, and silver trainers were on his feet.

Caroline Inshaw was staring at him. “Good morning, Mr. Winwood. How are you today?”

His father began to laugh. “Much as usual. What can I do for you? I don’t know why I ask. I know already. Ask away.”

“I would like you to tell me if you are aware of what I’m talking about when I ask you about a tin box containing a man’s hand and a woman’s hand and dating from about the year 1944.”

John Winwood sighed. “You’re a very good-looking woman. Seems a pity you have to spend your time talking about severed hands and buried boxes.”

Michael saw a flush mount into her face. “Mr. Winwood, would you answer the question, please?”

“Yes, I am aware. I put the hands in that box. I cut them off. I must have had a reason, but I’ve forgotten what it was. The woman’s hand was my wife’s, the man’s a chap called Johnson, Clifford

Johnson, who was her lover. I couldn't have that, could I?"

He looked pleased with himself, supremely contented. "I found them in bed. I strangled him first because if I'd killed her first, he might have killed me. Then I killed her, cut off his hand and then her hand. I said I don't remember why; just for fun, I suppose."

Caroline said, "Mr. Winwood, is this true or is it some sort of joke?"

"You mean you find it funny? Well, there is no accounting for tastes. I turned a bunch of kids out of the foundations of a house, including my son there, and once I was alone, I buried the box in a place where I thought no one would find it for years. And I was right. Shall I go on?"

"Yes, please."

"I got rid of him after that. Had him sent down to my cousin Zoe, a soft, sentimental woman who couldn't have kids or didn't. My wife was dead. I sold the house as soon as the war was over and married again. No one asked any questions. I said I was a widower, which was true, and they accepted it. I married a woman called Margaret Lewis. Her husband had been killed in the war, in North Africa, in a place called Mersa Matruh, and he left her a house, a great big country place, and a mint of money, never mind how much. A hundred thousand was a hell of a lot in those days. Everyone accepted that I was madly in love with her. It was as easy as falling off a horse.

"It was my looks that got her. I was very good-looking in those days, it gets them every time." He stared searchingly at Caroline Inshaw. "With your looks you want to remember that. 'Gather ye rosebuds while ye may.' I always did. I haven't worked since I was eighteen. Then a doctor told me I had a heart murmur. What happened to that, I wonder. Anyway, Margaret lived a long time, died at last, nothing to do with me. I married another rich woman, even richer, called Sheila Fraser. All the interests she had were nothing to me. I never cared about butterflies or—what are they called? Moths? The things that eat clothes—wildlife, trees, that sort of thing. I couldn't stand hearing her talk about leaves and fishes and otters and whatever while we were having dinner. She died—that was something to do with me, but we needn't go into that. I was by then a lovely old gentleman, people called me. I didn't want to live alone anymore, so I found the best place in this country to be looked after in. That was here and I've been here ever since. I sold the house, I've still got plenty of money. It'll last me out. And when I go, the hedgehogs will have it. Who would have thought I'd live to be a hundred—well, nearly a hundred. Are you going to charge me?"

Michael's father suddenly looked much younger, could have been taken for eighty, though eighty was hardly young.

"I am. But I want to talk to you some more. I have questions to ask you. I should like you to have a lawyer with you. Are you able to come to London with me? Now, preferably?"

"I haven't been out of here for eighteen years. I used to go out. I had a girlfriend in the village and I used to visit her. Those were the days. There's an old song my mother used to sing about when he thinks he's past love, 'tis then he meets his last love. Those were the days." He sang the lines of the song and now his voice cracked. "I don't think I can go to London. It's too far. I must think. Michael, pass me that glass of water that's on the bedside table."

Michael's legs felt as if they wouldn't move. They were heavy as if made of stone.

His father growled, "I said to pass me that glass of water that's on the bedside table? Come on, look sharp. I don't want to have to ask the lady, do I?"

Michael managed to lift himself onto his feet, felt he would overbalance but didn't. Swaying a little, he made his way to the table, lifted the glass, and carried it to his father. John Winwood's eyes were on him, an unflinching stare. Michael turned away, sat down again, but instead of looking once more at his father, turned his eyes down to his hands, which lay in his lap. The room was silent and then Caroline made a sound, a little gasp. Michael looked up. His father was drinking water out of the glass, not only drinking it but swallowing something.

"Lock the door," John Winwood said. He had a small bottle in his hand.

Michael said, "I don't . . . I can't . . ."

"Too late. It's too late now."

The bottle dropped out of his father's hand, fell onto the carpet, and rolled an inch or two. The almost-hundred-year-old man slumped over the arm of his chair, his face contorted. He began to choke, a dreadful rasping yet liquid sound. Caroline jumped to her feet. Michael flung open the door and cried out, "Is anyone there? Come here. We need help."

DARREN CAME QUICKLY, then Imogen, then a man Michael had never before seen. It had all taken five minutes and it was too late now. The man, who was a doctor, said, "What did he take?"

"He told me it was cyanide. He had it with him when he came to live here. I didn't believe him. I should have believed him."

The doctor asked Imogen to take Michael and Caroline Inshaw downstairs. He would come to them in ten minutes. They were shown into an austere, pale grey room. Neither of them said a word but sat down in silence and waited.

The doctor came in a little before the ten minutes were up. Michael liked him better than Stefani. "The autopsy will show," said the doctor, "but what he took was aspirin. Death from cyanide would look quite different." He sighed and shook his head. "It was probably a heart attack."

"So it had nothing to do with the pill he swallowed?" Caroline Inshaw sounded disappointed but was likely only shocked.

"Nothing. It wasn't the first heart attack he'd had, but it was the last."

Michael said, "He thought he'd had a heart murmur since he was young," but no one took any notice.

THOUGH VERY ILL and not expected to live, Norman Batchelor had survived, seemed well, and came to see his brother Stanley because it was now *his* life that was likely at an end. He had pancreatic cancer, and little could be done for him. Stanley often spent a day in bed, and he was in bed with Spot lying beside him when Norman arrived. John Winwood's death was announced in a tiny item in the newspaper because he was only a few days short of a hundred. Stanley read it in the *Mirror* but Helen had read it first, and Norman told him all over again.

Norman ate heartily of Helen's cooking. He had thought that Stanley would have passed away before January 5 when he had a seat booked back to France on the Eurostar, but things worked out differently. He was sitting on Stanley's bed, though he had been asked both by Stanley and

Helen not to do so, and when he got to his feet to fetch himself a cup of tea, he was assailed by the worst pain he had ever known. Clasping his left arm with his right hand, he was doubled up by pain. His legs gave way; he groaned and fell to the floor. Spot barked and ran downstairs, Helen came running up, but nothing could be done. It was another instance of too-lateness. Norman was dead. Stanley swore later that the last thing Norman had said before he died was that he had been born on the kitchen table.

WHEN IT GOT to Twelfth Night or some such time-honoured day soon after Christmas, Lewis told Melissa that he must go home. Everyone else had gone and he should go too.

"Why?" said Melissa. "No need to go unless you've something important to do at home."

"Well, I haven't. No, I haven't."

He stayed. That night he moved from the bedroom he had been sleeping in since Christmas Eve to her bedroom. In March, Noreen Leopold phoned and he was told to invite her to Chiswick. Noreen, who was a quiet, rather sentimental woman, told them they were so romantic, it went straight to her heart. She told Lewis that James Rayment had been turned down by Anita Winwood. Lewis wanted to know if his uncle had had a "proper love affair" with Anita, but Noreen would have been considered old-fashioned if she had been living in London and said that she "wouldn't know about things like that." He was her father, he wouldn't have mentioned something like that to *her.* He did say he was glad Anita had refused to go off with him because if she had, he'd never have met "the very sweet lady" who became Noreen's mother.

Noreen called her father an engineer. More like a motor mechanic, Lewis thought. Still, James did well, started his own business, and reared a flourishing family. "He often talked about you," said Noreen. "Said you were the only one of his British relations he missed."

Lewis thought that was a bit mean considering James had had a room in Lewis's parents' house for months in 1944 and used it—he was thinking of the goings-on in the air-raid shelter—in a way you couldn't use a hotel in those days, all rent-free. Still, he liked Noreen, and once she was safely back in the Tottenham Court Road hotel, he and Melissa took her about to see all sorts of sights, the Tower of London, the National Gallery, Madame Tussauds—they were the oldest people there—Harrods (twice), and first-class on the train to Brighton. After that Noreen went on a five-day tour to Cornwall, and Lewis and Melissa got married.

STANLEY BATCHELOR DIED in St. Margaret's Hospital, seven days after his brother Norman.

"That makes two more widows," said Maureen briskly. She wasn't sorry to find a sister-in-law sharing her plight. The family survivors all met at Stanley's funeral. Old people attend funerals far more than younger ones. You would suppose that such rituals would be too near the bone for the elderly, but it appears not to be so. Perhaps they go because funerals are so personal to them. They have experienced many of them, they know all about the way these things go. There are no surprises.

Most of those who survived went to Stanley's funeral, as did those widows, Maureen and, of course, Stanley's own widow, Helen. Rosemary was there and so was Lewis with his new wife, Melissa. Everybody stared at her and pretended to be looking at some piece of decoration on St. Mary's walls. The men's verdict was that old Lewis had done well for himself, and the women's that she had had at least one face-lift. Michael turned up, a rather unexpected guest. His father had died in his care home and in Michael's presence, everyone knew that, and to some people his appearance seemed in bad taste. How did he know about the funeral? No one found out. The answer was that Maureen had phoned and told him. No, Daphne wouldn't go. Alan would likely be there, and it might be awkward for both of them to meet on such an occasion.

Alan intended to go. Daphne had sent his other

suitcase some weeks before, and in it was his charcoal-coloured, almost-new suit, which he meant to wear. In the time he had lived alone, his feelings for Rosemary had changed. He longed to return to the flat in Traps Hill. He longed for *her.* Many aspects of her recurred, coming to him in the night, in dreams, and in the daytime when he was out food shopping or while he sat alone in the studio flat he was renting; the sound of her sewing machine, the sight of some new dress she had made, her always slightly wrong fish pie, returned to him. It troubled Alan that most of those who attended the funeral and knew him asked after Rosemary. Was she unwell? Didn't they know he and she had been apart for months? He replied noncommittally and went home before anyone could carry him off to the graveside.

The studio flat he rented in Buckhurst Hill wasn't much more than a room, its kitchen being some small pieces of equipment built into a panel on the wall where the door to the shower (no bath) room was. He tried to get out of it whenever he could. Therefore his attendance at Stanley's funeral. Back at home, he sat down to think about trying again. Just go to the flat in Traps Hill and ask to come back? Go further than that and tell her he loved her, he always had, and must have been mad to leave her? After a while he fell asleep, as he often did in the afternoons. This time he dreamt that he was back with her, it was eight on a Saturday morning, and she was bringing him a cup of tea, telling him it was going to be a fine day and how would he feel about going to see Freya and baby Clement? He thought it was real, that dream, and when he woke up and found it wasn't, he lay in the armchair and felt two tears run down his cheeks.

HAPPY ROSEMARY HAD rediscovered a couple of girls she had been at school with. Sylvia and Pamela were both widows and "well-left," as such women used to be described when husbands had died and left them a stack of shares and a considerable income. Now the three of them were friends again and had taken to attending the cinema together, going to the theatre, signing up for French-conversation lessons—age was no bar—going on weekend trips in luxury coaches and riverboats and buying tickets for book festivals.

While Rosemary was away at one of these, Alan made his carefully planned trip to the flat he longed to return to. The suitcase he left in the studio. Daphne had sent it on but his key wasn't inside. It was lost. Perhaps he had never put it in there. He called round to the flat as any male visitor might, but without the flowers such a man would have brought. Anyway, no one was at home. It was a bitter disappointment. He tried again, in the afternoon this time, on the following Wednesday. Rosemary was at a matinee of a play called *Once*, and this time with a man also called Alan, whom she had met at the Harrogate Literary Festival. The Alan that she was married to decided that to call in the morning might be wiser, and he did so on a Monday.

He was sick with trepidation. Like some young lover, he had woken up at 4:00 a.m. and lain in a sweat of dread. Suppose she turned him away again? Suppose she saw who it was through the window and refused to open the door? But he must do it, he must go there. She opened the door to him, all smiles, in a new dress that plainly wasn't one she had made. She looked years younger than when he had last seen her, and that wasn't a cheering thought.

"Rosy. Can I come in, Rosy?"

She nodded, the smile still there. No changes had been made to the flat. It was just as it had been when he left it. He sat down and she said she would make coffee. It was going to be all right, more than all right. She brought in the coffee and he noticed at once that it was far better than it used to be. She had learned how to make coffee in his absence. Grown slimmer since he'd left her, she had become cleverer and somehow more charming. She sat down, began to talk about some play she had seen and some literary festival she had been to in Yorkshire.

"You took yourself to a theatre on your own? Well done."

"I wasn't on my own."

It was a simple sentence. It sent a shiver through him. He drank his coffee, said he was living in a studio flat but now he thought he would give it up. There was no point in keeping it. Rents were so high, he had had no idea.

She picked up the tray and carried it to the kitchen. When she came back, she told him she thought he had a key "to this place."

"I did have but I've a confession to make. I seem to have lost it."

"Well, it doesn't matter, does it? You don't need it. Better not give up this studio of yours. Not till you've bought something bigger, I should think."

"Rosemary. Rosy, I thought I should come back here. I want to come back to you."

"Don't bother to sit down again. It's been nice to see you, but I have to go out in ten minutes. Back to the studio, eh?"

"Rosy, let me come back."

"I don't think so. It won't do. You left me for no reason and now I'm leaving you." She opened the front door. "Bye-bye, Alan. I'm sure we'll meet again someday."

He sat down on the same seat he had sat on those weeks ago when he had been turned away by the woman with the cat. This eviction, he felt, was final. He had no idea what he was going to do, now or in the future.

28

WHILE JOHN WINWOOD was alive and Zoe was in touch with him, Michael thought about his father with dread and tried more or less successfully to forget about him. Once she was dead and the duty fell on him, the ancient man had spoiled his life just by existing, as he had spoiled it when Michael was a child. Now he had gone. Michael felt happier than he had perhaps for ever. For even when he had Vivien, his father was *there,* was in the world, a threatening presence that might descend upon them, himself, his wife, and their children, and carry out some frightful acts of destruction. But not now, no more. Even he couldn't come back from the dead.

With no father there, a brooding presence, he found he liked his children better. When one or the other came to stay, he began to enjoy their company. He returned Jane's hugs with tender enthusiasm, enquired about Richard's business, asked after his new wife, the newly arrived baby. When would Richard bring this new family to see him? Jane was getting married again? He didn't add the once inevitable suffix, *at last*. He said good, he was happy. When was she going to bring her fiancé to meet him?

Some two or three months after he'd heard from Rosemary that Alan was now living in a house he had bought in Epping, Michael encountered Daphne Jones in the Café Laville. He always thought of her as Daphne Jones, but this was his first visit to the Café Laville. He had never belonged to that great sect whose doctrine is to buy, as a habit in the middle of the morning, a mug of coffee with a lid on and drink it on the premises or take it home or to work. He did it now, getting off the 46 bus on his way to Warwick Avenue station, because he saw Daphne inside. She was sitting at a table on that balcony bit of the café that overhung the canal and enjoyed a magnificent view of a glittering stretch of water all the way to the distant bridge beyond. Little Venice, it was known as.

She welcomed him to her table with the kind of smile he hadn't seen on a woman's face since he lost Vivien. "If Venetians come here on holiday, do you think they're flattered or disappointed?"

"I don't suppose they come," said Michael.

"You were the boy next door for years, but I don't think we ever spoke, not even in the qanats. What brings you down here?"

" 'A wonderful bus is the forty-six. It takes you right out to the sticks.' I was going to the tube station but I've forgotten why. Have lunch with me?"

So she did. Three months later he was spending half his time with her in the house in Hamilton Terrace and half at home. He was happy. Vivien's room he had locked up, opening it only when Jane and her husband came to stay.

About the Author

Ruth Rendell has won numerous awards, including three Edgars, the highest accolade from Mystery Writers of America, as well as four Gold Daggers and a Diamond Dagger for outstanding contribution to the genre from England's prestigious Crime Writers' Association. A member of the House of Lords, she lives in London.

Center Point Large Print
600 Brooks Road / PO Box 1
Thorndike, ME 04986-0001 USA

(207) 568-3717

US & Canada:
1 800 929-9108
www.centerpointlargeprint.com